C000016101

APOCALYPSO

ROBERT RANKIN

Apocalypso

Doubleday

LONDON · NEW YORK · TORONTO · SYDNEY · AUCKLAND

TRANSWORLD PUBLISHERS LTD
61–63 Uxbridge Road, London W5 5SA

TRANSWORLD PUBLISHERS (AUSTRALIA) PTY LTD
15–25 Helles Avenue, Moorebank, NSW 2170

TRANSWORLD PUBLISHERS (NZ) LTD
3 William Pickering Drive, Albany, Auckland

DOUBLEDAY CANADA LTD
105 Bond Street, Toronto, Ontario M5B 1Y3

First published 1998 by Doubleday
a division of Transworld Publishers Ltd
Copyright © Robert Rankin 1998

The right of Robert Rankin to be identified
as the author of this work has been asserted in accordance
with sections 77 and 78 of the Copyright Designs and
Patents Act 1988

All of the characters in this book are fictitious, and any
resemblance to actual persons, living or dead is purely
coincidental.

A catalogue record for this book is available from the British Library.

ISBN 0385 409435

All rights reserved. No part of this publication may
be reproduced, stored in a retrieval system, or
transmitted in any form or by any means,
electronic, mechanical, photocopying, recording,
or otherwise, without the prior permission of
the publishers.

Typeset in 11½/13pt Bembo by Kestrel Data, Exeter, Devon.

Printed in Great Britain by
Clays Ltd, Bungay, Suffolk.

APOCALYPSO

1

Porrig was lying in the gutter, but he wasn't looking at the stars. He was rubbing at the lump on his forehead and bewailing his lot. Bewailing his lot was something Porrig did on a more or less regular basis. It came naturally to him. He was good at it.

Porrig sighed as he rubbed and wondered exactly where he'd gone wrong this time. It did not take him long to reach a conclusion. Porrig had unwittingly stepped across the path of the common man's arch enemy. Political Correctness. He had said the wrong thing in the wrong company and he had paid the price for so doing.

He had received the thrashing.

He had missed the pudding course.

The dinner party had, until Porrig said his wrong thing, been going rather well. The five people present had all been enjoying themselves. Porrig's fiancée, Ellen, had been enjoying herself. Her two girlfriends from college had been enjoying themselves. And Collette, Ellen's sister, whose dinner party it was, had been enjoying herself also. Porrig, perhaps, had not been enjoying himself quite so much as the rest of them, because he hadn't seemed to be able to get a word in very often. But he had been enjoying himself up to a point, which was better than not enjoying himself at all.

And not enjoying himself at all was something Porrig did almost as often as bewailing his lot. In fact the two walked hand in hand. So to speak.

The dinner party conversation had revolved about 'Sisterhood' and the Feminist Movement. Much of this was lost upon Porrig, who did not have a sister and who normally associated the word *movement* only with the word *bowel*. But at least the conversation seemed to be about women and Porrig was always happy to talk about women.

And so, when there was a momentary lull in this conversation (it being either twenty past or twenty to the hour, those mysterious times when rooms unaccountably go silent), Porrig took the opportunity to remark casually that when it came to women he was very much a 'tit' man himself.

The strangled gasps and horrified expressions informed Porrig that he had committed a social gaffe.

Porrig grinned foolishly. 'Did I *really* say "tit" man?' he asked.

Four female heads nodded grimly.

'I do apologize,' said Porrig. 'What I meant to say was "tit" *person*.'

But it hadn't helped.

Porrig was taken to task. Cruel words were spoken and for a moment or two it seemed to Porrig that he was no longer Porrig at all, but some vile embodiment of all things that were male and therefore loathsome.

But he took it like a man. Well, *person*. Because, after all, he had been in the wrong.

And then, for some reason that was quite beyond Porrig, one of his fiancée's college friends brought up the subject of men's socks. About how 'fetching' men looked when wearing nothing but their socks. This got a big laugh around the table.

Porrig, sensing a lightening of the situation, responded by stating the practicality of men's socks. How rarely they needed changing, for instance. And this got a big laugh too.

Feeling that he was now in safe territory, Porrig continued. Men's socks triumphed over certain articles of feminine attire, he explained, in that they were so easy to put on and take off. And he went on to illustrate this by relating a humorous anecdote concerning the difficulties he had once encountered when trying to get a young woman out of her tights in the back of a taxi.

Porrig wasn't certain who had thrown the first punch, but he was sure that it hadn't been him. He sighed once more and picked himself up from the gutter. Was his wedding still on? he wondered. It seemed to be off more times than a prossie's knickers. Porrig groaned. That was wrong too, wasn't it! He hadn't meant to think that. *Sex therapist's* knickers, that was probably it.

Porrig dusted down his trousers. Were those stains red wine, or were they blood? Most likely they were both. Porrig took the opportunity to bewail his lot once more. It wasn't his fault that he got himself into these situations. Well, it was, but it wasn't . . . OK then, perhaps it was.

Porrig wasn't a bad person, he was kind and he was caring. But he lacked for a certain something. Some social gene had not been encoded into his make-up. He said the wrong things and he did the wrong things, but not through malice or badness.

Just *because*.

He tried so very hard to get things right, but his well-intentioned arrows always fell a little bit short of the mark. He was always that little bit out of step. Always that little bit *wrong*!

By day Porrig cleaned and polished used motor cars for a man of doubtful integrity who was known locally as Mad Jack. Porrig had learned early in his life that it is always best to tread warily whilst in the company of any man who has the epithet 'Mad' attached to his name. When at work Porrig chose his words with the utmost care. Mad Jack referred to his lone employee as Dumb Porrig. Both seemed happy with this arrangement.

By night, however, things were different. By night the *real* Porrig emerged from his daytime chrysalis. The *real* Porrig was a cartoonist. A graphic novelist. A creator of comic-book heroes.

Not that he had, as yet, managed to get anything published. But he kept trying. Oh how he kept trying. And he was careful too. Very careful that all his comic-book heroes should be politically correct. His latest, for example, was the very exemplar of political correctitude, being a small black boy, who, in the company of his lovable pet pooch, righted social wrongs and put bad guys to flight.

Exactly why *The Adventures of Johnny Foreigner and Dildo the Dog* had so far failed to impress prospective publishers was also quite beyond Porrig.

Still, perhaps they'd go for his new hero, who was not only black, but wheelchair-bound. *Jazz the Spaz*.

Porrig wandered home. He lived quietly with his mum and dad in Moby Dick Terrace. 'Quietly', because his mother had forbidden him from speaking in the house, and 'with his mum and dad' because no-one else seemed keen to offer him lodgings. The Brentford house stood directly opposite to that once owned by the now legendary Archroy, renowned world traveller and discoverer of Noah's Ark. Archroy's house had a blue plaque above the front door. Porrig's didn't.

But it will one day, thought Porrig, although *why* was any-body's guess.

Porrig did not enter by the front gate but climbed carefully over the fence. The reason for this *outré* behaviour was that Porrig's neighbour, Mrs Chisholm, was in the habit of setting traps for him. She had recently joined a Pentecostal Church, The Twenty-third Congregation of Espadrille, and become con-vinced that Porrig was an agent of the Antichrist.

Porrig had tried to put her right, but strangely his pleas of innocence had gone unheeded and his kind offer to pluck the hairs which sprouted from a mole on the lady's face had been misconstrued. Further wary treading was now necessary in his own front garden.

Porrig stepped over the piano wire that was stretched between the rose bushes, turned his key in the front-door lock and went inside.

He was now forced to shin over the armchair that blocked the hall. This was not a barricade to keep him out, nor was it the work of Mrs Chisholm. This was only his mum having another bash at *feng shui*.

On the hall table was an envelope. Porrig observed that it had his name written upon it. The writing was in green ink. The writing was in a careful hand. Porrig took the envelope and went upstairs.

Porrig's bedroom was not without interest. It contained many books, as Porrig was an avid reader, devouring the works of such luminaries as Johnny Quinn and Hugo Rune with great gusto. Whether or not he actually took in much of what he read was a matter for debate (though not for a particularly serious one).

There was Porrig's drawing table, of course, to which were pinned his latest efforts at penmanship. And it did have to be said that he was a fine artist: skilful and delicate, with a lightness of touch which captured perfectly the mood and disposition of his characters. Sadly, however, this was buggered all to hell by the excruciating phrases that issued in speech bubbles from their mouths.

Porrig sat down on his bed and perused the envelope. It was definitely his name on the front, but as there was no address and no stamp, it had certainly been delivered by hand. Which might not be such a good thing. A letter bomb from next door, perhaps? Porrig shrugged this off. Many faults had he, but the duffel-coat of paranoia did not hang in the wardrobe of his failings.

Porrig read aloud his name. It was spelt Padraig, but as it was pronounced Porrig that was what everybody called him.

'Padraig,' read Porrig. 'Padraig Arthur Naseby'. Porrig shook his head; he really hated that name. No matter how you read it, it always sounded like 'The Accused'. 'Padraig Arthur Naseby, you stand before me accused on ten counts of Political Incorrectness. How do you plead?' Guilty. Always guilty.

Porrig's name was a lot he constantly bewailed. He would change it by deed poll as soon as he could get around to it. And as soon as he could make his mind up as to a replacement. He fancied something posh. One of those double-barrelled lads so beloved of the aristocracy. Screen-Saver perhaps, or Sellby-Date.

Padraig Arthur Naseby indeed!

Porrig opened up the envelope. Inside it he found, of all things, a letter, similarly addressed to himself. Porrig unfolded it. Top quality paper, all waxy, with a watermark and everything.

11

From a solicitor's office: Ashbury, Gilstock and Phart-Ebum, Grand Parade, Brighton, Sussex.

'Brighton, Sussex,' read Porrig. 'I've never been to Brighton, Sussex. And Phart-Ebum, that's a good name. I rather fancy that. Porrig Phart-Ebum, it has a definite ring.'

Having got that over, Porrig read the letter.

> Dear Mr Naseby [it read],
>
> I am instructed by the executor of your late uncle's estate to inform you of your inheritance.
>
> As you must surely know, your uncle entered into many different fields of endeavour subsequent to his retirement from the stage. Not all of these were entirely successful, and the full extent of his debts, along with the rightful ownership of certain properties have yet to be established.
>
> However, his will is most clear upon one point: that the full ownership of ALPHA 17 be passed on to you and you alone.
>
> In order that we may facilitate matters apropos and a priori, it is requested that you present yourself here at your earliest convenience.
>
> Please bring proof of your identity. We look forward to meeting you.

'Et cetera,' said Porrig.

And, 'Cheeses of Nazareth,' said Porrig.

And, 'Uncle *who*?' said Porrig.

And, 'ALPHA 17,' said Porrig. 'An uncle I know nothing of has died and left me a planet.'

Said Porrig.

2

Porrig's father, Augustus Naseby, lurked in the standing room. This had, until recently, been the sitting room, but, with his wife's *feng shui* on the go again, the armchairs were now distributed about the house and the only furniture that remained in the sitting room was a low coffee table with a flowerpot on the top and a drawerless chest of drawers. But these *were* beautifully positioned.

Porrig's father lurked behind the drawerless chest. Lurking was something he excelled at, he had it down to an art. At his son's appearance in the doorway he shrank down and kept very still.

'Father,' said Porrig. 'I must speak with you.'

'To wit to woooo,' went Porrig's father.

'No,' said Porrig. 'You cannot fool me by doing that. You are not an owl, you are my father.'

Augustus Naseby straightened up and addressed his son. 'Is it yourself then, Porrig?' he asked.

'It is,' said Porrig.

'And sure would you look at yourself there.'

Porrig shook his head. 'Why the Irish accent?' he enquired.

'I'm thinking of converting to Catholicism. I just wanted to know what it felt like before I commit myself.'

'And what does it feel like?'

'Pretty good. If you do a Northern Irish accent you get served much quicker in pubs. But why are you speaking at all, son? You know it's not allowed in the house.'

'I have something very important to say. It's about your brother.'

'God rest his soul.'

'Ah. Then you know already.'

'Know what?'

'That he's dead.'

'Who's dead?'

'Your brother.'

'I don't have a brother.'

'But you said, "God rest his soul." '

'It's an Irish expression. They say it all the time.' Augustus Naseby crossed himself.

Porrig sighed.

'Don't do that,' said his father. 'You know it depresses me.'

Porrig sighed again and his father flinched. 'Do you or do you not have a brother? Or *did* you? Yes or no?' Porrig folded his arms. 'Come on, I want to know.'

Porrig's mother, Myra Naseby, now entered the room carrying a goldfish bowl with a piece of cheese in it.[1] 'Shut up, Porrig,' she said.

'Mother, this is important. An uncle has died and left me a planet.'

Myra Naseby burst into tears. 'You wicked boy,' she blubbed, 'with the cruel and evil things you say. Why can't you be like your brother?'

'I don't have a brother.'

'And whose fault is that?'

'Don't look at me,' said her husband. 'I did what was expected of me on our wedding night. Once was enough, surely?'

---

[1]The cheese was not from Nazareth.

14

Porrig sighed once more. His mother shrieked and his father ducked back down behind the drawerless chest.

'I intend to get to the bottom of this,' said Porrig. 'One of you must have had a brother. He couldn't have been my uncle otherwise.'

'Go to your room,' said Porrig's mother. 'And don't ever come out of it again.'

Porrig's arms were folded and they stayed that way. 'Which one of you had a brother?' he demanded to be told.

Augustus Naseby stuck his head up from his hiding place. 'Look, Porrig,' he said, 'there's something your mother and I have been meaning to talk to you about and now would seem to be the right time.'

'Oh yes?' said Porrig.

'Oh yes indeed to be sure.'

'In an English accent might be nice.'

'Quite so. You see, Porrig, you aren't our real son.'

'I'm not?'

'You're not. You were created in a laboratory as a cure for the common cold.'

'No,' said Porrig, shaking his head.

'No?' said his father.

'No. I have heard all that stuff before. How the fairies left me on the doorstep. How Mother was artificially inseminated during an alien abduction. How I came in parts from a toy company and was brought to life by some magic dust that a witch woman gave you for pulling her out of the canal. How . . .'

'How we opened up a can of sardines and—'

'That too. Why do you insist on making these things up?'

Porrig's father shrugged. Porrig's mother said, 'It's because we don't like you, dear. It's nothing personal. Well, actually it is.'

'All right,' said Porrig, 'that's fair enough.'

'You mean you don't mind?'

'Why should I mind? You can't be expected to like everyone you meet. I certainly don't like everyone I meet. In fact, there are some people I really hate. For instance—'

15

'No,' said his mother. 'Please don't. That's one of the things, you see. I know you're only being honest, that you mean no actual harm by what you say, but you offend everybody you meet. Ellen was on the phone before you came in. She said you'd offended her friends and that the wedding was off and she never wanted to see you again.'

'Oh,' said Porrig.

'I'm sorry if that's upset you, dear.'

'I'm not upset. I know she only wanted me to father her children.'

'What?' said Porrig's mum.

'I don't think women really enjoy sex at all,' said Porrig. 'I think they're driven by their hormones to reproduce and they—'

'Shut up, Porrig!'

'Sorry, Mother.'

'Actually, I think he might be onto something with that one,' said Porrig's dad.

'And you shut up too and stand by the window where I told you. You're messing up my *feng shui* and I won't have it.'

'Look,' said Porrig. 'It's quite clear that you don't want me around any more. Ellen doesn't want to marry me and as I've been left this inheritance, now would probably be as good a time as any for me to go off and make my way in the world.'

'Inheritance?' said Porrig's mother.

'ALPHA 17. The planet. I told you.'

Porrig's mother began to laugh.

'Why are you laughing?' Porrig asked.

'Oh, no reason, dear. Sometimes I just break into spontaneous laughter due to the sheer joy of being alive.'

'Hm,' said Porrig.

'It's quite true,' said Porrig's dad. 'It used to happen every time I took my trousers off. That's probably why we never had any more children, now that I come to think about it.'

Porrig's mother shushed her husband into silence. 'Porrig's right,' she said. 'Now would definitely be the time for him to leave home and make his way in the world. What with him being left a . . . left a . . .' She crumpled once more into laughter.

'Planet,' said Porrig.

16

'Planet, dear, that's right.' And Porrig's mother collapsed onto the carpet, where she rolled about, laughing hysterically and kicking her legs in the air.

'I am going upstairs,' said Porrig. 'I am going to pack my bags and I will be leaving first thing in the morning.'

'Sleep well then, dear,' howled Porrig's mother, gasping for breath and drumming her fists on the floor.

Porrig went up to his room, pulled his battered suitcase from beneath his bed and packed.

He slept very badly that night. His dreams were full of spacecraft and of alien ambassadors who came in peace but left in a right huff after his welcoming speech. There was a magistrate who said things like, 'Porrig Arthur Naseby, you stand before me accused of causing intergalactic war, how do you plead?' And Porrig's mum was there laughing and shouting, 'Guilty! Guilty! Off with his head!'

Porrig was awoken early by a scream, a thud and a shattering of bottle glass, as the milkman, tripping on the piano wire, dropped his crate and struck his head on the front door.

Porrig shook himself fully awake. 'Time to be off, I think,' he said.

In the bathroom he showered and dried and dressed. And gathered up his razor, comb and toothbrush. He thrust these into a pocket of his jacket and stood for a moment before the bathroom mirror, considering his reflection.

A young man gazed back at him. A young man of nineteen years, moderately handsome, firm of jaw and twinkly of eye. It was not the face he would have chosen, had he been given the choice, but it was not a face to be bewailed. Porrig grinned at the face and the face grinned back at Porrig. Simultaneously.

'Right then,' said Porrig to his reflection. 'This is it.'

And it was.

His parents were still asleep and so Porrig left a note which thanked them for having him and wished them all the very best for the future. He closed the front door quietly behind him, stepped over the prone body of the milkman and set off to the station with a whistle.

17

The sun rose over Brentford, beaming blessings on the borough. Sparrows sang their simple songs. Chaffinches chewed cherries on chimney-pots and a dark dog did a doo-doo in a doorway. Pete the parish pervert was probably playing with his pecker in the park, but as Porrig wasn't passing by that way he didn't see him.

Porrig did, however, pass by Mad Jack's Used Car Emporium. And here he paused to push a postcard through the letter-box. On this postcard were written words of apology, explaining that Porrig had, through no fault of his own, been forced into taking an early retirement. Porrig had been very careful indeed when penning this missive to couch it in terms that would not be likely to cause offence or risk retribution.

He had only used the word 'fuckwit' twice in describing his employer.

Porrig went a-whistling on his way and the sun rose ever higher over Brentford.

Ahead lurked trouble with a capital T.

In the ticket office at Brentford Central Station sat Russell The Railwayman. He had originally been christened Russell Hubner, but had changed his name by deed poll. Working on the railways can do strange things to a man (as will certain women if you pay them enough). But this aside, Russell had changed his name with a definite purpose in mind: to pursue a career as a stand-up comedian. There had once been a singing postman. There had also been a singing nun. A laughing policeman had been sung about, as had a fisherman called Pedro who was always whistling. But where were all the railwaymen, eh? Working on the bloody railways, that's where! Russell meant to change all that. Well, for *himself* at least.

But so far things hadn't worked out all too well. In fact they hadn't worked out at all. His attempts to take the world of comedy by storm had been met with indifference. And when not with indifference, then with outright hostility. His regular appearances at The Flying Swan's Thursday Talent Night were received with catcalls and the throwing of furniture. The world of comedy did not seem ready for a ribald railwayman.

But why?

Well, it did have something to do with Russell's 'delivery'. He was a natural mumbler. And when it came to stage presence, you either have that or you don't.

As for his material, limited as it was to Russell's specific interests, the bogie arrangements on pre-war locomotives and the music of Abba, it did not appeal as widely as it might have done. Russell's only real fan was his mother.

And so Russell festered in the ticket office of Brentford Central Station, bitter and resentful and taking his spite out on the travellers.

And one was approaching even now. A young man with a bulging suitcase. Evidently off on his holidays.

Russell peered through the grimy glass of the ticket office window. 'The first of the day,' he mumbled. 'And with only five minutes to catch the Victoria train. He's going to have to hurry if he doesn't want to miss it.'

Porrig dragged his suitcase into the booking hall and set it down upon the tiled floor. Squaring up before the counter window, he said, 'A single to Brighton please and . . . er . . . Hello, where have you gone?'

Beyond the range of Porrig's vision, Russell had sat down in a corner and opened up the latest edition of *Bogie World*. 'Shan't keep you a moment, sir,' he called.

'Fair enough.' Porrig stuck his hands into his trouser pockets and gazed all about the booking hall. The station was Grade Two listed, as were most of the older buildings in the borough. When Sir John Betjeman allegedly wrote of Brentford, in his famous poem 'Town I do thee love':

> Oh beauteous borough, fairest jewel
> Set in the crown of London's west
> By the Thames so coolly cool
> And blah de blah and beer is best.

he might well have had a few pints under his belt, but he certainly wasn't pissing on his boots. When it came to tasteful architecture, Brentford had it. And then some.

Porrig idly perused the railway timetable.

The trains that ran to Victoria, where he must make his Brighton connection, ran on the hour.

Porrig idly perused his wrist-watch.

It was now four minutes to the hour.

'Oh,' said Porrig, and, 'Excuse me, please, but can I buy a ticket?'

'Won't keep you a moment, sir.'

'Hurry up. I'll miss my train.'

In his hidden corner Russell smiled. 'A live one,' he whispered. 'Be with you in a minute, sir,' he called.

Porrig scuffed his heels upon the tiled floor. He had always considered himself to be an easy-going fellow. And it could be truthfully stated that, as with the duffel-coat of paranoia, the red cagoule of anxiety did not hang in the crowded wardrobe of his failings.

The double-breasted blazer of impatience did though. In fact it took up much more than its fair share of space.

'Hurry up,' cried Porrig, 'get a move on.'

A lady in a straw hat now entered the booking hall.

'Good morning to you, young man,' she said. 'Do you know what time the next train goes?'

'Any minute now,' said Porrig. 'I'm waiting to get a ticket.'

'Do you mind if I wait with you then?'

'Eh?' said Porrig.

Russell's smiling face now appeared at the window of the ticket counter. 'So then, madam,' he said, 'how may I help you?'

'Oi!' yelled Porrig. 'I was here before her.'

'Come now, sir,' said Russell. 'Ladies first.'

'I'll miss my bloody train.'

'No need for bad language, there's plenty of time before the train gets in.'

'No there isn't.'

'Yes there is, sir. Now, madam, what can I do for you?'

'A return please,' said the lady.

'Return to where, madam?'

'Return to here, of course.'

Russell laughed.

The lady laughed.

Porrig did not laugh.

'The old ones are always the best,' said Russell.

'I prefer the young ones myself,' said the lady. And they both laughed again.

'The train's coming.' Porrig pointed up the track. 'I can hear it.'

'Long way off yet,' said Russell. 'Now, madam. Where did you want to travel to, before you returned to this station?'

The lady in the straw hat cocked her head on one side. 'I can't really make up my mind,' she said. 'Where do you think would be nice at this time of year?'

'*What?*' went Porrig.

'Well,' said Russell to the lady. 'It all depends on how much you want to spend. The West Midlands are very nice. Particularly the town of Harcourt, which was noted for its steel mills. Before the war they produced many of the 4-2-4 bogie couplings that were used on the old LNER.'

'That takes me back,' said the lady.

'It's coming into the station,' shouted Porrig, jumping up and down.

'Have a care, sir, that floor is Grade Two listed.'

'Perhaps you'd better serve this chap first,' said the lady. 'He's getting himself in a bit of a state.'

'If you're quite sure,' said Russell.

'I am,' said the lady.

'All right then, sir, what do you say?'

'A single to Brighton and make it quick.'

'Not to me, sir. To this lady.'

'What?'

'Two little words, sir.'

'*What?*'

'Thank you, sir. Say *thank you* to the nice lady.'

'*WHAT?*'

'I'm waiting, sir. Courtesy costs nothing, you know.'

'The train's in the station. I'm going to miss it.'

'They'll be taking on the mail. There's plenty of time. Come on now, sir. Say thank you to the lady for letting you push in front of her.'

Porrig clenched and unclenched his fists. 'All right,' he gasped. 'All right. Thank you. Thank you. Now give me a ticket to Brighton.'

'I don't think you said please then, did you, sir?'

'Aaaaaaaaaagh!' went Porrig.

'I'm prepared to accept that,' said Russell. 'After all, it's not compulsory for passengers to be polite to us. Only that we be polite to them.'

'A single to Brighton. Please, please, please.'

'A single to Brixton. Coming right up.'

'Brighton,' said Porrig.

'It certainly is a bright'n today, yes, sir. But I expect it will cloud over later.'

'Brighton!' shouted Porrig. *'Brighton! BRIGHTON!'*

'Oh, Brighton. I thought you said Brixton. I'm a bit deaf in my left ear, you see. Actually, it's quite a funny story how it happened. They were doing these tours of the engine sheds at Crewe and I—'

'Give me my ticket. Give me my ticket.'

'Quite so, sir. Now what kind of ticket was it that you wanted? Was it the super-saver, the value-variable, the weekend-wonder, the mmmmmmmmble bmmmmmlemmm—'

'I can't understand what you're saying. You're mumbling! I . . . look, just give me anything, anything, the train isn't going to wait.'

'First class or second class?'

'Anything! Anything!'

'The choice is yours, sir. I can't influence you either way. It's more than my job's worth to do that.'

'Second class then, the train's going to go. It's going to go.'

'Second class it is then, sir. Nine pounds, seventeen and sixpence.'

Porrig flung a ten-pound note across the counter.

'I don't think I can change that, sir. Do you have anything bigger?'

'Bigger?'

'It's these new computer tills.'

Porrig snatched back his tenner and rummaged in his trouser pocket. He had brought with him all his savings. He produced a twenty-pound note and flung this across the counter. Russell handed him his ticket. 'Now,' said Russell, 'let's see if I can get the hang of this till. I think you have to press this button, or was it this one?'

'Wasn't that the guard's whistle?' asked the lady in the straw hat.

'Aaaaaaaaaagh!' went Porrig, abandoning his change, snatching up his suitcase and making a dash for the platform.

Russell and the lady watched him go.

'A good turn of speed,' said the lady in the straw hat. 'Do you think he'll catch it?'

'Oh yes,' said Russell. 'Just. I've never had a passenger miss one yet. I pride myself that I can get it down to the very last second. That's the humour of it, you see. It's all in the timing. It wouldn't be funny if they missed their trains.'

'You're a comic genius, Russell,' said the lady in the straw hat. 'And you're wasted here. But your day will come, son. Your day will come.'

'Thanks, Mum. And I really do appreciate you coming down here each morning to work on these routines with me.'

'A boy's best friend is his mother,' said the lady in the straw hat. 'And the extra money comes in handy. Give me my share of the young buffoon's change and I'll get off up to the shops. Pork chops be all right for you tonight?'

'Magic,' said Russell The Railwayman.

3

The station master *had* blown his whistle and the train *was* leaving the station. Porrig rushed across the platform, puffing and blowing and bewailing his lot. In the last compartment of the very last carriage some Good Samaritan espied Porrig's plight and opened the door for him. Porrig scrambled onto the train.

He slammed the door shut, swung his suitcase with difficulty onto the rack and threw himself down onto one of the bench seats.

'Thank you,' said Porrig in a breathless fashion.

The Good Samaritan smiled in reply. 'That was close,' he observed.

Porrig made a bitter face. 'Bastards,' he said.

'Excuse me?'

'Bastards. Some officious twat in the ticket office and some old cretin of a woman who pushed in front of me. I don't know about making pensioners resit their driving tests. They should make them do their O levels again. And swim ten lengths of the local baths. And if they can't – Porrig drew a finger across his throat – 'euthanasia,' he said. 'The best thing for them.'

'That is perhaps a tad extreme.'

'You've got to be cruel to be kind,' said Porrig. 'Put them out of *our* misery.' Porrig grinned up at his fellow traveller. 'Oh shit,' said Porrig.

The Good Samaritan grinned at Porrig. He was a very *old* Good Samaritan. *Very* old. He was small and he was wiry, a bit like an ancient whippet. In fact there was a definitely canine look to him altogether. He had a shock of white hair that stuck up in two earlike tufts and his face had the appearance of a bloodhound that had been given cosmetic surgery in some vain attempt to pass it off as a poodle.

'No offence meant,' said Porrig.

'None taken, I assure you. But then I *can* swim ten lengths of the local baths and I *do* have an IQ of one hundred and ninety. The only way you could offend me would be by attempting to mug me. And I wouldn't recommend that.'

'Why not?' Porrig asked.

'Because I am a master of Dimac, the deadliest form of martial art known to mankind, and I'd kick your bollocks right up your arse.'

'I'll bear that in mind,' said Porrig. 'Thanks again for opening the door and I'm sorry about the tactless remarks.'

'Forget it, lad. You're still young and youth is its own excuse for stupidity.'

'I'll bear that in mind too.' Porrig settled back to gaze from the window. The train was gathering speed now and the picturesque town of Brentford was falling away behind. Ahead lay the big metropolis, another train and Brighton.

And then what?

Porrig really had no idea at all. But something. Something different. Something new. A new beginning.

'Do you believe in fate?' asked the old fellow.

'Fate?' Porrig shrugged. 'If you mean do I believe that things are preordained, then no, I don't. Things happen because things happen.'

'How old did you say you were?'

'I didn't. I'm nineteen.'

'And how old would you say that I am?'

25

Porrig idly perused the ancient. 'You look pretty knackered,' he said. 'Eighty, perhaps.'

'A great deal older than that.'

'You'll be dead quite soon then.'

'Not for some time yet I fancy. Would you care for a cigarette?'

'No thanks, *I* don't feel like dying.'

The old fellow laughed. 'Then you do believe in fate. You believe that if you smoke cigarettes your fate would be an early death.'

'Fate has got nothing to do with it. Cigarettes are toxic. I wouldn't drink poison, so why should I smoke it?'

'Fate brought you into this carriage,' said the old fellow. 'Fate decreed that an old woman would delay you and an old man would open a door for you and then you would find yourself here talking about fate.'

'I think *you* brought the subject up.'

'Only because you were thinking about it. You were gazing out of the window wondering what fate would bring you. Something different? Something new? A new beginning?'

'How did you know I was thinking that?'

'Call it an educated guess. Would you like me to tell you a little story concerning fate? It would pass the time and I think it might amuse you.'

'Oh yes please,' said Porrig, in a tone that lacked all conviction.

The old fellow leaned towards Porrig. 'Do you often find yourself being smashed in the face for your sarcasm?' he asked.

'All the time,' said Porrig. 'You'd think I'd learn, but I don't seem to.'

'Well, just be advised on this occasion. I've a very short temper and despite my frail appearance I could easily knock your nose clean through the back of your head.'

'About this story,' said Porrig.

'Indeed,' said the other, settling back onto his seat with a creaking of bones and a crackling of ancient flesh. 'It begins long ago in the days of my youth. I was born of humble working stock and grew up in the kind of poverty which, although not so bad at the time, has, with the constant retelling of this tale, grown into something so awful that many who hear of it scarcely believe it to be true.'

'Eh?' said Porrig.

'Folk cannot bring themselves to believe that anyone could have endured the kind of hardships I tell them I endured. And why should they, eh?'

'Eh?'

'But endure these fictitious hardships I did. And although a sickly child, all gone with the mange and the ringworm, the rickets and the bloat, I laboured fifteen hours each day in the fields, drawing turnips and bringing in the sheaves. My mother died giving birth to my elder brother and my father lived out his final years a broken man, made barmy and blind through drinking fermented cows' urine, which in those days you could get on prescription from Boots the Chemist.'

'I think my stop's coming up,' said Porrig.

'I thought you said you were going to Victoria.'

'I'm sure I didn't.'

'But you are.'

'Go on with your story.'

'Hard times,' said the old one, 'hard times. Though not without joy. We had no television sets in those days, we had no electricity, but we made our own amusements. We would hollow out a dead rat to make a glove puppet, or hold maggot races, or simply engage in acts of anarchy and arson.'

'Happy days,' said Porrig.

'Are you taking the piss?'

'No, of course not. Well, just a bit. Perhaps. I mean, what is the point of all this? It's just nonsense you've made up.'

'So far it is, yes. But I'm leading you on to the good bit. Have you ever seen an angel, Porrig?'

'How did you know my name? I never told you my name.'

'Didn't you? Well, I must have just guessed that too, mustn't I? So have you ever seen an angel, *Porrig*?'

'Of course I haven't. There's no such thing.'

'No such thing as fate. No such thing as angels. What a lot

27

you think you know. Well, I *have* seen an angel, Porrig. I've seen one and I've touched one. So what do you think of that?'

Porrig eyed the old fellow warily. 'I'd rather not say,' he said.

'Very wise of you. In our yard.'

'In your yard?'

'In our yard, up against the cottage wall, was an old lean-to shed. We used to keep the chickens in it. Rotten, it was and it smelled real bad. Well, one night there was a big storm, thunder and lightning and winds and roaring rain. We brought all our livestock into the cottage and the wind tore tiles from the roof and ripped up trees and blew down the landlord's barn. People were killed in our village: a young family who lived in a cellar. The rain flooded down the high street and through their room and lifted the baby out of its crib and the parents tried to save it and they were all washed away and drowned. People could hear their screams above the storm but could do nothing to save them.'

'Oh,' said Porrig. 'This is true, isn't it?'

'Yes, Porrig, this is true. But in the morning after that terrible night, the storm had blown over and there was peace. There was wreckage everywhere, trees down, hedges ripped away, dead cows in the fields, and three dead people too, but they found them later when the water went down. All curled up together, they were, with their arms about each other.'

'Oh,' said Porrig, once more.

'Yes, oh. And I remember that light, that first light, when I went outside. Everything seemed to be different. Clearer somehow, more defined. As if the rain had washed clean the air, made it like glass. I waded out through the mud to see if there was anything that could be salvaged. Anything valuable that might have blown our way. And I found something valuable all right, in fact something quite beyond value.

'You see, somehow the old lean-to had survived the storm. The door was gone but it was still standing and as I looked inside I could see something odd. Something sort of glowing. Like a dim lamp, or the light that shines through your fingers when you cup your hands about a candle. And I leaned in through the doorway and there, crouched in the corner, was a

28

man. But he was not a man. He was like a man, but he was too small, the size of a three-year-old child. Perfectly proportioned though. A miniature man. And he was quite naked as he crouched there in the corner, shivering, and the light came from him, it shone all about him, as if he were lit from inside.

'And where we have hairs on our bodies, under our arms and on our chests and so on, he had these tiny feathers, like the soft down on chicks, and on his back and curled right under him he had wings. Wings, Porrig, curved like eagles' wings, but more complicated somehow, and these wings were golden, or silvery-golden, and they shone too. They glittered. They were the wings of an angel.

'But this light about him, it sort of came and went. Faded and then came back. Because he was ill, you see, he was wounded. His wings were wounded. The feathers were all broken at the bottom. And the smell of him. How I remember that smell.'

'That smell?'

'The smell of lilacs. The odour of sanctity, it's called. The perfume that issues from the incorruptible bodies of the saints. Sanctity, you see, perfection, it has its own smell. Not like anything in this world, this world where everything corrupts and dies. Not like ordinary lilacs, oh no.

'And I stared down at this tiny naked man with the wings, this angel, and he looked back at me with his eyes so pale and pleading, but he didn't speak. I don't know if he could speak. Perhaps they don't. Perhaps there are no words in the perfection of heaven. Perhaps words themselves are corrupt. Perhaps to put a name to anything given by God, to label it with a word, perhaps that is blasphemy.

'But though he didn't speak, I knew that he was begging me, begging me to protect him and not let him be seen. You see, somehow, in that great storm, he had fallen to Earth. I don't know how it happened, he never told me, because he never spoke, but somehow he let me know that he had come for the souls of that poor family who died. Come to take their souls to paradise.'

Porrig's mouth was open, but no words came from it.

'I nursed him,' said the old fellow. 'I hid him and I nursed him. I kept him secret in the old lean-to. I brought him out a blanket and I fed him milk. He didn't drink it like we do, he held it in the palms of his hands and it evaporated, or sank into the skin, or something.

'So I looked after him and I protected him. I straightened out the feathers on his wings as best I could. There was this dust on the broken ones, this light dust that came off on my fingers when I touched them. And the smell was on that dust and on my fingers and all through the day, when I sat at school in the classroom, I could smell that smell. I would sit there and sniff my fingers and smell that marvellous perfume.'

Porrig looked at the old man. His face was shining and there were tears in his eyes.

'Go on,' said Porrig. 'Go on with your story.'

'He went,' said the old fellow, 'upped and went. One day I got home from school and he'd gone. Without a word of goodbye, or of thank you.'

'But he never spoke.'

'I would have known, he would have let me know. But he was gone, just gone. I searched all over the place, and I cried, I can tell you. I sat there in that old lean-to and I wept. But I never saw him again. I don't know what happened to him.'

'He was well again,' said Porrig. 'So he had gone to . . . you know.'

'To perfection. He had gone back to perfection. But he left me with something.'

'He did?'

'Oh yes. But then, no, he did not. I took it, you see. I know now that I shouldn't have and I know now that I must return it to him. Find him and return it. I must do that, I know.'

'I don't understand what you're talking about.'

'While he slept,' said the old one. 'He slept a lot at first, while he was so very ill. And while he slept I took it. Just a little piece to carry with me, so I could smell that marvellous perfume. I didn't think it would matter.'

'A little piece of what? What did you take?'

'A piece of a feather from his broken wing. I've kept it with me ever since. Until the day comes when I can return it to him.'

The old fellow slipped a wizened hand beneath his jacket and delved into the pocket of his tweedy waistcoat. From here he drew out an old snuff box. It was a shallow ebony cylinder, perhaps an inch and a half in diameter, shining with a rich patina.

'I bought this box brand new,' said the old fellow. 'Saved up my pennies and bought it. To keep my treasure in. And I've carried it with me ever since. Would you like to see what's in it, Porrig?'

Porrig stared at the box and then into the eyes of the old man. What was all this, he asked himself. Some elaborate hoax? Some almighty wind-up? The old man's foolish talk and then this incredible tale that he told with such conviction. Could such a tale be really true? And if it was, what would it mean? A feather from an angel's wing?

The sunlight flickered through the window and the carriage wheels click-clacked on the track beneath. But somehow here, here in this compartment, there was silence. And stillness.

And sanctity.

'You may see it,' said the old man. 'Although you may not touch it, you may see it.' He held the box forward and his ancient fingers lightly brushed the polished lid. And Porrig saw that on that lid there was a date engraved in silver. Engraved when the box was new, in the year that the old man had bought it.

And the year engraved upon that lid was 1837.

'That is my fate,' said the old man. 'I will not die. I cannot die, until I have returned what I have stolen, do you understand?'

And gently, gently, he unscrewed the lid.

'You gotta get out now, love. The train don't go no further.'

Porrig jerked up on his seat, eyes blinking.

A large Jamaican lady in the costume of a cleaner smiled down upon him. 'Sorry to have to wake you up, love. But it's the end of the line, Victoria, and I gotta clean the compartment.'

Porrig gaped all about. But for the smiling cleaner he was all alone.

31

'Did you see an old man?' Porrig asked. 'Getting off the train? He was sitting just there and—'

'I see lots of people. Thousands of people. One old man's much the same as another.'

'Not this one.' Porrig shook his head and clicked at his jaw. 'Never mind,' he said, as he dragged himself to his feet. 'It was just a mad dream or something.' And he pulled down his suitcase from the rack and turned to take his leave.

'You look after yourself,' said the cleaner. 'You mind how you go.'

'I will,' said Porrig, climbing down from the train.

'And, love,' called the cleaner.

'Yes?'

'That's a real pretty aftershave you're wearing. It fills up all the compartment. It smells just like lilacs, it does.'

4

It was a somewhat ashen Porrig who boarded the Brighton-bound train. A chastened Porrig. A quiet one. He took himself off to the buffet car and ordered a cup of coffee.

'Not till the train leaves the station,' the attendant told him. 'And that goes for the bog too.'

Porrig sat down in the nearest compartment and waited for the train to leave. He was confused, Porrig was. Confused and upset. He didn't know what to believe. He knew he had met the old man. The old man had held the door open for him: he'd have missed the train otherwise. But how much of the rest had been real?

Probably only the first part. The stupid story about hollowed-out rats and maggot races. He must have dreamed the rest. Fallen asleep and dreamed it. And the smell of lilacs? Well, *he* hadn't actually smelled that himself. But perhaps it had wafted into the carriage from the outside and he'd smelled it in his sleep and sort of incorporated it into the dream.

That all made sense. After a fashion.

That's how Scully would have figured it out. Though possibly not Mulder.

Satisfied that it did all make sense, after a fashion, Porrig returned to the buffet car, for the train was now leaving the station. Here he was met by an unruly scrum fighting for attention at the counter. Porrig went back to his seat.

The train rushed forward, passing by houses and streets, houses and streets, further houses and further streets. Porrig looked out at them and wondered, as many have before him, just who were all these people who lived in these houses and drove along these streets. There were so many of them, all going about their daily lives, their ordinary lives. These people didn't meet angels, they just went to the shops and watched television and brought up children who did just the same. That was the real way of it; that was how it really was.

At length the scrum cleared and Porrig was able to get himself coffee and something that vaguely resembled a roll. And the train rushed on to Brighton and Porrig rushed on with it.

Brighton Station is still a thing of wonder and beauty: a triumph of Victorian ironwork, curving for a quarter of a mile. The great arched roof, with its countless skylights and its many pigeons, echoes with life. It's a Grade Two listed building, but it could use a lick of paint. Porrig humped his suitcase across the concourse and out to the rank where the taxis, distinctively tasteless in their pale blue and white livery, stood, surrounded by another unruly scrum.

Porrig decided he would walk.

'Grand Parade?' he asked a pimpled youth.

'*Big Issue?*' this fellow replied.

'Bless you,' said Porrig.

'Bless you?' said the youth. 'You the flipping Pope, or something?'

'No,' said Porrig. 'It's a joke. You said "*Big Issue*" and I said, "Bless you," as if you'd sneezed, you see. *Big Issue* sounds like Atishoo. It's really not funny if you have to explain it.'

'So you think homelessness is funny, do you?'

Porrig put down his suitcase. 'Well, obviously not *all* homelessness,' he explained. 'Homelessness brought on by deprivation, need and abuse wouldn't be too funny. But homelessness chosen as an alternative lifestyle, that's another matter.'

'I see,' said the youth.

'Not that I've got anything against alternative lifestyles,' Porrig went on. 'I'm all for them. If anyone wants to buck the system that's all right with me.'

'Most enlightened of you,' said the youth.

'It's everyone's right to rebel,' said Porrig.

'Here here,' said the youth.

'But not at my expense.'

'You flipping bounder!'

'Eh?' said Porrig.

'Life on the street is hard, mate. It's no laughing matter. I don't do this by choice.'

'Then get yourself a job,' said Porrig.

'I'm homeless, you flipper!'

'Well, get a job with a home thrown in. Caretaker, or light-house keeper, or North Sea oil driller, or performing in a circus or something.'

'Get real. There ain't any jobs like that. I'm a free spirit, me. The only jobs I could get would be unskilled slave labour. Washing dishes, or cleaning out toilets. And I'm not doing those.'

'You could get other jobs, you're not a loony or a cripple.'

'I'm not a slave either, mate. I'm not selling my soul to the work ethic. I'm a free spirit, I told you.'

'So hawking magazines on the streets in all weathers is your idea of being a free spirit?'

'You flipping flipper!'

'And what's all this "flipping" stuff? Don't you know how to swear?'

'I'm not allowed to swear. I'll lose my licence if I swear at people.'

'Oh, very free spirit.'

The youth headbutted Porrig and Porrig fell down on the pavement.

'Welcome to Brighton,' said the youth.

By the time Porrig regained consciousness the youth had departed. And so too had Porrig's suitcase. On the bright side, the unruly scrum surrounding the taxis had also departed and so Porrig was able to get himself a cab.

'Grand Parade please,' he said, in a dazed and dismal tone. 'The offices of Ashbury, Gilstock and Phart-Ebum.'

Grand Parade, as it happened, was only a few hundred yards from the station, although it did take the taxi driver nearly fifteen minutes to get there, by a route which took in the seafront and many places of local interest.

Porrig paid up the excessive fare and accepted his short change without complaint.

As irony would have it, the offices of Ashbury, Gilstock and Phart-Ebum were on the first floor, above a job centre that specialized in work for the homeless. Porrig gazed up at the building. It was Georgian. It was Grade Two listed.

Porrig went inside and humped his suitcase up the stairs. Then, recalling that his suitcase had been stolen, he thrust his hands into his trouser pockets and humped himself up instead, bewailing his lot as he did so.

He knocked on the door of the solicitors' office and it was opened by a young woman dressed in white. She was beautiful, pale and ethereal, with large dark eyes and Pre-Raphaelite hair. Her slender body was sheathed in a dress that seemed spun from sugar and Porrig was drawn at once to contemplate the glory of her breasts.

'Yeah?' said this vision of loveliness. 'Wotcha want?'

'I am Padraig Arthur Naseby,' said Porrig.

'Oh yeah. Your case comes up next week, don't it?'

'No,' said Porrig, shaking his head. 'I've come about my legacy.'

'Sorry. It's just your name, it sounds like—'

'Yes,' said Porrig. 'I know what it sounds like. But I'm here to claim my rightful inheritance.'

'You'd better come in then.'

Porrig followed the vision into the office and observed that she had a nice bum too. The vision placed her nice bum upon her office chair and began to root about through a lot of paperwork. 'It's in 'ere somewhere,' she said.

Porrig stood before her desk, feigning an interest in the

bookshelves while casting many a furtive glance towards the breasts of glory.

The vision looked up from her sifting of paper. 'Like the look of my tits, do you?' she asked.

Porrig, taken somewhat by surprise, could only mutter that he did.

'Well, don't get your hopes up. Unless you've inherited a million quid.'

'You'd have sex with me for a million quid then, would you?'

'Sure I would.'

'What about for half a million?'

'Yeah.'

Porrig dug into his trouser pocket. 'What about for twenty quid?'

'*Twenty quid?* What do you think I am?'

'I think we've established *what* you are. I thought we were just haggling over the price.'

'You're quite a comedian, ain't ya?'

'Not really.' Porrig grinned. 'I think Oscar Wilde said it first. Or perhaps it was Winston Churchill. It's usually one or the other.'

The vision dug into further papers and finally unearthed a file with Porrig's name on. This she opened to have a good old nose inside. At length she looked up and smiled. 'Well, you ain't inherited a million,' she said. 'So it looks like you'll have to go on wanking.'

Porrig eyed the outspoken vision. Could this be a match made in heaven? he wondered. Probably not, he concluded.

'So who do I have to see?' he asked.

'You'll have to see Mr Phart-Ebum.'

'Ah,' said Porrig. 'So that's how it's pronounced.'

Mr Phart-Ebum was about as broad as he was long. He wore a suit of orgone blue and a flower in his buttonhole which might have been a Sumatran dogwort, but was probably only a Cambodian marsh lily. He waved Porrig into an overstuffed chair and paced to and fro before the casement.

37

Porrig gazed approvingly about the elegant office. It looked just the way a solicitor's office should look. All those mahogany bookshelves and leather-bound legal tomes. And the Persian kilim and the partner's desk and the humidor and the Victorian drinks cabinet and the framed certificates and charters and—

'It's a sad old business,' said Mr Phart-Ebum.

'Is it?' Porrig asked.

'Death,' said the solicitor.

'No,' said Porrig. 'I can hear you just fine.'

Mr Phart-Ebum raised an eyebrow. 'Was that supposed to be funny?' he asked.

'I'm sorry,' said Porrig.

'You have blood on your nose.'

'I was attacked at the station. My suitcase was stolen.'

'Then we must call for the police.'

'No, don't bother with that. It was all my fault. I got what I deserved.'

'That's a most philosophical attitude.'

'Not really. It's just that I've had dealings with the police before. I have a tendency to say the wrong thing. It does not endear me to policemen.'

'Well, let us get down to business. You have the letter I sent you and some form of identification?'

Porrig had both and he showed these to Mr Phart-Ebum who nodded his head. 'All is in order then,' said he.

'Good,' said Porrig. 'So, about my planet . . .'

'Your planet?'

'ALPHA 17. That's a planet, isn't it?'

Mr Phart-Ebum shook his head. 'No,' he said. 'It's not.'

'Oh,' said Porrig. 'But it does *sound* like a planet.'

Mr Phart-Ebum nodded. 'But it's *not*. A breezeblock sounds like a bunk-up in a draughty alley. But it's *not*. You have *not* been left a planet.'

'Oh,' said Porrig. 'What a bummer.'

'You have been left a bookshop.'

'A bookshop?' said Porrig.

'Not a very large bookshop I hasten to add, and not a particularly successful one.'

'I would have preferred a planet,' said Porrig. 'And a bunk-up as well.'

'I'm sure that you would. But a bookshop it is, you can take it or leave it.'

'I'll take it.'

'Good man. Now there's some paperwork for you to sign and then I'll take you down and show you the premises.'

Porrig shrugged. 'All right,' he said, 'but I wonder if you wouldn't mind clearing up a couple of things that have been puzzling me.'

'Such as?'

'Such as exactly who this uncle of mine was. Neither my mum nor my dad will own up to him.'

'He was your mother's brother. They were not a close family, there was some acrimony. Although she did attend the funeral.'

'Did she? Then why wasn't I invited?'

'Because you weren't even born. Your uncle died thirty years ago.'

'I'm not getting this,' said Porrig. 'If he died before I was born, how could he leave me his bookshop?'

'He left it to the first-born son of his sister. Should she ever have a first-born son.'

'Then how come it's taken all this time for me to get it?'

'Legal complications.'

'You mean fat cat solicitors lining their pockets.'

'Would that be an example of the wrong things you say?'

'Fairly typical,' said Porrig.

'But in this case wholly justified. Your uncle did leave a great deal of money, but it was all swallowed up by legal costs. This was before my time here, of course. Such practices would no longer be tolerated. You will find that I am utterly scrupulous and quite beyond reproach.'

'I'll just bet you are,' said Porrig. And Mr Phart-Ebum raised his other eyebrow.

'Do you want to sign the papers and see your property?' he asked.

'I do.'

'Then here they are.'

Porrig signed what he was given. Naturally he neglected to read the small print. He'd had a rough day. Rougher so far than any he could remember. He just wanted to sign the papers and get a look at his bookshop. And perhaps get some lunch and a pint or two of beer. He was going to have to find somewhere to stay, too. He had quite a lot on his mind.

And so he didn't read the small print and he signed away a substantial sum of money into the Swiss bank account of Mr Phart-Ebum.

The solicitor smiled solicitously and then gathered up all of the papers.

'Will I get copies of those?' Porrig asked.

But Mr Phart-Ebum did not reply.

The vision in white had gone out for a bite, which, although poetic, meant that Porrig was denied another opportunity to ogle her breasts. But he wasn't too fazed. He was a man of substance now. A man of property. A man who owned a bookshop. And although he had not exactly received the flags-out and ticker-tape welcome, he felt that this town would be lucky for him. That he could make a new start here.

Something different. Something new. A new beginning.

He would work hard, he would change his ways, he would try not to offend and he would succeed.

In the words of Oscar Wilde he would 'live long and prosper'.

And so Porrig followed Mr Phart-Ebum as he led him through the streets of Brighton, a-whistling once more and completely unaware of the utterly horrendous things that fate was even now preparing to chuck in his direction.

It was going to have to be a good long chuck, because the events which would lead to these horrendous things occurring were presently unfolding in a far and distant place. But it would certainly be an accurate chuck, and although it would ultimately affect the lives of half the people living on the planet, it would affect no life more than that of Padraig Arthur Naseby.

And so, without further ado let us leave Brighton and travel south to far and distant climes.

To the island of Gwa'tan Qua Cest'l Potobo.

Yes indeed.

5

The tropical island of Gwa'tan Qua Cest'l Potobo lies in the Pacific Ocean, roughly three thousand miles north-east of the Tuamotu archipelago, and enjoys the benefits of both the equatorial counter-current and the south equator drift.

It is one of those earthly paradise lads, fringed about with waving palms, all dreamy sunsets and dazzling dawns. The natives enjoy a simple life of fishing and fornication. They shun material possessions and formalized religion, speak a basic language consisting of 352 words and engage in weekly *bluggas* (or 'piss-ups'), where they all get commode-hugging drunk on a local brew called *blug*, a cocktail of island fruits and fermented cows' urine.

Exactly why the likes of Thomas Cook and Richard Branson have so far failed to capitalize on this primitive people might well be explained by a translation of the island's name.

The first Westerner ever to come ashore was the infamous pirate captain Leonard 'Legless' Lemon in the year 1692. His ship, *The Shagger*, dropped anchor in the bay and lowered a longboat. Leonard was met on the beach by a fishing and fornication party and enquired the name of the island.

Gwa'tan Qua Cest'l Potobo, he was told. Which means:

'Bugger off back to where you came from, you white bastard, or we'll bung you in the cooking pot'.

The mistranslation of this by Leonard's Maori interpreter, who took the phrase to mean: 'You're all welcome ashore for a spot of the old jigger-jig and a slap-up fish supper', led to some unpleasantness and the origin of Leonard's nickname.

But that of course was long ago and since then many men have visited the island. Certainly few in the early days left with the requisite number of limbs, but over the years the natives have come to embrace certain aspects of Western civilization: nylon fishing lines, fruit-flavoured condoms and a selection of pharmaceuticals to stave off the more debilitating effects of *blug*. There is also now a small religious community dedicated to the worship of Carol Vorderman. The members of this cult hold that the shapely presenter with the laughing eyes and the calculating personality is a three-fold divinity, capable of tri-location, owing to her ability to appear on three television programmes simultaneously.

But apart from this the islanders keep themselves pretty much to themselves and resist the temptations of the outside world. And so it was only after much persuasion and negotiation, coupled with the promise of a signed photo of Carol, that a three-man party was finally allowed permission to fly out to Gwa'tan Qua Cest'l Potobo.

And thus it came to pass that even as Porrig toiled through the streets of Brighton, these three men, whose collective fate would soon become entangled with his own, were unloading supplies from a seaplane and rowing them ashore.

Of the three, one stood out immediately as being the leader, by virtue of his bearing and his height. Sir John Rimmer, the famous paranormal investigator and celebrated biographer of (amongst others) Hugo Rune, was a giant of a man. Nearly seven feet from toe to topknot, he carried with him an air of supreme authority.

It was rumoured that while still a child and not yet knighted by the Queen, his teachers had called him Sir. It was a good rumour and one of many that Sir John had put about himself. It wasn't strictly true, in fact it wasn't true at all, but it *was* a good story and it added to the image.

Sir John's boyhood had in truth been a time of torture and torment. His father had been the now legendary Sebastian 'Ringpiece' Rimmer, playboy adventurer and mucker to the late King George. And while Crowley was being damned by the yellow press as 'the wickedest man on Earth', 'Ringpiece' Rimmer was having at it with man, beast and backgammon board, frigging away the family fortune and indulging in practices which would have had even Crowley averting his eyes.

The difference between Aleister Crowley, self-styled Great Beast of the Apocalypse, and Sebastian 'Ringpiece' Rimmer, philanderer and ne'er-do-well, was that 'Ringpiece' did it with charm. And charm is like charisma, which is somewhat like stage presence. You either have it, or you don't.

'Ringpiece' had it, big time. So 'Ringpiece' had it good.

He was fêted. Folk loved him, forgave him, cancelled his debts and increased his credit line. He rubbed his tailored shoulders against the good and great and, though many times he put a foot wrong, he never stepped in the doo-doo.

The son was dwarfed by the father: although he outgrew him physically, he could never outgrow him in charm. Sir John was a charmless child who grew into a charmless adult. And those who lack for charm, make up for it in bluster.

With height to his advantage (and some advantage that was), Sir John took to looking down upon the world. Aloft, aloof and alone, he sought to make a name for himself and one that would be remembered.

Sir John Rimmer.

Just plain *John* wouldn't do. And, as it was unlikely that he would ever actually be knighted, John changed his name by deed poll to *Sir John*. It was perfectly legal and made up for any lost time.

And it carries quite some clout in certain circles.

Much time might be spent and much ink shed in setting down a record of Sir John's exploits. They lacked not for adventure, nor for courage, nor for self-publicity. But where the fact ended and fantasy began, who can truly say? It was certainly true that he was presently employed by a mysterious government department known as the Ministry of Serendipity. This body's currency was 'The Strange'. It had fingers in many odd pies and very long arms indeed. But exactly what Sir John's involvement was with the ministry, is something that will soon be explained.

For now, what more of the man?

Of his looks: they were impressive, with his great height and practised noble bearing. But to these he added a finishing touch: the beard. Many a great man has had a great beard. Karl Marx, Ernest Hemingway, Giant Haystacks, ZZ Top. But Sir John Rimmer's out-greated them all. It was a blinder of a beard, a magnificent piece of face furniture. Ruby red and teased and twirled into a riot of beribboned ringlets, it was a beard to reckon with and it reached right down to his dongler.

On this particular day, and in this particular region, the beard was in company with 'tropical kit'. Sir John wore a solar topi and one of those *Sir* Richard Attenborough safari suits. And it does have to be said that few men living can dress like that and carry it off.

Sir John was accompanied upon this occasion, as upon many previous, by his two loyal, although singularly less famous companions. The first of these was Dr Harney, Fellow of the Royal Society and advisor to certain covert government operational units on the retrieval and study of downed alien spacecraft. All governments have such advisors, because most governments have one or two downed alien spacecraft knocking about in their military aircraft hangars. Not that they'll own up to it, and why should they, eh?

Dr Harney's upbringing was somewhat different to Sir John's. He came from a normal background. All right, so what's *normal*? Well, how about *average*? How about *functional*? How about *ordinary*?

Dr Harney's dad was ordinary. He had an ordinary job at an ordinary factory. His mum was an ordinary mum, who, in those days when ordinary mums didn't go out to work, stayed at home and brought up her ordinary children in an ordinary house in an ordinary street in an ordinary town. One of those houses in one of those streets that Porrig had gazed upon as he travelled down to Brighton on the train.

Ordinary. Everyday. Safe.

Well, that's what it looks like if you don't screw up your eyes.

Dr Harney had been an ordinary child. Not too dim and not too bright. Good enough at games to avoid ridicule, but not good enough to shine. He drifted along through his ordinary childhood into ordinary adolescence. And he would no doubt have drifted into ordinary adulthood had not someone bunged him a tab of acid.

It was his sixteenth birthday party, it was 1967 and ordinary folk were turning on. Someone turned on Dr Harney and Dr Harney screwed up his eyes, then opened them very wide.

Dr Harney took the hippy trail. Dr Harney sought enlightenment. Dr Harney fell in with strange folk and took many strange drugs. And Dr Harney was no longer ordinary. No longer everyday. No longer safe. He took a doctorate of parapsychology at Cal Tech. He became Dr Harney.

Now he was middle-aged, a jolly freckle-faced fellow, whose conical head, enveloped in a froth of white hair, had the appearance of a mountain peak capped by cloud. He was far from ordinary, and he was here. And very much the brains behind Sir John.

The third member of this redoubtable party was Danbury Collins, the psychic youth and masturbator. Danbury was a furtive-looking individual with hollow red-rimmed eyes and hairs upon the palms of his hands. Although frequently to be found engaged in his favourite pastime, he possessed certain rare gifts which made him invaluable to Sir John: the ability to programme video recorders, for instance, and to know which queue to join at a supermarket checkout. Danbury had never once stepped in dog poo, nor been fouled by pigeon guano. His giro always arrived on time and if he ever visited the shoe sales, no matter which style he chose, they always had his size in stock.

Bastard! And done with no charm whatsoever!

But more than this, young Danbury had a nose for impending

45

danger which had saved his two companions' lives on more than one occasion. So even though they didn't like him very much, him being such an inveterate pud-puller and everything, he was worth his weight in mucky mags in a tricky situation.

And so what, it might well be asked, was this notable trio doing on Gwa'tan Qua Cest'l Potobo?

Had they come for a holiday, perhaps? To enjoy the dubious pleasures of *blug* and a bit of the old F and F? Or could it be possible, just possible, that they were here upon some secret mission? Some psychic quest? Some investigation into an ancient mystery that would lead them into danger, peril and high adventure?

Well, yes, it could.

Danbury Collins hauled the final weighty wooden crate up the beach and sat down heavily upon it. 'I notice,' he said as he did so, 'that all these boxes bear government seals.'

'MoS,' said Dr Harney, dropping down beside him on the sand. 'Ministry of Serendipity, Mornington Crescent. They are funding this expedition.'

Sir John's gaunt shadow fell across the doctor. 'I think it might be a sound idea for us to arm ourselves with a few stout sticks,' he said. 'I spy a number of natives skulking amongst the palm trees. One of them is wearing a chef's hat and another has a bag of charcoal.'

'Just let them try something,' said Danbury, patting at the bulge in his red cagoule. 'I came tooled up.'

'Is that a gun in your pocket?' asked the doctor. 'Or are you—'

'My old man's service revolver. I smuggled it out in the diplomatic bag.'

'Most enterprising.'

'I had a "certain feeling" that it might come in handy.'

Sir John nodded approvingly. 'I have come to rely on your "certain feelings",' he said. 'The guide I have engaged should be with us in about ten minutes. He speaks pidgin English and he has arranged accommodation for us. In the meanwhile we had best be on our guard.'

'No sweat, Sir John,' said the psychic youth. 'And while we're waiting, perhaps Dr Harney would like to fill us in on all the details of what exactly we're doing here.'

'I would,' said that man. 'I would indeed.'

'Then please do,' said Sir John.

'It is a most incredible business,' said the good doctor, rising to his sandalled feet and patting the sand from his strides, 'and has been pieced together, partly from speculation, partly from historical records and partly from physical evidence. All may not be entirely correct, but I believe I can offer an overview of the situation.

'Let us begin with a degree of speculation. Let us envisage a super-civilization somewhere in a distant galaxy. This civilization is technologically advanced, it is benign, it is sophisticated. The folk here have eradicated illness and put an end to war. There is no poverty, there is no want. These folk live long and prosper.'

The doctor paused on the off chance that some running gag concerning Oscar Wilde was about to be slipped in here, but as none was, he continued.

'Utopia,' the doctor said. 'Or so it would appear. But disaster looms. Population growth is outstripping food production, natural resources are being depleted. In short, time is running out. It is reasonable to surmise that should our civilization continue, we will encounter these very problems and sooner rather than later.

'And so, what is to be done? As I said, this is a technologically advanced civilization. These people have the ability to construct spacecraft. Migration and the colonization of new worlds would seem a viable option.'

'If they had the ability to locate these worlds,' said Danbury. 'Had they?'

'No, they had not. But they had the capability to mass produce the craft. By the hundreds, by the thousands. And they found no shortage of volunteers to risk a voyage into the unknown.'

'Your Thomas Cook and Richard Branson types,' said Danbury.

'Quite so. The idea was that they would be put into cryogenic suspension inside the spacecraft and then shot off into the void. The spacecraft were equipped with sensors that would scan for suns of a suitable magnitude, then automatically monitor any orbiting planets, searching for vital signs, radio emissions, favourable atmosphere, gravity, whatever.

'If it came up trumps, the spacecraft would land and defrost its occupant. And if he found that all was well he would radio his position back to the home planet.'

'Hum,' said Danbury. 'I do foresee a few flaws in this. Such as how far one would have to travel and how long the journey might take.'

'Exactly. And it was understood that most of the spacecraft would probably speed on for ever and ever. But the future of their civilization depended upon it. What other option did they have? And if one single astronaut were to strike it lucky, then all the rest would have died in a worthy cause.'

'A noble enterprise,' said Danbury. 'And did one strike it lucky?'

'Yes, one did. His spacecraft came upon a golden sun lighting up a circlet of planets, and amongst these planets it found one that was perfect. The one we call Earth.'

'I had a certain feeling this would be the case.'

'Our chap's spacecraft drops down onto Earth. He defrosts, but, oh calamity, one hundred thousand years have passed, his civilization is gone into dust and he is all alone.'

'How sad.'

'There's worse.'

'There's worse?'

'Far worse. Our chap is damaged, both mentally and physi-cally. Cryogenic suspension is an untried science. No-one can predict what will happen to a being that is deep frozen for a thousand years, let alone one hundred thousand. Our chap went in as a benign adventurer, he has emerged as a crippled psychopathic monster.'

'Oh dear.'

'And he has developed powers.'

'What powers?'

'Telepathic powers. Although the freezing had damaged his

physical brain, his mind had developed over the long years. He was now capable of imposing his thoughts physically upon others. He could hurt them with his mind. Inflict mental and physical anguish upon them. Force them to do his bidding.'

'I don't like the sound of that one bit.'

'I'm sure you don't. But nevertheless it was true. In fact all over the world we have evidence of this being's existence. Works of monumental masonry dating back to the megalithic period. He forced thousands into his service, driving them with mental torment to achieve his ends. Our old friend Stonehenge for example. Massive stones dragged for many miles across rugged terrain. Not dragged there by choice, or at the bidding of a priesthood. Dragged by *his* slaves and hoisted into place to provide a shelter for *him*.

'And he survived. He lived for centuries. Carnac, the pyramids; all his doing, the work of his will. People were cattle to him; he drove them until they died.'

'Why didn't they revolt?'

'How could they revolt? His will was too strong. The mental control he exerted, the pain he could inflict was too great. Unbearable. None could stand against him.'

'So what happened to this tyrannical monster?'

'Mu,' said Dr Harney.

'Meow,' said Danbury Collins.

'Not *mew*, you stupid boy, *Mu*! The lost continent of Mu. It went down, like Atlantis. Natural catastrophy.'

'*Cat*-astrophy,' said Danbury, 'ha ha ha.'

'Smack him,' said Sir John. 'I find it helps if he gets silly.'

Dr Harney smacked the psychic youth and Danbury made a sour face. 'So he went down with Mu,' he said. 'Then that is that and a good thing too.'

'It is not the end of the story.'

'It's enough for me,' said the lad, his right hand straying once more to his trouser pocket. 'Down with Mu will do for me.'

'I will, however, tell you the rest. What I have told you so far regarding his rule on Earth has been pieced together from ancient texts and hieroglyphics. Allow me to quote to you from one of the last.

'And as the ground shook and the temple fell The God did enter into His shield. And His shield was as a seven-pointed star and at its heart a tomb of ice. And the shield did close upon The God and did rise into the heavens.

'So he took off in search of other worlds to conquer.

'But the heavens were troubled and all about a storm did rage. And The God fell once more to earth a great way off and never was He seen again.'

'Crash bang wallop,' said Danbury, 'and a good thing too.'
'There's a little bit more.'
'Go on then.'

'And the people that did dwell behind, those who had served The God, did cry out in a loud voice, saying, "Bloody good riddance," and did bare their bottoms in the direction of His passing and make with gestures that were lewd and most profane.'

'As well they might.'
'Agreed,' said the doctor. 'And there for the most part you have it. Part conjecture, part historical account and please would you not do that while I'm talking to you.'

Danbury untrousered his hand. 'I recall,' he said, 'that you mentioned "partly physical evidence". By that did you mean the monumental architecture?'

'No, I meant the satellite photographs from a recent geophysical survey. It was carried out by the Ministry of Serendipity to map the movements of the continental shelves and record undersea activity, volcanic and the like. Plate tectonics, you know the kind of business. Allow me to show you this.'

Dr Harney took from his case a large transparent sheet of film, not unlike an X-ray plate. 'Take a look and tell me what you see.'

Danbury examined the sheet. 'An area stretching from the

western coastline of South America to the Tuamoto island chain. These would appear to be undersea fault-lines and we would be about . . .'

'Here,' said Dr Harney, pointing. 'Now allow me to show you a blow-up of this area.'

Danbury examined this. 'I see,' said he. 'We're just here.'

'And that?'

The lad squinted. 'Just off the southern coast. It looks to be . . .'

'A star with seven points.'

'I see.'

'It's there, my boy. Out there.' The doctor gestured to the open sea. 'Half a mile away and in less than fifty feet of water. Thrown up by recent volcanic activity, and waiting . . .'

'For us to recover it? That's why we're here, to recover it?'

'Before the Americans do. Steal a march on the blighters, eh?'

'I see.'

'Think of the technology. This spacecraft would appear to be intact. This would make it the first ever to be recovered in one piece. The advances in technology to be gained from an examination of it are inestimable. This is a salvage operation, Danbury. This is history in the making.'

'I see,' said Danbury once more. 'Now just let me get this straight. You are suggesting that we haul up an alien spacecraft and ship it back to England. An alien spacecraft that in all probability contains a mad alien in cryogenic suspension. A mad alien that, were he to get thawed out, has the mental power to control human beings. To drive them to fulfil his every wild demand. To drive them like cattle until they die. That is what we are here for.'

Dr Harney nodded. 'Do you have a problem with that?' he asked.

'Well . . .' said Danbury Collins.

6

'Well,' said Mr Phart-Ebum. 'Here we are and this is it.'
Porrig looked up. 'Oh,' he said, and, 'Wow, and I mean,
oh yeah! All right!'

The shopfront was magnificent. All pastel colours and under-
stated elegance. Above the broad window hung a chromium and
pink enamel winged pig motif.

'But I thought you said that it wasn't successful.' Porrig stared
awestruck and all overwhelmed. 'This is a Flying Pig bookshop.
One of the great chain that began in Crow Street, Dublin, with
the now legendary O'Mealoid and Bacon partnership. These
shops carry the finest selection of sf, paranormal, cult, occult
and God-knows-what-altogether books in the world. They're
internationally famous.'

Porrig peered in through the window. Sophisticated custom-
ers, those smart young types who still read books, browsed
amongst the stylish shelves. Music that could only be described
as 'cool' came drifting through the doorway.

Porrig's heart rose towards the heavens. He had really
fallen on his feet this time. This was the big one. To own a
branch of the Flying Pig chain. This was wonderful. Incredible.

'Now, I have your key here,' said Mr Phart-Ebum. 'Where exactly did I put it?'

'Never mind about the key.' Porrig rubbed his hands together. 'Let's go inside and see how much money they've taken today.'

'How much what?' Mr Phart-Ebum stared at Porrig and followed the direction of his eager gaze. Then Mr Phart-Ebum began to laugh.

'What are you laughing at?' Porrig asked.

'Oh, nothing. I mean, well . . . you didn't think that . . . Oh, you did . . . Oh, I am so sorry.'

'What?'

'You thought that *that* was your bookshop. I really am so sorry.'

'What?'

'That isn't yours. Yours is the one next door.'

'*What?*'

'That one there.'

Porrig stared. 'What one where? What shop?'

'Right here.' Mr Phart-Ebum pointed.

'But there isn't any shop. Just a derelict building with posters plastered all over it.'

'The shutters are a might gummed up, I suppose. But then they would be. No-one's opened them for thirty years.'

Porrig's heart went sink

sink

sink.

'Ah yes,' said Mr Phart-Ebum. 'Here's your key. Will I do the honours, or will you?'

Porrig looked up at the building. It was tiny. It was wretched. Paint hung from its front wall in scabious flakes. The upper windows were fogged by the grime of three decades. Most were broken. Pigeons cooed from roosts within.

A low and dismal groan arose from Porrig's throat and issued through his mouth.

'I will then,' said the solicitor, approaching the door. A fetid mattress lay across it. The smell of urine hung in the air. Mr Phart-Ebum prodded the mattress with a polished toe-cap. 'Best left alone, I think,' he continued, as he eased the old key into the lock. 'I might need a hand here getting this open.'

Porrig stood in the sunshine, shaking his head. 'Not from me,' he said slowly. 'Not from me.'

'Oh come on, Mr Naseby.'

'No,' said Porrig. 'I think I'll just stand here and bewail my lot, if that's all right with you.'

Mr Phart-Ebum was shouldering the door. 'It's giving,' he said. 'I've got it open a bit.'

'Leave it,' said Porrig. 'Forget it.'

'But aren't you anxious to take a look inside?'

'Are you jesting? I know what will be inside. A lot of rotten, mouldy old rubbish and no doubt the floorboards will collapse and plunge me to my death.'

'Ah,' said the solicitor, who now had the door half open. 'You might well have a point there.' He tugged the key from the lock and presented it to Porrig. 'Well, I have conducted you to the premises and given you the key. My duties are therefore con-cluded. Do you wish me to send the bill for my services to your home address, or will you be taking up residence here?' Mr Phart-Ebum caught the eye of Porrig. And a bitter eye it was.

'Just one thing,' said the lad, 'before you go.'

'Oh yes?'

'I don't even know the name of this dead uncle of mine.'

'You are thinking perhaps of putting up a blue plaque?' Mr Phart-Ebum had a real smirk on.

'Not that.' Porrig shook his head fiercely. 'It is just that in order to curse the soul of someone properly, you have to know their name.'

'Indeed? Well, in all truth I don't know his original name. He had it changed by deed poll when he first went on the stage. All I know is his professional name.'

'Which was?'

'Apocalypso The Miraculous.'

Porrig choked. 'The Miraculous?'

'With a capital *T* in the *The*. He was very famous in his day. You can look him up in books.'

'Not in this shop,' said Porrig bitterly.

'Well, in the one next door then.' Mr Phart-Ebum made throat-clearing noises. 'And so, I must be off about my business and leave you to yours.' He took Porrig's dangling hand between his own and shook it. And then, chuckling like a bad'n, he went on his way.

Porrig gave a deep and heart-felt sigh. He should never have got his hopes up really. Good things never came in his direction. He was just one of life's losers, doomed ever to disappointment and blows to the skull.

Porrig squinted in through the half-open door. It looked pretty grim in there. Dark and dank and quite without a welcome.

Was it worth a look inside, or should he just get back on the train and go home?

'Home,' said Porrig. 'I don't think I can take any more.' He turned the old key on the palm of his hand. He would lock the place up and go home. He could call Mr Phart-Ebum later. Tell him to put the building on the market. Property was always worth something, even if you just knocked it down and levelled the ground for a car-park.

Porrig stepped nimbly over the mattress and tugged at the ancient door. It was all jammed up with rubbish now and Porrig fought to close it. The door seemed disinclined to close. 'I am an open door now,' it seemed to say, 'and I will stay that way.'

'Oh no you bloody won't.' Porrig struggled and strained and sweated and swore. And then he slipped upon something unspeakable and plunged headlong through the doorway.

Porrig now found himself lying face down on the floor. A sad and sorry sight was he. A glum and gloomy grizzler. Porrig thrashed his legs about and drummed his fists on the floor. Only the previous night his mother had behaved in this same fashion. She, however, had been all convulsed with laughter. Porrig now knew why that was. Porrig thrashed and Porrig drummed, but laughter wasn't in it.

'Aaaaaaaaaagh!' went Porrig, wishing not only that he was dead, but indeed that he never had been born. Although not a one for religion, he now prayed hard that the angel the old bloke

55

on the train had told him of might fly down from heaven this very instant and carry him off to a far better place.

'Aaaaaaaaaagh!' he went once more.

Passers-by in the street made the sign of the cross and hurried on by with their shopping.

'God's bollocks!' Porrig kicked about and tried to gain his feet. He stumbled up, put out his hand to support himself on the wall and in doing so pressed down the light switch.

Lightning flashed and tore about the shop and Porrig ducked his head. 'I'm sorry, God,' he mumbled. The lightning stopped and Porrig blinked his eyes.

Not lightning.

Neon ceiling lights.

The lights had come on to illuminate . . .

A stunningly beautiful bookshop interior, all polished ebony bookshelves and Victorian leather-bound books.

Sadly, no.

The lights had come on to illuminate a long, low-ceilinged room, furnished all about with shelves. But not one book upon them.

'Not a single sodding book,' said Porrig. 'Not a single one.'

But plenty of cardboard boxes.

Porrig managed one more sigh, straightened himself up as best he could and peered at the boxes. There were dozens of them on the shelves. All open-topped and packed with something or other. Porrig dug into the nearest one and pulled out . . .

'A comic book,' said Porrig. He moved along the shelves, peeping into the boxes. 'They're all packed with comic books. And they're . . .' Porrig examined the one in his hand. It was Marvel Comics' issue number one of *The Silver Surfer*.

Porrig gaped at it, then gaped at it again. 'Issue number one,' he gasped in a very choked kind of a whisper. 'Issue number one.'

This shop was full of thirty-year-old comic books. And if they were all like this one, all in mint condition . . . untouched and unread, pristine, perfect . . .

Porrig stared at the treasure in his hands. He didn't need to strain his brain to know what this was worth. If there was one thing he did know about, it was comic books. He had the price guide at home, but this was easy stuff. Your starter for ten.

Magnus Magnusson: The price please of Marvel Comics' issue number one of *The Silver Surfer*?

Padraig Arthur Naseby: One thousand, four hundred and fifty quid!

'Oh, dear God,' prayed Porrig. 'Please let it be true. Please don't let me be lying unconscious on the floor dreaming this.'

Porrig dared another look at the comic. If he were dreaming it would probably change into a pork sausage. Things often did in his dreams, although he had never been able to find out why. The comic book was not a sausage. It was still *The Silver Surfer*.

Porrig's hands began to tremble; he glanced about in sudden fear. Fear that someone might burst in and steal it all away.

Porrig rammed shut the door and locked it from the inside. Then he took a great breath. Turned slowly to survey the room. And then went just a little mad.

He rushed along the shelves, going from box to box to box, pulling out comics (though with great care) and letting free cries of delight.

The Mighty Thor, Dr Strange, The Fantastic Four, Spiderman, the entire early Marvel back catalogue. All new. All unread. All in mint condition.

'I'm rich!' Porrig danced a silly jig. 'I'm rich. I've done it. I've hit the mother lode.' He found himself now at the rear of the shop and here he came upon a big plan chest.

Porrig eased out a drawer, bringing to light something beautiful. Porrig stared down at it. A poster. A 1960s poster. A Martin Sharp poster. The famous Bob Dylan 'Blowing in the Mind' poster, printed in black and red on gold card. Porrig dug into the drawer. There were five copies. And beneath this, five copies of the 'Putting together of the Heads' 1967 legalise cannabis classic.

'Jesus' Jumpsuit!' Porrig had seen photos of these in an auction catalogue. How much had they gone for?

'Lots,' said Porrig. 'Lots and lots.'

And the ones in the auction had been second-hand, and these

were perfect. Perfect. Porrig opened further drawers and revealed further wonders. Mike English posters. The Hapshash and the Coloured Coat ones of Hendrix and the Floyd and The Incredible String band. Porrig pushed in the bottom drawer and sat down on the floor.

This was it. The collector's dream come true. The place that every collector fantasizes about. The warehouse no-one has opened for a century. Great-granddaddy's attic. Aunty Nora's cellar.

Uncle Apocalypso's shop!

And this *was it*. He'd found it. He, Porrig the no-mark. He'd hit the jackpot. And why? Why him?

'Because I deserve it,' said Porrig. 'Because I am the only person in the whole wide world who really truly deserves it. I have been sorely tried and cruelly tested and I have been found not wanting. It is my destiny to be wealthy and successful. It is my fate.'

And satisfied with this load of old tosh, Porrig actually offered up a prayer of thanks. A real one. 'Thank you, God,' prayed Porrig. 'And thank you too, Uncle Apocalypso The Miraculous, with the capital T.'

Porrig wept a little tear for his defunct uncle and also for himself, because he was now a man of possessions and a man of possessions can be a worried man. Porrig's first reaction upon seeing his treasure had been to slam and lock the door, which had worried him at the time. The sheer instinctiveness of the act. Instant covetousness and instant paranoia. All of this was all too much. Half of it would have done. A quarter. But all? What was he to do with it? How could he sell it? Whom could he trust? One of the big auction houses? Anyone?

Porrig now felt a wee bit wobbly. He climbed slowly to his feet and took another look around. 'Pull yourself together,' he whispered. 'Don't go to pieces.'

Then he spied the staircase. More upstairs? More stock? The stair light also worked and Porrig peered up the narrow stairway. 'Easy now,' he told himself. 'Don't rush it. One rotten stair and you'll be joining your uncle.' But the stairs looked safe and

Porrig took a step or two before he paused and looked back into the shop.

Something wasn't right about that shop.

Something that should be there, wasn't.

And Porrig now knew what that something was.

'Dust,' said Porrig. 'There's no dust.'

He examined his hands.

They were clean.

Porrig returned to the shop. He ran his finger along the nearest shelf. Dust free. Not a speck.

Now that did not make any sense at all. A shop locked up for thirty years and not a trace of dust?

'Let's check upstairs.'

Porrig checked upstairs. He did tread with considerable care, but the stairs held. The stairs, with their nicely well-swept carpet, held. On the first floor he was met by another surprise. Another working light displayed a room full of machinery. It was all most impressive. All buffed up brass and steel. It was . . .

'A printing press.' Porrig whistled. 'It's a printing press.'

He circled the machine, admiring all its polished bits and bobs. This was a real deluxe jobbie. Ideal for . . .

'Printing comics.' Porrig whistled once again. 'Why, with a rig-out like this I could print my own comic books. No more rejection slips from publishers.'

This was bliss. Oh perfect day. And Porrig engaged in another foolish jig.

Then he explored a bit more. He came upon a small bath-room and a tiny kitchenette. They were nothing special. But they were both impeccably clean.

'Still no dust.' Porrig shook his head. So what about the front room with the broken windows and the roosting pigeons? Porrig opened the door and switched on the light.

The curtains were drawn. The room was pristine. A bed of burnished brass, covered by a colourful quilt. A pitch pine wardrobe and a matching dresser. Landscapes in gilded frames and a very nice rug indeed.

Porrig crossed the room and flung aside the curtains. Pigeons fluttered up in a panic, but didn't fly into the room. A sheet of glass barred their way. It was sealed to the bedroom wall a foot inside the outer broken panes.

'Clever,' said Porrig, nodding his head. 'A clever deception to make it seem from the outside that . . .' He paused and a little chill ran down his spine. 'That this is a derelict building, which clearly it is not. Someone's living here.'

Porrig returned to the kitchenette and opened the fridge. It was packed with food. He took out a carton of organic milk and sniffed at the top. It was fresh.

'Oh shit!' said Porrig. 'I've got a squatter.'

And then he heard a sound downstairs.

Porrig froze.

Someone was entering the shop, and not by the front door. This someone was whistling in that carefree 'this is my house and I'll whistle in it if I want to' kind of way.

'Oh shit,' said Porrig. 'Shit shit shit.'

So what to do? Confront the squatter? Order him off the premises? Use force if necessary? How much force? And how big the squatter? The *one* squatter, was it? Or maybe there was more than one . . .

Porrig sought a weapon: a rolling pin or a big kitchen cleaver. Porrig found a diminutive pink plastic dish-washing brush. He took it up and held it in a menacing fashion. No dirty squatter was going to deprive him of his inheritance. He would fight to the death to protect what was his.

Well, maybe not to the death, but he'd give the bastard a sound brushing up for his trouble.

'Try and steal from me, will you?' whispered Porrig.

But then a thought struck him. It was a thought so terrible that Porrig tried at once to force it from his mind. But the thought wouldn't budge. It stayed and it grew. And it grew.

'Now what,' said this thought, 'if all that stuff downstairs doesn't actually belong to you at all? What if it actually belongs to the confident whistler who's just walked in? He could well have come across this empty untenanted building years ago and taken up residence here. Which would mean that none of it's yours, Porrig.

'None of it, you useless no-mark loser!'

'Oh no.' Porrig's knees became weak and he sank onto the kitchen chair. It couldn't be true. It just couldn't.

But oh yes it could. It would all make sense that way. All of it. Someone living here and carrying on their own business. It was probably those swine from The Flying Pig next door, using the place as an annexe.

Porrig sought a knife to end it all. Enough was enough. He had suffered much more than any man should suffer. It was time to take the gentleman's way out.

As no knife was forthcoming Porrig solemnly took up the pink plastic brush and began to rake at his wrist.

And then he heard the footsteps on the stairs.

And the whistling grew louder.

And—

'Hello there,' said a voice.

Porrig abandoned his suicide attempt. He looked up and he stared.

In the doorway stood the pimpled youth from the station. He was holding Porrig's suitcase.

'Aaaaaaaaaagh!' Porrig leaped for the throat. 'You thieving bastard. You're gonna die.'

He caught the youth off balance and the two tumbled out of the kitchenette and onto the landing. Porrig was no fighter, but his mind was now so scrambled up that he fought like the madman he was. The youth, however, was not without some martial skills; he parried Porrig's every blow and countered with no small number of his own.

In fact, to use the parlance of the fighting fraternity, he kicked the shit out of Porrig.

'No more.' Porrig curled up in a ball on the landing floor. 'I give up. Let me crawl away to die.'

The youth, who'd been putting in the boot, straightened up. 'Are you absolutely sure you've had enough?' he asked.

'I am,' whimpered Porrig.

'Only I really do enjoy a bit of violence. It's in my nature, you see. I come from a broken home.'

'I'm sorry about that,' moaned Porrig. 'I really am.'

'Oh, don't be. It was me who broke it.' The youth made unpleasant sniggering sounds. 'Come on, take another pop at me. You never know, you might strike lucky.'

'Lucky?' Porrig gave a sickly laugh. 'Me, lucky? I don't think so.'

'Oh well, as you please. Do you want a cup of tea then?'

'A cup of tea?' Porrig uncurled a little and peeped up at his tormentor. 'You're offering me a cup of tea?'

'Or coffee, whichever you prefer. It's decaff, of course. Gotta look after your health.'

'My health?' Porrig clutched at his ribs. They were broken, he was sure.

'I stick to a wholefood diet,' said the youth proudly. 'Strictly vegetarian and macrobiotic.'

'That's probably why you have such a spotty face,' observed Porrig and the boot went in again.

'Oh, I'm so sorry,' said the youth in a genuine tone. 'You've got a lairy mouth and I've got a short temper. Not a very good combination, is it?'

'No,' Porrig groaned.

'So we'll both have to try a little harder. Would you like a cup of tea?'

'Yes please,' said Porrig, through gritted teeth.

The youth helped Porrig up, led him into the kitchenette and set him down on the chair. 'I'll put on the kettle,' he said.

Porrig sat and hugged at his ribs. The youth filled up the kettle. 'My name's Wok Boy,' he said. 'Though I won't tell you why. And yours is Porrig, of course.'

'You what?'

'I'm sorry I had to nut you at the station. We got off to a bit of a wonky start, didn't we?'

'How do you know my name?'

'Well, I was supposed to meet you and extend you a warm welcome.'

'You what?' said Porrig once again.

'Meet you and bring you here. But I didn't know it was actually you until I had a look in your suitcase. But then when I went back to the station, you'd gone. I figured you'd show up here eventually, so I just dossed about for a bit. I didn't want to be here in case that slag Phart-Ebum came inside. He didn't, did he?'

'No he didn't. Look, what's going on?'

'I really am sorry I had to nut you at the station, but you did ask for it, didn't you?'

'What is going on?' Porrig asked once again. 'What are you doing here? Why were you supposed to meet me? How do you know about Phart-Ebum? Why—'

'One thing at a time. What sort of tea do you like? Orange Sunset or Peach Truffle?'

'Peach Truffle?'

'Oh good, that's my favourite too.'

'Stop fucking me about,' said Porrig.

'Easy, pal,' said Wok Boy, displaying a well-made fist.

'All right,' said Porrig. 'Just one question. The stuff downstairs. Who does it belong to?'

'You, of course.'

'It's really mine?'

'It's really yours.'

'I don't get this.'

'It's really simple,' said Wok Boy. 'There's no great mystery.' He lit the stove and put the kettle on to boil. 'This old bloke employed me to clean up the shop. Clear out all the old crap that was in it. Give the place a lick of paint. Bring down all these cartons of comic books he had stored in London. Restore the printing press. I've been working here for months getting everything prepared for you.'

'For me?'

'He wanted everything to be exactly as you'd have wanted it to be. It's all yours, all of it. All he wants you to do for him is draw him a comic.'

'What comic?'

'I don't know *what* comic. He didn't tell me everything. But it's something very special. He's got a real bee in his old bonnet about it. You are an artist, aren't you? You can draw?'

'Of course I can draw. Didn't you see my stuff when you nosed through my suitcase?'

'Oh yeah. Gyp the Crip, wasn't it?'

'Jazz the Spaz.'

'You wanker,' said Wok Boy.

'How dare you!'

'Well, get a grip. Jazz the Spaz? Whatever goes on in your head?'

'Look, forget about my head. It's confused enough as it is. This old bloke who's done all this for me. Who is he? What's his name?'

'He never told me his name. The people round here all call him the wizard. But he doesn't look much like a wizard to me. Actually he looks more like a dog. He's got these two white tufts of hair that stick up like big ears and—'

Porrig's eyes grew wide. 'Two white tufts of hair,' he said slowly.

'And he's well hard,' said Wok Boy, popping two pink teabags into cups. 'I wouldn't want to piss around with him, even though he's old and frail-looking. He says he knows—'

'Dimac,' whispered Porrig.

'Yeah, that's it. Oh yeah, and he said I was to give you this.' Wok Boy dug into the pocket of his greasy jeans and brought out a crumpled envelope.

Porrig took it and tore it open.

'What's in there?' Wok Boy asked.

'A business card,' said Porrig. He took it out and stared at it.

On the card was printed a seven-pointed star.

A seven-pointed star and a name.

Porrig read the name aloud.

The name was *Apocalypso The Miraculous*.

7

' Nuke it,' said Danbury.
'Pardon?' said Sir John.

'Nuke it and I'm not kidding.'

Sir John Rimmer diddled with his twiddly-diddly beard.
'What exactly are you trying to say?'

'I'm trying to say nuke it.' Danbury threw up his wandering
hands. 'I have been on edge ever since I stepped down from the
plane.'

'And fell in the water,' said the doctor.

'All right, yes. But I knew that there was something very
wrong here. And it's not just the blokes with the knives and
forks. Clear the island. Call up the MoS. Get them to nuke the
alien.'

'Nuking is not an option,' said Sir John.

Danbury threw down his wandering hands. 'Look,' said he.
'Don't you ever go to the movies? This is standard sci-fi fare.
Spaceship is brought up from the depths, mad alien thaws out,
hell and horror all around, thousands flee in terror and a bloody
big explosion at the end. Why not cut around all the bad stuff
while we have the chance? Nuke the bastard now.'

Dr Harney shrugged. 'The pud-puller does have a point, you

know. If the alien were to thaw out, there's no telling what might happen.'

Sir John ceased to diddle with his twiddly bits. 'There will be no nuking and that is that,' he said in a very firm tone.

Danbury's hands returned to his trouser pockets. 'Then leave it,' he said. 'Just leave it where it is. Call up the MoS. Tell them we have checked it out and it's not a spaceship at all, it's a big starfish, or a rock formation or something.'

'Or something?'

'Or anything. Bluff it. Just do it.'

Sir John Rimmer shook his hirsute head. 'No,' he said and, 'no no no. It just wouldn't wash. For all we know the Americans are already on their way.'

'Stuff the bloody Americans. In fact, let the bloody Americans have it. They were so gung-ho in *Independence Day*, let's see how smart they are when they come up against the real thing.'

Sir John gazed out at the ocean blue.

Dr Harney scuffed sand with his sandally shoe.

Danbury played with his old plonkeroo.

And a crab scuttled sideways, well what a to-do.

Sir John turned sharply to avoid things slipping off on some poetic tangent. Shaking his noble head, he paced back and forwards, making 'quack quack' noises and doing a passable impression of Max Wall. At length he performed a cartwheel and a double back somersault and came to rest in the splits position. 'What if we were to retrieve the spacecraft and then carefully dispose of its occupant?' he asked. 'Remove him from the craft, still in cold storage and—'

'Nuke him,' said Danbury. 'It's the only way to be sure.'

'I have told you, nuking is *not* an option. But we might take the alien in its cryogenic unit, weight it down with stones and drop it into deep water.'

'I want to go home,' said Danbury. 'What time does the next plane leave?'

'You are not going home.'

'I have a suggestion,' said Dr Harney. 'How would it be if we retrieved the spacecraft, removed the alien still in its cryogenic unit and let Danbury here put a bullet through its head with his daddy's gun?'

'*What?*' Danbury's hands flew out of his trousers and waved all about in the air. 'Are you seriously suggesting that we raise this spacecraft, root out this mad alien and then I, *I* end up with the sole responsibility for killing it? That the entire burden of sparing the human race from this thing rests upon *my* shoulders? That *I* take my father's gun and shoot it? Blast an alien from another world out of existence? *Me?* That is what you're suggesting?'

'Do you have a problem with that?'

Danbury pulled out the pistol and grinned at it. 'Fucking hey!' he said. 'Let's haul the bastard up.'

'Then we are agreed?'

'Big-fala, him blong Godlady picker-pick?'

The three men turned to confront a smiling native.

The smiling native caught sight of Danbury's gun and took a dive for cover.

'Put that away,' Sir John ordered, stooping from on high to pacify the native.

Danbury twirled the pistol on his finger and blew across the barrel. 'Your move, creep,' he said as he tucked it into his red cagoule.

'No shoot'm,' begged the native from the foetal position.

'No shoot'm,' said Sir John, helping him up.

The native dusted sand from his T-shirt. It was a nice new T-shirt. It had the words '*Virgin* coming soon to this island' printed on the front.

'Bugga-dat,' said the native. 'Godlady picker-pick. Her blong you, blong me, pronto-Tonto.'

'Dr Harney,' said Sir John. 'I think he wants the photograph.'

'Of course.' Dr Harney dug into his case and brought out the picture of the lovely one. He passed this with due reverence to Sir John, who handed on the sacred item to the native. 'Oh Carol,' said Sir John.

The native smiled at the ten by eight glossy and then smiled at Sir John.

'What very pointy teeth he has,' said Danbury.

The native's smile froze. 'One hundred dollar-pounds,' he said.

'What?' asked Sir John.

'One hundred dollar-pounds, yes-siree, by Jingo.'

'Dr Harney,' said Sir John. 'You understand pidgin, what is he trying to say?'

'Spit'm it out,' said Dr Harney.

'Shoot'm,' said the native. 'Heart-bump'm fair-had-me-going. One hundred dollar-pounds.'

'He's demanding compensation,' said the doctor, 'because Danbury pointed the pistol at him. He has a bad heart, he says.'

'Outrageous,' said Sir John.

'Godlady picker-pick.' The native pointed to the photo. 'Brown-bots blong stone-bonker. No-way-Hosay, big-fala blong stone-bonker, dig deep long-pockets, ya boo sucks.'

'Ah, I see.' The doctor now smiled. 'What he is saying is that if we are daft enough to believe that he and his fellow islanders worship Carol Vorderman, then we're also daft enough to cough up one hundred quid for pointing a gun at him.'

'Well, is that so?' Sir John reached into a safari suit pocket pouch, withdrew a set of brass knuckles, fitted these over his right fist and then dealt the native a weltering blow to the skull.

The native collapsed in an untidy heap and lay on the beach a-rubbing at his head.

'Do *I* make *myself* understood?' asked Sir John.

The native nodded soberly.

'Right then, no more of your nonsense. Lead us at once to our accommodation. Danbury, you stay and guard the supplies until our chap here returns at the hurry up with some native bearers. Up and at it then, Mr Brown-bot, there's work to do.'

Danbury chewed upon his lip. 'There'll be tears before bed-time,' he said.

'Chop chop,' said Sir John. 'Pacey pacey.'

The native rose and led Sir John and Dr Harney up the beach and off into the palms. His smile soon returned to him and he engaged the doctor in conversation. He was eager to know all about England. Were New Labour living up to their election promises? Had the Spice Girls released a 'concept' album yet?

What exactly did the word 'oxymoron' mean? How tall did you have to be to join The Twenty-third Congregation of Espadrille?

Dr Harney, who knew when the piss was being taken, answered these questions politely and then posed a few of his own, regarding life on the island.

The native explained that his name was Monty and that he was head man of the nearest village. He apologized to Dr Harney about the business of the hundred dollar-pounds, but excused himself by saying that, as one who had travelled widely, he had always found ripping off the gullible foreigner to be the rule rather than the exception. He would just have to work a bit harder at honing his skills.

Dr Harney asked what duties were expected of a head man and was told that the post was largely honorific, as the local populace recognized few laws and fewer leaders. The head man was, none the less, empowered to impose three laws of his own choosing, for which the penalty was death. Death by slow torture, followed by being eaten.

However, said Monty, as a humanitarian himself, he had imposed three laws that were unlikely to be broken. Impersonating an Egyptian was one, and goosing an elephant was another. And so he therefore maintained an air of authority and the goodwill of his people, without the need to participate in torture, butchery and anthropophagous gut-fillings.

At length Monty led Dr Harney and Sir John into a clearing.

'You said that there were three offences punishable by death,' said the doctor. 'You told me the first two, but you didn't mention the third.'

Monty put his fingers to his lips and whistled. From all sides sprang natives. They were heavily armed natives, bearing stout sticks and pointy spears. They surrounded Dr Harney and Sir John in a scrum that was far from unruly.

'Third law,' said Monty. 'No hit'm head man.'

Danbury Collins sat on the beach, his back against a wooden crate, his shoe and sockless feet dug in the sand. Danbury gazed out over the beautiful bay, from the palm-fringed shore to the sea of deepest blue. It really was paradise here and no mistake. One hundred yards off the coast four long canoes moved easily across the water, each manned by ten long-limbed and finely muscled natives. They went about their noble task and paid no heed to Danbury.

The lad sighed gently as he watched them. What a life that must be. Fishing and fornication. No mobile phones, no motor cars and no McDonald's Big Macs. If it hadn't been for the presentiment of doom that clung to him like an unwanted lover, he could quite have gone for it. Whipped off his kecks and leaped into the water.

But the water was not really a good place to be. Something lurked out there. Beneath the waves a monster dwelt. A monster that should never be allowed to surface.

But, of course, it could all be rubbish. Perhaps there was no spacecraft. Perhaps it was just an odd rock formation. Perhaps the whole shebang was a pile of poo.

But Danbury knew better. He had the 'certain feeling' that big bad trouble lay out there and although shooting an alien did have its fun side, the responsibility was no laughing matter.

The fishermen had cast their nets and were now rowing home. Danbury looked on as they applied themselves to their oars. It was all perfect unison and great heroic strokes. They would certainly have put the wind up an Oxford or Cambridge crew. As they reached the beach they clambered down into the water, took up the stern-lines and pulled on them with a will.

The lines stretched out into the sea, where nets bulged big with jumping fish. Ring-tailed spromlings, diamond-finned loonbellies, rainbow snoutmaskers and bum-waggle gin-pit splay-jawed grum-doodlers.

Danbury rose and stretched and viewed the fishermen. There was such dignity to them: a proud people fishing as their fathers had done before them. And their fathers' fathers. And their fathers' fathers' fathers. And their . . .

My, how they sweated and strained. And my, how they still paid no heed at all to Danbury. The lad broke wind and watched and wondered.

The nets drew ever closer and the natives plunged in thigh

deep, shouting and cheering and hauling their catch towards the land.

The nets now broke the surface to display their shining bounty. Danbury saw a silver dome-like body crest the waves.

A flat-tailed chufgrumbler, was that? Or a bandy-browed hooleyplop?

Surely not a rare duck-loined blanket-shark?

Danbury squinted.

The native fishers hauled and dragged and cheered and shouted, as up from the depths and onto the beach came a silver-grey metal object of considerable size.

Danbury's jaw dropped open and his bowels began to move.

'Oh no,' said Danbury. 'Oh no no no.'

But it was, *yes*, and up it came, to the cheers and shouts and hauls and pulls: an elegant aeroform resembling a star with seven points.

'Put it back!' shrieked Danbury. 'Get it back in the water!'

The natives ignored him. They were poking it with their spears. Poking, prodding, laughing and joking. They were not to be bothered by a stone-bonker white-fala jumping up and down.

As Danbury looked on in horror, he could see the steam starting to rise. As the massive craft lay there on the baking sand, the seawater was beginning to evaporate on its hull. The seven-pointed spacecraft was already warming up nicely.

'Put it back! Put it back!' Danbury unholstered his weapon and fired it into the air. 'Stand away from that spaceship,' he ordered. 'No, I mean, get it back in the water. Quick. Pacey pacey. Get a hurry up.'

And then someone struck him from behind and Danbury Collins said no more.

He had plenty to say though when he regained consciousness.

Like 'Aaaaaagh!' and 'Ow!' and 'Oh my head!' and 'Where am I?' and 'What is going on?'

'Be at peace there,' said the voice of Dr Harney.

'I've gone blind. I've gone blind.'

'No, you haven't. You're in the dark.'

'Why am I in the dark?'

'Because you're locked in a shed.'

'Oh, I see. No, I bloody don't. Why am I locked in a shed?'

'There's been a spot of bother,' said the doctor.

'A spot of bother? A spot of . . . Oh shit, I remember. The spacecraft. They've brought up the spacecraft.'

'We know,' said the voice of Dr Harney.

'You know?'

'There's been a lot of chit chat going on outside. A lot of chit chat in American accents. It would seem that the MJ 12 mob from Area 51 got here before us. They paid the natives to bring up the spacecraft. It's been taken aboard a tramp steamer and is being shipped off to an American naval base.'

'Well, well,' said Danbury. 'The things you can hear through the walls of a locked shed.' The lad tried to get up, but he couldn't. 'I can't get up,' he observed.

'That would be the ropes,' said Dr Harney. 'They do somewhat impede movement.'

'Somewhat. Oh my poor head.'

'You'll be all right.'

'Oh no I won't.'

'No, you're probably right about that.'

Danbury groaned. 'Will someone please tell me just what is going on?'

'I told you, a spot of bother.'

'You couldn't perhaps be a little more specific?'

'Well, you know how Sir John clumped the native?'

'I do recall that, yes.'

'Well, the native was the head man of the village and clumping the head man is a punishable offence.'

'I suppose it would be.'

'Punishable by death.'

'Help!' screamed Danbury. 'Let me out. I didn't clump anyone. I'm innocent.'

'I tried that myself,' said the doctor. 'They weren't having any. "All white-falas guilty," the head man said. Apparently he's inviting his cousins over for the big blow out.'

'What big blow out?'

'After they've tortured us slowly to death, they are going to cook and eat us.'

'Do you remember me saying that I had a "certain feeling"?'

Dr Harney made a grunting noise.

'What about the Americans?' Danbury asked. 'They won't let these savages eat us, surely?'

'I think the Americans have all buggered off in their boat.'

'Oh shit!'

'And so I was rather hoping that you might favour us with something. You being the lad who never steps in dog doings and always comes up with a rose between his teeth.'

'We'll just have to shoot our way out.'

'I think you'll find that they've taken your father's revolver.'

'I think you'll find that they've missed my mum's Luger. It's strapped to my left ankle.'

'What foresight you do show.'

'Well, I did have a "certain feeling".'

'Bravo.'

'But I've just had another.'

'What exactly do you mean?'

A key turned in a padlock and the door to the shed swung open. Sunlight beamed in and so did Monty the head man.

'Chow time,' said Monty.

'*That's* what I mean,' said Danbury. 'But *that* ain't the half of it.'

Chow time on a certain tramp steamer was at 1800 hours, southern Pacific time. And it was shortly before chow time that the radio operator called in a message to the American naval base to say that the ship was steaming smartly along at forty-five knots in a north-north-easterly direction and that the 'consignment' was safely stashed in the forward hold.

It was shortly after chow time that he called in to say that a fault had occurred with the refrigeration unit in the forward hold, but that the engineers were working on the problem.

About an hour later there was one further message, although those who heard it at the American naval base could not make out exactly what this message was. It appeared to be a lot of incoherent babbling, followed by a terrible high-pitched scream.

And then all communication with the tramp steamer *Apocalypso* was lost for ever.

8

'Apocalypso The Miraculous,' read Porrig, somewhat earlier. 'That's what it says on the card.'

'I read about him in a book,' said Wok Boy. 'He was very famous in his day. He's dead now, of course.'

'But if he's Dog-face the Dimac Man, the old bloke I met on the train this morning, and that's the same old bloke you've been working for here, then—'

'Then he's not dead. But it won't be the real Apocalypso, the real one is definitely dead.'

'How can you be so sure?' Porrig sipped at the tea he'd been given. 'This tastes like cat's piss,' he observed.

Wok Boy took the cup and sniffed at it. 'Smells like cat's piss too. That would probably be the cat.'

'Oh, there's a cat, is there? How charming.'

'You like cats then?'

'No, actually I hate them.'

'Me too.'

'Then why do you keep one?'

'I don't. It's not mine. It gets in somehow and pisses about the place. I have to use a lot of bleach and air freshener. Pine, for preference; the others smell too synthetic, in my opinion.'

'Yeah, right.' Porrig shook his head wearily. 'I asked you how you could be so sure that the real Apocalypso is dead.'

'Because it said so in the book I read. And there was a picture of his funeral with all these famous stage magicians standing around in top hats. And there was a picture of his tomb. This amazing marble obelisk and sort of stone masonic temple affair. It's in the local churchyard, you can go and see it yourself.'

'And were there photos of Apocalypso in this book of yours?'

'Of course there were.'

'Well . . .'

'Well what?'

'Well, was it the same bloke?'

'Oh, I see, right.' Wok Boy made a thoughtful face. 'No,' he said. 'Not the same bloke. Although . . .'

'Although what?'

'No.' Wok Boy shook his head. 'Not the same bloke, I'm sure.'

'Well, I'm buggered if I know where that leaves me. I get left a bookshop in the will of an uncle who died thirty years ago. Some old bloke, who may or may not be this dead uncle, employs you to do this place up and move all this stock in for me . . .'

'And wants you to draw this very important comic book.'

'Oh yeah, and that. But if this uncle is dead, then who is the old bloke? And if he's not dead, why all this pissing around?'

'More tea?' asked Wok Boy. 'In a fresh cup?'

'Something less pink this time. I've never liked my tea pink.'

'Blue Bayou is rather special.'

'I'll just bet it is.'

Wok Boy brewed blue tea. 'The old bloke will probably explain everything when he sees you. Do you want me to unpack your case?'

'No, just make the tea and sling your hook.'

'Such gratitude, after all I've done for you.'

'All you've done? You beat me up, you bastard. Twice.'

76

'The first time you were asking for it and the second time I was only defending myself.'

'Just make the tea and take your leave. I have to think about all this.'

'I can't go yet. I don't finish till six.'

'You finish now. You're fired. Just go away.'

'Then you don't want me to work for you in the shop?'

'No-one is going to work in the shop. Those comic books are far too valuable to sell over the counter. I'm going to put the lot up for auction.'

'I don't think that's what the old bloke had in mind. I think he wants the shop reopened.'

'It's my shop now and I'll do what I like with it.'

'But I think he wants me to work in the shop, while you work on his comic book. I think it's something pretty important, that's the impression I got.'

Porrig accepted a cup of blue tea. 'Well, I'll discuss it with him when I see him. Please give me your key and I'll see you out.'

Wok Boy produced the back-door key and threw it onto the table. 'I can see myself out, thank you.'

Porrig rose rubbing his ribs. '*I'll* see you out,' he said. 'I wouldn't want any valuable first editions accidently falling into your pockets.'

Wok Boy took Porrig by the throat. 'Now just you listen to me, you shithead,' he growled. 'I am *not* a thief. I've been working here for months. I could have nicked anything I wanted. But I didn't, because the old bloke trusted me.'

Porrig shook himself free. 'Well *I* don't,' he said.

Wok Boy looked him up and down. 'I don't like you, Porrig,' he said slowly. 'You've a real bad attitude. I've a good mind not to tell you now.'

'Tell me what?'

'Something very important that you have to know.'

'Then don't bother to tell me. Just go.'

'No,' said Wok Boy. 'The old bloke said that I had to tell you, so I will.'

'Well, make it fast, my tea's getting cold.'

Wok Boy made a bitter face. 'The old bloke said that I was to impress upon you the importance of what I'm going to say.'

'Go on.'

'OK: when you go to bed here, be in bed *before* midnight. And bolt the bedroom door. Don't come out before six in the morning, no matter what you may hear.'

'You *what*?'

'That's what I had to tell you and now I've told you. And now I'm going.'

'Hold on, hold on. Don't come out of my room after midnight? And I'm supposed to take this crap seriously? What do you take me for?'

'A total wanker. But the old bloke told me to tell you, so I have. Personally I don't give a toss, you can do what you like. But if I were you, I'd do what he says and if you really *have* met him, you'll know what I'm talking about when I say that *I* wouldn't cross him.'

Porrig did some thoughtful lip-chewing. 'All right,' he said. 'So now you've told me, please go away.'

'OK, I'll go. But just do me one favour. If you use the front door early in the morning, try not to step on me.'

'Come again?'

'The mouldy old mattress in your front doorway. That's where I sleep.'

'You mean that you haven't been sleeping in here?'

'I'm not a thief and I'm not a squatter.'

'Oh,' said Porrig.

'Yes, oh. I sleep rough in the doorway. It's cold and it's wretched and drunks piss on me in the night. But that's how it is when you're homeless.'

'Oh.'

Wok Boy turned to leave.

'Hold on,' said Porrig.

'What?'

'About you sleeping rough in my doorway. That's not right. It shouldn't be like that.'

'Well, it is like that. When you've got nowhere to stay it's all you can do.'

'But with people pissing on you and that. I mean . . .' Porrig cleared his throat. 'I mean, I don't want you to have to do that any more.'

'You mean . . .' Wok Boy looked about the kitchen.

'I mean,' said Porrig, 'I want you to sleep in someone else's doorway. You lower the tone of my establishment.'

Wok Boy took a swing at Porrig. But Porrig, who had anticipated such a swing, side-stepped it and brought Wok Boy down with the kitchen chair. 'You can sleep here in my kitchen,' he said. 'But don't go out after midnight or the bogy man will get you.'

And, as Wok Boy *was* down, Porrig kicked him.

To Porrig's surprise, and also his relief, Wok Boy declined his kind offer of accommodation. He did, however, make the ominous remark that, 'I wouldn't sleep in this place if you offered me a million quid.' Then he shook Porrig by the hand and left.

Leaving Porrig more confused than ever.

The man of property sat at the table staring into space. To the weight of responsibility had now been added a nebulous 'something'. A sinister subtext. The darkness at the top of the stairs.

'Frankly,' said Porrig. 'I wish I'd never got up this morning.'

He sought to make himself some lunch. He dug about in the fridge and in the cupboards and came across a lot of unwholesome-looking wholefoods. These he cobbled together into a semblance of sustenance and stuffed into his face. He passed on the blue tea though. As he munched, spitting out little seeds, he pondered on how best to spend the balance of the day.

Then there was the worrisome matter of all the valuable stock. That would have to go off to the auction. He'd have to catalogue it and then call up a big London sale-room.

So what should he do first?

'Finish eating this rubbish and then have a couple of pints,' said Porrig.

His lunch concluded, he left the dishes unwashed and

departed by the rear door. He took great pains with the locking up and gazed about the rubble-strewn back yard. Quite a nice little sun-trap this could make.

A nasty little alley led him back to the street. Porrig glanced into his doorway. The mouldy mattress had gone.

Porrig felt a twinge of guilt. He also felt a twinge of bruising around the ribcage. Porrig shrugged and looked up at the building that was now his own. It looked no less ghastly than it had upon his first perusal, although that now seemed a lifetime ago. He'd have to get the outside done. Put a new sign up, the old one had gone to buggeration. He'd have to come up with a new name. That was something to think about. But then there was so much to think about. *Too* much to think about. He needed some time to plan out just what to do.

Porrig looked along to the smart shopfront of The Flying Pig. That was how a real bookshop should look. A real bookshop that was full of wonderful books.

Magic.

'Magic,' said Porrig, which gave him an idea.

Porrig strolled into The Flying Pig and took in big breaths of the place. The music was certainly 'cool'. Sonic Energy Authority's sixth album, *Requiem for a Drowned Pope*, welled from hidden speakers and all around were books books books.

As one might reasonably expect in a bookshop.

But then these weren't just any old books. These were the books that you couldn't get anywhere else. The small press publications the major bookstores wouldn't touch. The rare books they couldn't get their hands on. The imports they never got around to ordering. The 'out-of-print' stuff that really wasn't 'out of print' if you knew where to look for it.

And where else would you look for it but in The Flying Pig?

Porrig scanned the nearest Bookshelf. *Snuff Fiction*, by Johnny Quinn. They even had books in stock that didn't really exist. What a class act!

Porrig drifted over to the art section. Here were all the big boys: Dave Carson, Matt Humphrey, Savage Pencil. Porrig spied a Carson portfolio he didn't have. He pulled it out with care and cast an eye across the price. Then he pushed it back with care. That one would have to wait until he sold a few first editions.

Porrig's eyes moved along the spines and came to rest on the breasts.

Porrig's eyes went blink blink blink.

Porrig recognised those breasts.

Those were the breasts he'd seen earlier in the day.

Behind the counter stood the vision in white from the solicitors' office. Porrig offered her a smile.

The vision did not receive it with grace. She turned her head away.

Porrig hastened over. 'Hello,' he said. 'I didn't know you worked here.'

'How would you? I didn't mention it.'

'Great shop,' said Porrig.

'Better than yours.'

'For now, yes.'

'Thinking of opening up in competition, then?'

Porrig hadn't been. 'I just might,' he said.

'In your dreams.'

'Perhaps.'

'Well, it's fifteen quid. You can take it or leave it.'

'Fifteen quid?'

'That's the price. I won't go any lower.'

'Oh,' said Porrig. 'Well, that's very fair. Should we go to my place, or do it here behind the counter?'

'For the book. Fifteen quid for the book.'

'What book?'

'The one you came in here for.'

Porrig shook his head.

'About Apocalypso The Miraculous.'

'What?'

'That's what you came in here for, isn't it?'

'Yes it is. But how did you know?'

'Just because I have big tits doesn't mean I'm stupid.'

Porrig almost said 'Shame' but somehow he controlled himself.

'I read your file in the office, didn't I? So I knew you'd

81

inherited the building next door. And Phart-Ebum told me that Apocalypso was a stage magician and how he'd read about him in a book. And you obviously hadn't got a clue who this uncle of yours was, so eventually you were bound to come in here to see if we had the book about him. And this is it and it's fifteen quid.'

'Jesus' jockstrap!' said Porrig. 'You really are more intelligent than you look.'

The vision in white shook her beautiful head. 'You wanker,' she said.

'I'm really getting fed up with people calling me that.'

'Then get your act together. Do you want the book or not?'

'Yes, please.' Porrig fished out the money. He examined what he had left in his pocket. It wasn't much.

The vision put the book in a bag and handed it to Porrig. 'Piss off then,' she said.

Porrig tried another smile. 'Look,' he said. 'I'm sorry if I offend you. I offend everyone, but I'm trying to change. There's a lot of really good gear in my shop, it's going to make me a lot of money. Would you care to come out with me later for a celebrational drink?'

'I'm working later.'

'Here?'

'No, in the pub across the road.'

'How many jobs have you got?'

'Quite a few. All part time. People keep offering them to me. I've no idea why.'

Porrig's eyes were back upon those breasts. 'I think I have some idea,' he said.

'Yeah, well, I reckon I do too. But I need the money.'

'Would you have a drink with me later? At the pub where you work?'

'I might.'

'Brilliant. What time will you be there?'

'Any time after seven.'

'Brilliant. I'll see you later then.'

'OK.'

Porrig left The Flying Pig. That had been a bit good, hadn't it? He might be on a winner there. Take her back to his place and rock'n'roll till dawn.

With the bedroom door bolted. Of course.

Yeah, well, he could dream.

Porrig returned to his shop, went upstairs to the bedroom and lay down on the bed. As he didn't have much money, the pub would have to wait. Until after seven.

Porrig pulled the book from the paper bag. *Beyond Doubtable Reason: The Biography of Apocalypso The Miraculous*, by Sir John Rimmer.

Porrig flicked straight through to the photo section. There was the young Apocalypso, looking every bit the business in his top hat and tails. And here he was dressed in the habit of a monk. And here he was impersonating an Egyptian!

Porrig stared hard at the faces and the faces stared hard at Porrig. But neither of the either recognised the other of the other. As it were.

There was the funeral. Very impressive.

And the tomb. Even more impressive.

Porrig flicked back to chapter one.

'Chapter one,' he read. And immediately his eyelids started to close and soon he was fast asleep.

Which was a bit of a shame, as it went. For reasons numbering three. The first being that Porrig would now never get to finish that chapter. The second, that he would sleep right through the evening and miss his 'date' with the vision in white. And the third, that Porrig had *not* bolted his bedroom door.

It is said that great events oftimes cast a shadow before them and also that there are folk, such as Danbury Collins, who can sense approaching danger. And who amongst us can honestly say, with a hand upon the heart, that there has not been a time when they have just 'known' that something was *not quite right*?

Porrig awoke with a start at one minute to midnight.

'Shit,' said Porrig, looking at his watch. 'Oh shit shit shit.'

And then he said, 'Oh dear me,' because the handle of the bedroom door was slowly beginning to turn.

Porrig leaped from the bed and flung himself with vigour at

the door. He pushed the bolt home and leaned back against it. His heart was going bump bump bump and a fine cold sweat was breaking on his brow.

'Who's there?' shouted Porrig, when he could find his voice. 'Who's out there? Is that you, Wok Boy? Are you having a pop at me?'

Little hairs were now standing up all over the place on Porrig. Little hairs that normally stayed in the down position. He felt seriously scared and he had absolutely no idea why.

Something had jerked him awake. Something had warned him that he was in danger. What was that something?

Porrig dithered at the door. 'Come on, Wok Boy,' he called. 'I know it's you. Don't piss about.' He pressed his ear to the polished pitch pine. A nasty rat-like scuttling sound had his ear go jerking back. Jerk jerk jerk.

'Get a grip, Porrig,' said Porrig. 'Look at yourself, you're trembling like a silly big girl.'

'I'm coming out,' he shouted. 'And I'm armed.'

Porrig returned to the bed and sat down. 'Get a grip,' he told himself again. 'What *is* the matter with you?'

THUMP! went a thump right over his head. And THUMP! it went again.

Porrig covered said head with his hands. 'I don't want to be here,' he whispered. 'I want to go home.'

A bright light shone under the bedroom door and the door began to vibrate.

'No,' wailed Porrig. 'Whatever it is, I don't want to see it. Help. Help!'

The light flashed off and the door became still. There were no more THUMPings to be heard.

'It's got to be a wind-up,' said Porrig to himself. 'Some sort of stupid prank. To see if I can be frightened, or something.'

Or something.

'Someone's been hiding all day in the loft. The old bloke, probably.'

Porrig took his fingers from his face and blew upon them. It had suddenly got rather cold. Porrig glanced at the door. 'I'm not going out there,' he mumbled. 'I've been to the movies. I know what can happen. If I step out of that door I'll end up with my face sawn off. It happens every time. It must just be a mistake that the woman with the great tits isn't here. She should have her face sawn off first.'

Porrig now chewed upon his chilly fingers. 'But,' he said, between chewings. 'That *is* the movies, of course. In real life it's more likely that a burglar has broken in and is . . .'

Porrig didn't finish that sentence. If he had, then the words he would have chosen would probably have been: STEALING MY STOCK!

Porrig was up from the bed in a flash. And he was across the room in another flash. And in a third flash he had the bolt drawn and the door open. And in a fourth flash he was standing on the landing with his fists raised and a furious look on his face.

There might well have been a fifth flash, but this one would have been particularly fleeting as it involved Porrig looking down and seeing that he no longer had a landing to stand on and was falling very fast into something deep and dark.

A hole, perhaps?

'Aaaaaaaaaagh!' went Porrig, which is what you do when falling into something deep and dark (a hole, perhaps). Then, 'Oh,' as he was standing now upon a wooden floor, unscathed. And dark it was no more, because a light shone all around. And Porrig looked and Porrig saw and Porrig did not then believe at all in what he was seeing. As it were.

Porrig stood on the polished floor of a bookshop. But it was not his bookshop, neither was it The Flying Pig. This bookshop was old, centuries old, if a bookshop it was. It had more the look of one of those monastic libraries. Ancient leathern tomes with burnished hasps and locking bits. Scrolls of parchment. Vellum pages bound with silk.

Porrig caught what breath he could. He wasn't dreaming, he was sure of that, but he wasn't at the bottom of his stairs. He was somewhere or other that he shouldn't be and he knew, just knew, that he wasn't alone.

Porrig peered down a long aisle of musty old volumes. Something was moving, and it was a *something*, rather than a *someone*.

Porrig screwed up his eyes. 'No,' he whispered. 'I'm not having *that*.'

The something had a quality of not quite being there. It wavered and it wafted, it went in and out of focus. It was wraith-like, it was ghostly, it was—

'It's a pig,' said Porrig. 'It's a fucking pig.'

The pig, for such it evidently was, turned its snout towards Porrig, made a most obscene noise and vanished.

'Who did that?' someone shouted. 'Who has offended the pig?'

Porrig ducked away behind the nearest stack of books. 'I am dreaming,' he whispered. 'Pig equals pork sausage. It's always pork sausages in my dreams. And I don't even like pork sausages.'

'Who offended the pig?' The voice was louder. The voice meant to know. Porrig ducked and slunk away. There was quite a lot of away to slink to. The bookcases and tables of scrolls and racks of paper and piles of old parchment went on and on and on.

Porrig broke into a run and, some time later, breathless, scared and quite pissed off, he sat down on the floor. 'Just reason it out,' he said, between gaspings. 'What has happened to you? Have you fallen into some parallel world, or down a hole in time, or through a crack in the clouds—'

'Or up your own arse,' said a voice.

Porrig jumped to his feet. 'Who said that?'

'I did.'

'Where are you?'

'I'm here, but I'm not coming out.'

'Then don't. Just tell me where I am and how I get back to where I came from.'

'Use your key. You did bring your key, didn't you?'

'What key?'

'That would be a "no", I suppose.'

'Where are you?'

'I'm up here. But I'm not coming down.'

'Why not?'

'Because you'd get yourself all in a state if I did.'

'Of course I wouldn't. I mean, you're not a pig, are you?'

'Of course I'm not a bleeding pig. How dare you?'

'Then come out.'

'Okey-dokey.' There was a scuffling amongst the books above Porrig's head and then something small and definitely on the strange side climbed slowly down and stood before Porrig.

Before and a good way beneath.

Porrig stared down and his mouth dropped open.

'It's very rude to stare,' said the something. 'You ought to be taught some manners.'

Porrig's head bobbed slowly in agreement, but words would not come to him.

Before him and beneath stood a creature so queer and oddly formed that Porrig was completely lost for anything to say.

In height it barely topped eighteen inches. Its skin was dry and dull and breeze-block grey. Its head was high and domed and almost hairless. It was insect-thin and naked; it was weird and it was fey.

> It had no nose to speak of
> And its eyes were like a cat's.
> Its lipless mouth was boasting just three teeth.
> In the fingers of its left hand
> It held a magic wand
> And it was male (it had a willy underneath).

'Poetic, aren't I?' it said. 'The name's Rippington, what's yours?'

'Mine is Porrig,' said Porrig, in a silly shaky voice.

'Pleased to meet you, Porrig.' And the thing stuck out its hand. 'And I'm not a *thing*, nor an *it*, I'm a dvergar.'

'I'm a Leo,' said Porrig.

'Was that supposed to be funny?'

'I expect it was supposed to be.'

'Well, it wasn't.'

Porrig shook the tiny hand. It was cold. It was very cold. 'Your tiny hand is frozen,' said Porrig.

87

'And yours is way too hot. What manner of being are you then? Clurichaun, are you? Gremlin?'

'Leave it out. I'm a person.'

Rippington sniffed at Porrig. 'I don't think you're supposed to be here,' he said.

'I just want to go home.'

'Well, use your key. Ah, no, you haven't got your key, have you?'

'What key? The shop key? I haven't any other key.'

'It's not that kind of key. It's a musical key. You don't know what key you're in, do you?'

'I haven't the foggiest idea what you're talking about.'

'I'm talking about harmonics, obviously. If you don't know what key you're in, no wonder you're out of tune.'

'Is this a theme park?' Porrig asked.

'A what?'

'A theme park. This isn't *Lord of the Rings* World, or something?'

'Or something.'

'Yeah, right.'

'This is ALPHA 17,' said Rippington. 'Seventeenth harmonic in the Alpha scale. But if you say you're a person then you most definitely shouldn't be here. Persons are a different scale altogether. Betamax, or something.'

'Betamax?'

'I could look you up in the big book.'

'You said ALPHA 17. That's the bookshop where I've come from.'

'They don't sell books in shops,' said Rippington. 'That really would be absurd. Imagine what would happen if just anything could get its mitts on a book. Chaos there'd be. Oh yes. No more harmony, everything out of key.'

'I'll bet this is all really cosmic stuff,' said Porrig. 'But personally I've never had too much of an interest in elves and goblins and all that sword and sorcery cack.'

'You're a bit of a rub-tugger, aren't you?'

'A rub-tugger?'

'One who tugs at his rubbing part.' Rippington waggled his willy about.

'Oh perfect,' said Porrig. 'Even the fairies have me down as a wanker.'

'Do you want me to look you up in the big book, or don't you?'

'I do, yes please.'

'Then follow me. But pretend that you're not. If you follow me.'

'Yes, I think that I do.'

And so Porrig followed Rippington, whilst pretending that he wasn't, down between the aisles of books, along stone corridors, around balconies that looked down upon further balconies and further corridors, through halls lined with more books and rooms lined with even more. And on and on and on some more.

'Are we nearly there?' Porrig asked.

'Are you following me?'

'Yes, but I'm pretending not to.'

'Then pretend not to speak to me either.'

'But are we nearly there?'

'Let's pretend that we are.'

'All right, I'm pretending.'

'Then we're here.'

'Absurd.'

'I do so agree. Help me up onto the desk.'

Porrig dithered a little. He did not like the feel of Rippington.

'I don't like the feel of you either. Just lift me up.'

'There you go, then.'

It was a great big old desk and it was covered by many big old papers, maps of unlikely places and manuscripts scrawled in fanciful lettering.

'Here's the big book,' said Rippington.

Porrig stared down at it. 'That's not a very big big book,' he said.

'Size is relative, you know. Now let's have a look. *Person*, you said, let's see. *Pergola*, I've got. It says, *see: Trumpet*. That's not even close, is it?'

'Let me have a look.'

Rippington waved his magic wand about. Porrig felt an

unpleasant itching sensation. He rubbed at his hand. 'Please don't do that,' he said.

'Then keep your mitts away from the big book. Ah yes, hold your fire, Mr Rub-Tugger. *Person*. It says, *see: human being*. Would that be the one?'

'Yes it would.'

Rippington leafed through the little pages of the big book. He paused now and then and looked sidelong at Porrig. Sidelong and up quite a bit. At greater length he ceased to read and closed the book, and sat cross-legged upon it. 'We have a situation here,' he said.

'We do?' said Porrig.

'We surely do. According to the big book, you are a mythical being.'

'I am?' said Porrig.

'You are and you come from a magical kingdom high above.'

'I do?' said Porrig.

'You do. And I am apparently now in a state of grace because I've met you.'

'You are?'

'I am. Well, no, actually I'm not. But I could pretend to be if it would make you feel more at home.'

'It wouldn't,' said Porrig.

'So what are you going to do? Are you going to grant me a wish? I'd quite like a larger rubbing part. Size being relative and all my relatives having bigger ones than me.'

'I just want to go home.'

'Back to heaven, do you mean?'

'I'm not from heaven. I'm from Earth.'

'Same place.'

'It's not the same place. Look, where's the exit? Is there someone in authority? Who runs this mad house?'

'That would be the curator.'

Porrig sighed. 'And would I be right in supposing that the curator is a bowed old gentleman with a long white beard, a conical hat and a gown all covered in stars?'

Rippington pointed to his willy. 'Tug tug tug,' he said.

'All right,' said Porrig. 'Then let me have another try. Would I be right in supposing that the curator *is* an old gentleman? That he doesn't have a long white beard, but that he does look a bit like a dog, with two white tufts of hair on the top of his head?'

'Well,' said Rippington.

'Well?'

'That's a pretty good supposition.'

'And would you be impressed if I went for the double and told you his name?'

'Very,' said Rippington.

'Apocalypso The Bloody Miraculous.'

Said Porrig.

'Well, tug my rubbing part.'

Said Rippington.

'So I'm right!'

Said Porrig.

'No,' said Rippington, 'you're wrong. But one out of two wasn't bad. Now, about my rubbing part . . .'

9

The largest rubbing part in the whole wide world belonged to Dilbert Norris. It was approximately a yard and a half in length and resembled a giant parsnip.

Now, whilst it is certainly true that there are few things the British public find more side-splittingly funny than a vegetable shaped like a willy, it is interesting to note that the man who possesses a willy shaped like a vegetable, especially one of such length, is rarely to be found waving the thing about in the high street in the noble cause of a good clean laugh.

It must also be said that the practical applications for such a monstrous member are few, other than for sticking it into your ear and going to a fancy dress party as a petrol pump, when the laughter would soon die away and horrid thoughts enter the mind.

Naturally opinions vary greatly regarding just what size the perfect penis should be. Most men would go for an eight-incher, although this man for one has no intention of lopping off a couple of inches to please anybody.[1]

Dilbert would have liked a bigger one. But then Dilbert was

[1]Humour (or is it?).

92

not as other men. Dilbert was, in fact, not a man at all. Dilbert was a vegetable. And whether a vegetable having a willy shaped like a vegetable, no matter what size it happens to be, is actually funny, is anyone's guess.

It certainly was not considered even vaguely amusing on the planet where Dilbert grew up: a planet called Eden in the constellation of Knob-end Major, which is not to be found on any earthly star map because it is a very very great distance away.

For those who prefer clarity to inference, let it now be said that Dilbert Norris was the creature in the seven-pointed space-craft that had recently been hauled from the depths of the Pacific Ocean.

And also, that although much of what Dr Harney had to say about Dilbert was correct, the appellation attached to Porrig's previous employer at the Used Car Emporium could not be applied to him. Dilbert was *not* mad, time had *not* addled his brain, he was neither stone-bonker nor space cadet. Dilbert Norris was a sentient vegetable, and sentient vegetables see and do things differently.

On Dilbert's home planet there had been no mammals, no herbivores to gorge themselves on nature's bounty and interfere with the true path of evolution: that of vegetable rather than mammal. On Dilbert's home planet the vegetable kingdom had become *the* kingdom, vegetables the rightful heirs to the earth in which they grew.

It was all peace and harmony upon Eden, where no serpent, or perhaps more appropriately, no cow, had ever entered the garden of paradise.

Now, it is surely self-evident that a universal truth must apply, no matter in which part of the universe you choose to apply it. And the universal truth that the highest life form on a planet with an atmosphere and a gravity similar to that of Earth will have man-like characteristics, is one of these very truths.

You can fiddle about a bit with the basic design features, but a head at the top end with eyes in the front, a pair of legs to get about on and those all-essential opposing thumbs are prerequisites. And willy in the middle has yet to be bested.

Dilbert Norris was man-like, as were all of his ilk. But

Dilbert's ilk possessed certain powers that humankind do not.

It has long been accepted that plants are capable of communicating with one another, although the means by which this is done are not fully understood. Nor, it can be said with some authority, are they ever likely to be, as man's inability to understand even his fellow man, let alone plants, and his basic attitude to the vegetable (which he sees foremost as a source of food rather than wisdom), puts the kibosh on this from the outset.

The relationship between man and vegetable is a very one-sided affair.

Vegetables communicate telepathically, as do some fish, most insects, yellow-handled screwdrivers, car keys, biros and small screws from the insides of pop-up toasters.

Only one man in history has ever come to terms with this and he is Hugo Rune and his is another story.

Dilbert's bunch, having evolved into their man-like forms, still retained their telepathic abilities, and it was by means of these that Dilbert found himself able to exert control over the beings he encountered here on Earth. Beings who, by the very nature of their eating habits, were his natural enemies. Or, in his case, unnatural, as none existed on his particular planet.

In describing Dilbert's physical appearance the word 'tricky' springs to mind. Not that he looked tricky (although he did), but more because it is tricky to find flattering prose when describing a creature some twenty feet high, weighing in at approximately two tons, that resembles a man-shaped sprout and possesses the aforementioned yard-and-a-half long parsnip donger.

No doubt Dilbert would have been considered a good-looker on Eden, a regular beau, a dandy, drop-dead gorgeous and hot to trot. But here on Earth, and casting 'tricky' to the four winds, there could be no hesitation in referring to him as one big fat ugly-looking son of the sod.

And he smelled bad too.

On Eden Dilbert had not amounted to very much, a verdant version of Tom Cruise perhaps, but a tad intellectually challenged. Or, as Porrig might have put it, thick as shit. A second-rate clerk in a town-planning department, he spent most of his days staring dreamily out of the window and planning plans of his own about what he might do if he ever won the National Lottery. For it is another universal truth that no matter where a civilization rises, there will always be clerks looking dreamily out of windows and there will always be a National Lottery.

For the most part these clerks must dream on, but in Dilbert's case fate had other plans. Dilbert came up trumps on the National Lottery and bought himself a spaceship.

And the rest is history.

Although not the history you will read about in many other books. Especially those of a religious nature.

In all fairness it has to be said that Dilbert never intended to set himself up as a god. Not originally. When he set out from Eden in his spacecraft it was with the intention of finding a new world for the folk of Eden and earning the big kudos that went with such a discovery. Had it ever crossed his mind that things would work out in the way they did, he would probably have stayed at home. Although home was getting *very* crowded. And had things worked out a little differently on his arrival here, he would probably never have acted in the way he did.

But it didn't, and they did, and he didn't and they didn't and so he did. As it were.

Location can often be everything and had not Dilbert's craft chosen the island later to be known as Gwa'tan Qua Cest'l Potobo as an ideal landing site things might have gone a little more smoothly and much unpleasantness been avoided.

But it didn't, and it wasn't.

The spacecraft dropped down out of the clear blue sky halfway through the ceremony to inaugurate the instatement of the new village head man. An omen if ever there was one.

The natives gathered about the seven-pointed craft, which bore to them an uncanny resemblance to a giant wok, and looked on in awe as it opened to reveal to them something that bore an uncanny resemblance to a giant version of a particularly toothsome local vegetable: the sand sprout.

It was as clear as clear was possible to be that the gods had sent down an offering. A food parcel from on high. And all they had to do was cook it up and tuck in.

They got a nice big fire going under Dilbert's spacecraft.

Now, to be awoken from one hundred thousand years in cryogenic suspension by a bunch of aliens roasting you up for dinner is no-one's idea of a good time and, rightfully miffed at this abhorrent circumstance, Dilbert arose in displeasure.

And also in pain.

Pain was an entirely new experience for Dilbert who came from a planet where thoughts are shared. For when thoughts are shared, then so is pain, which probably explains why, as a race, vegetables are so much nicer than people.

At that moment Dilbert didn't feel very nice. He was hurt and he was angry. He was all alone on a far-distant world, under attack from beings that, although basically the same shape as himself, were far smaller and far nastier and whose intentions towards him were hostile.

It was not to be a meeting of minds. Nor was it to be 'hands across the universe'. The die was cast, as they say. The battle lines were drawn.

And when Dilbert discovered within minutes of leaping hot-bummed from his spacecraft that he could mentally inflict pain upon his attackers, but that they were unable to do likewise to him, and when the sheer enormity of these beings' dining habits was brought home to him, it took him no more than a moment to decide their fate. If his race were to colonize this planet, then the indigenous population would have to be either exterminated, or brought under control.

In his vegetable wisdom Dilbert opted for the latter.

It might well be a very long wait before his spacecraft's homing signal ever reached Eden and a great deal longer before anyone arrived from there. So Dilbert thought he'd make the best of a bad job. He'd knock these beings into shape and, though it was clear that he wouldn't be able to change their eating habits, they would certainly learn who was the boss.

Who, in fact, was 'God'.

★   ★   ★

He travelled widely in those, his first days, and by many names they came to know Him. Names of Power. He was Wotan to the Nordic race and Dadga to the Celts. He was Zeus. He was Kronos. He was Jahweh. He was Amen-Ra. And all His people knew His power and worshipped at His temples.

He was kindly when He chose to be, forgiving when He chose to be, but those times were rare. They knew Him by His wrath and at His name whole nations trembled. For He used them and He squandered them, He ravaged and destroyed them and He gorged Himself upon them, for He'd learned to like the taste.

Great cities they raised for Him and, driven by the pain He could inflict, His armies marched across the world, subduing all. For all it seemed were His, to do with as He pleased and His excesses were awesome, spreading horror, and fear at His displeasure chilled the hearts of those who whispered His name.

All power corrupts, they say, etcetera, and, if there is time here for yet one more universal truth, it is this.

Most no-marks who win the National Lottery eventually return to no-mark status. And most do sooner rather than later. Fate is ever the bastard pup that bites its master's knob.

Dilbert's knob got bitten in Mu: His summer home, a Pacific paradise and very nice with it. Dilbert was lounging atop a mound of slave girls when the first tremor struck. Unseated from his cosy throne he tumbled headlong to the marble floor with a cry of 'Bollocks' (He had learned the tongues of Man) and a splattering of sprout flesh unpleasing to behold.

Shake shake shake went the ground and then, up from under, erupted the volcano. Dilbert hastened to take His leave. And as granite pavements sank and gilded towers collapsed, He lashed at His subjects with mental pain, forcing them to cart His horrid heavy body to the means of His escape.

But He didn't get far. The thrashing winds and the clouds of volcanic dust drove His spacecraft down from the sky and down down down into the ocean.[2]

[2]And only one hundred yards from the shore of Gwa'tan Qua Cest'l Potobo where he'd landed in the first place. Some coincidence, eh?

Rocks and rubble fell and Mu went down, to legend and to fable.

And that was that for Dilbert (or it bloody should have been!)

Back in cryogenic suspension and under hundreds of tons of volcanic debris, it could reasonably have been assumed that he had finally returned to no-mark status.

But no. Fate, the old knob-gobbler, had other knobs to nibble.

Many years passed, years that became centuries, that became millennia. The world forgot about Dilbert. The world had the legends and the religions and whatever, but the being behind them was forgotten. He was written out. He no longer applied.

But He was there all the time. Lurking like Porrig's dad. But lurking big time. Down all alone at the bottom of the sea. Frozen in time. Waiting.

Until one day.

Bang.

Or Boom. Or dull dank thud, or whatever you like. The sound that a nuke makes when tested under water. And if Danbury was to recall his science fiction clearly, he would recall that many a good yarn *begins* with a nuke, rather than ends with one.

Bang, boom, dull dank thud or whatever you like: American testing of nukes beneath the nice blue waves of the Pacific.

Then shift went the debris; switch on went the automatic controls of Dilbert's spacecraft. Unthaw went Dilbert. And quiet was He.

Hungry was He also. But still wise.[3] Many years had passed since His ship went down and before He rose again, God-like from the briny deep, Dilbert thought it best to test the water, sniff the air, judge the mood and generally make no rash moves whatsoever.

And so He sent out His thoughts to see what His people were up to. *His* people. Had they forgotten Him? Had they developed? How much did they now know? How much harm

[3]Wise as in 'mankind' wise. But still 'thick as shit' in vegetable terms.

were they capable of doing Him? And He sent out His thoughts to listen to theirs. And what He heard didn't please Him one bit.

They *had* forgotten Him. They *had* developed. They knew a whole lot more and they were certainly now capable of doing Him a great deal of harm. And there was still absolutely no sign of His real people, the people from his own planet. They had either not heard his call or they were gone for ever.

But Dilbert was back. And this time it was personal!

And so He listened in, to many thoughts. He swept the planet with His mind, gathering information. And the information He received surprised Him. At first He thought that the planet's power base lay in a land called America, a land He had once named Dilbert. But the more He listened and the more He screened out the interference caused by the babbling of millions, the more clearly did another truth emerge.

It was not a universal truth, but it was a truth none the less. The land of America was not the seat of world power. The real seat of world power stood upon a swirly-whirly-patterned carpet in a small office in a government department called the Ministry of Serendipity, beneath an Underground station called Mornington Crescent, in a city called London, in a country called England.

And so it was to here that He sent a little thought of His own. A little suggestion. That the someone who sat in the chair upon the swirly-whirly-patterned carpet might just carry out a satellite survey of a certain area in the Pacific Ocean and discover something star-shaped and wonderful.

Something that must be brought at once, intact, to that very seat of power.

And the rest was history?

Yes, it was.

Or, yes, it would be.

He quite liked the look of the native fishermen who dragged His spacecraft ashore. All those firm muscles beneath the brown skin. They recalled to Him His Nubian slaves, the chosen ones of most outstanding beauty, who had carried Him upon their straining shoulders and pandered to the needs of His body. Without and within.

As He viewed them through the porthole he nodded with approval. He would take two dozen with Him when He left the island.

Then He saw Danbury, lazing on a packing case with one hand in his trouser pocket. He didn't take to him. A shiftless idle type fit only to be used as a suppository. Didn't he jump when he saw the seven-pointed craft rising from the waves. And he fired a gun!

No guns were allowed. Dilbert threw out a thought. A compulsion. The need to obey. At once. And He smiled as He watched the shiftless youth struck down from behind. His powers had not deserted Him. If anything they were stronger than ever.

He was *not* impressed by the *Apocalypso*. Even though it was a metal boat and powered by engines rather than oars, it did not impress Him. He was used to far better. He liked the ships that bore Him to be large and gaily painted, like the barques that long ago had carried Him in luxury upon the waters of the Nile.

They lowered His spacecraft into the forward hold, down into the darkness and the dirt, and they set men there to guard it. Men with guns.

He studied their minds and once more He was not impressed.

And He heard them speak of Him. They called him alien.

Alien!

He, their God! They called *Him* alien.

He killed them. Killed them all. Flung agony into their minds and made them shoot themselves. Good riddance too.

He ate them.

And then, His repast over, He sensed something. Something large and near. Something splendid. And rising to the deck upon a ladder formed from men He spied it, riding upon the night-time ocean. Drifting gorgeously upon the moonlit sea.

A liner: *The Leviathan*, on its maiden voyage from New York.

'I'll have that,' He said. And He did.

There were three thousand folk aboard that ship. Three thousand carefree souls, exalting in their wealth and status. Three thousand who now were His.

They screamed as He was carried aboard and some tried to

100

fight and repel Him. So He drew Himself up and He stared down upon them and He entered their minds with His own and He hurt them. He drove them to the deck, clutching at their heads. Their heads that burst with the pain He threw at them. And they hastened to obey, to do as He commanded, to kneel and to worship and to welcome Him back.

He called for the captain and issued His orders. They were clear and they would be obeyed. The ship's radio was to be smashed and all communications severed. And the ship was to be brought about, to sail north-east, through the Panama Canal and across the Atlantic ocean.

The destination was to be the British Isles.

England, London, Mornington Crescent.

The Ministry of Serendipity.

The seat of ultimate power.

The man who presently sat in the seat that stood upon the swirly-whirly-patterned carpet in the office of this ministry knew nothing whatever of just what was heading his way.

He did not, as it happened, so much 'sit' in the seat, as 'lurk' in it. Because this man's name was Augustus Naseby.

Yes, indeed, and there you go. Augustus Naseby.

But more of him later.

For now let's return to his son.

10

Rippington jigged upon the little big book. 'Come on now,' he said to Porrig. 'Just one wish, that's all I want.'

'That's all *I* want,' Porrig said. 'Or maybe two, or three at a push.'

'Well, you're the angel, dish'm out.'

'I'm not an angel, I'm a person.'

'It's the same thing here, mush. You might be just a person up upon heavenly Earth, but here you're the old bee's bollocks.'

'Is that a good thing or a bad thing?'

'It's the bestest thing there is. Come on now, just one little wish.'

'I wish I was home,' said Porrig.

'No no no. A wish for me, you rub-tugging son of a—'

'*Rippington!*' The voice was that of the old bloke and Rippington drew up short when he heard it. Porrig turned and the old bloke was there. Just there. Of a sudden. In a magical way.

'Ah,' said Porrig. 'It's you.'

'And it's you,' said the old bloke. 'But it shouldn't be, should it? Should I praise you for your ingenuity, or punch your lights out for your disobedience?'

'Now just see here,' said Porrig.

'What, *here*?' The old bloke ceased to be there. 'Or *here*?' And now he was somewhere else.

Porrig stared in the direction of his latest appearance. 'I'm not impressed,' he said, which, although a lie, he made to sound convincing. 'You're a stage magician. You can do tricks like that.'

'Rippington's impressed,' said the old bloke. 'Aren't you, Rippington?'

'Not as impressed as I would be by a larger rubbing part.'

'I'll knock your rubbing part up your pooing part if you don't mind your manners.'

'Oh, turn it in,' said Porrig.

'You want some of this?' asked the old bloke, making a fist.

'I just want to go home. It's been a long day.'

'You spent half of it asleep.'

'I won't ask how you know that.'

'Then don't. But, as you're here now, I suppose I'd better fill you in on all the details, as it were.'

'Oh goody,' said Porrig.

'Was that a "tone" in your voice?'

'Please stop bullying me,' Porrig said. 'I know I shouldn't be here. I'm sorry that I've come here. I just want to go home.'

'And so you shall. Once I've told you what you have to do.'

'Then please tell me and I'll be off.'

'Quite so. Follow me.' The old bloke turned and strode away.

'Help me down from the table,' said Rippington.

'Leave him there, Porrig,' called the old bloke. 'And get a move on.'

Porrig shrugged towards the imp and followed the old bloke.

'And make out you're not following me.'

'God's gonads,' said Porrig.

The old bloke led Porrig down further corridors, across further balconies that looked down on to further corridors, through further rooms all filled with books and up a natty staircase wrought from decorative silk.

'You can't have a staircase made out of silk,' observed Porrig.

'*You* can't,' said the old bloke.

'Are we nearly there?'

'Would you like us to be?'

'I would.'

'Then we are.'

'Absurd.'

'Yes, isn't it.' The old bloke turned a key in a lock and swung open an ancient door. 'My office,' he said.

Porrig caught up and peered in. 'It's upside down,' he said.

'Why yes, so it is.' The old bloke closed the door and reopened it. 'That's better.'

Porrig shook his head.

'Follow me.' And Porrig did so.

The room itself was small and lacked for windows. Porrig realized that he hadn't actually seen a single window since he'd arrived in this curious place. But as he had assumed that it was all underground, he hadn't really been surprised. The fact that there was at least something he hadn't been surprised about gave him some comfort.

But not very much.

As to the furnishings, this room held many and various.

There were chairs of the vintage persuasion
And a table of Romany caste.
A throne for a special occasion,
A desk with a shadowy past.

A rug that was woven from feathers,
A tapestry woven from cheese.
Some pictures of ladies in leathers,
And Porrig was taken with these.

A view of a bay in a frame made of gold.
A brown nodding dog that was not very old.
A lamp with a bulb, though it wasn't electric.
A collection in all, that was somewhat eclectic.

'A very poetic room,' said Porrig.

The old bloke grinned. 'There's lots of poetry down here,' he said. 'It escapes from the books and drifts all over the place.'

'Poetry can't escape from books,' said Porrig, 'that's just plain stupid.'

The old bloke shrugged. 'Fair enough,' said he. 'I'm sure you know what you're talking about. I'll bow to your superior wisdom.'

'I'll bet you will.'

'That "tone" again . . .'

'I'm sorry,' said Porrig. 'But I really *have* had a long day.'

'And it's far from over.' The old bloke sat down in a chair of the vintage persuasion at the desk with the shadowy past. 'Sit over there in that throne,' he told Porrig. 'After all, this is a special occasion.'

'Is it?' Porrig asked as he sat himself down.

'Perhaps more so for me. But then I have been waiting a very long time.'

'Who are you?' Porrig made himself comfortable. 'Are you my uncle, and if so—'

'I'm not your uncle, Porrig.'

'I didn't know I had an Uncle Porrig.'

The old bloke sighed. 'It's a nervous habit, isn't it?' he said. 'You do it when you're ill at ease. Like when you were in the solicitor's office. "Death," said Mr Phart-Ebum. And you said, "No, I can hear you just fine." '

'You were there?'

'In a manner of speaking. I put myself about, keep an eye on things.'

'Please tell me about my uncle.'

'Apocalypso The Miraculous. Greatest stage magician of his day. The master of legerdemain. He made the Impossible, possible, although many said that demons whispered at his ear. There is a biography about him, written by the eminent para-psychologist Sir John Rimmer, but you won't find any other mention. His name has been stricken from the records of the Magic Circle. The old playbills have been destroyed. No-one even knows what his real name was.'

'Why all the mystery?' Porrig asked. 'Or is this just part of the mystique?'

'I think it had something to do with the demons speaking at

his ear. It gave him an unnatural edge on the opposition. You see, stage magic is just that, *stage* magic. Tricks, sleight of hand, special effects, but it still holds a fascination for the public at large. They like to be fooled.'

'They wouldn't vote if they didn't.'

'Don't be cynical, Porrig. But they *do* like to be fooled. And they love the wonder of it all. And they actually like, secretly of course, because they'll never own up to it, to believe that some of it might just be *real* magic. That real magic might actually exist.'

'And does it?' Porrig asked.

'It all depends on what you mean by *real*. But you see it fascinates people, intrigues them, obsesses them. It obsessed your uncle. He set out to discover whether real magic existed. And now you're sitting here, and I'm sitting here, which probably means that it does.'

'And who *are* you, exactly?'

'I'm your great-great-grandfather, Porrig.'

'Oh,' said Porrig.

'Is that all you have to say, *oh?*'

'For the time being, yes. No, hold on, it isn't. If you're my great-great-grandfather, then that would have made you my Uncle Apocalypso's grandfather, wouldn't it? And if that was the case, you'd know his real name.'

The old bloke shook his old head. 'No, Porrig, I wouldn't. I'm your father's great-grandfather, not your mother's.'

'Yes, but—'

'Yes, but, nothing. I was Apocalypso's apprentice, I didn't even know he had a sister until after he died. But your mother wouldn't tell me his real name and there are absolutely no existing family records, she saw to that.'

'But why? I don't understand.'

'Because of what he discovered. Because it was a secret that no-one wanted ever to be revealed.'

'And you know this secret?'

'For my sins, yes.'

'Tell me then,' said Porrig. 'I promise I'll keep it to myself.'

'But I don't want you to keep it to yourself. I want you to tell everyone about it. This secret has led to a worldwide conspiracy and the whole world must know about it.'

'So, tell me.'

'All in good time.'

'Look,' said Porrig. 'This is all very fascinating and I would love to hear this big secret of yours, if it's really true. But I'm not entirely certain what I should or shouldn't believe—'

'Believe in this,' said the old bloke and he took from his waistcoat the polished ebony snuff box he had showed to Porrig in the train. 'This is true. The feather from the angel's wing. I am doomed to wander this planet until I can return it. This is the curse that was laid upon me.'

'I don't see how immortality can be a curse.'

'At your age, no you wouldn't. But I'm getting on for two hundred. It aches, Porrig. It hurts. I hurt.'

'I'm sorry.'

'Thank you. During my long life I have seen more than any one man should see. We were not created to live so long. To see so much. I want only to rest. I have done my best to atone for my sins. When I met your uncle and saw the danger of what he was doing, I tried to help him. But he would not be shaken into sense and now he is gone and I am left alone. Alone, but for you, Porrig.'

'Why me?' Porrig asked.

'Because you are the beneficiary of your late uncle's will.'

'I wasn't even born when he died.'

'No, but he knew you would be. He divined it. You can do that kind of stuff here, you know.'

'I'm so confused.' Porrig shook his weary head. 'Just where is *here*? You still haven't told me.'

'Rippington told you. ALPHA 17 the—'

'Seventeenth hows-your-father of the Alphonic whatsaname.'

'It's all in here.' The old bloke made a magical pass and a book appeared in Porrig's hand. It was a bigger book than the little big book had been. But not so big as some of the big big books Porrig had passed by on his journey through wherever he was. As it were.

'Is the secret in here?' Porrig asked.

'Everything's in there. Everything about me and about this place and about what I want you to do. I have gone to a great deal of trouble setting this all up for you, I hope you won't disappoint me.'

'I still don't know what you want me to do.'

'I want you to draw and print and distribute a comic book. I want the secret spread amongst the young. I don't want another generation living in ignorance of the truth.'

Porrig lifted the front cover.

'No,' said the old bloke. 'Not here. You read it when you get back to the shop. And keep it safe.'

'All right, I will.' Porrig tucked the book into his pocket. 'Can I go back now?'

'Indeed. We've said enough for the time being. You read the book and then we'll have another talk. All right?'

'All right.' And Porrig shook the old bloke by the hand.

'Ouch,' said the old bloke.

'I'm sorry,' said Porrig.

The old bloke led the way and Porrig followed. There was more of the same: the corridors and the rooms and the balconies. But Porrig was getting the measure of it. He pretended not to follow and when he'd had enough (which was really quite soon) he said, 'Are we nearly there?'

'Would you like us to be?'

'Yes, I would.'

'Then we are.'

They stood ·before a little door. 'You'll have to stoop,' the old bloke said.

'And does this come out in the shop?'

'No. I think it comes out under the pier.'

'You *think*?'

'I'm reasonably sure.'

'Oh goody,' said Porrig.

' "Tone",' said the old bloke. 'Now get a move on, we don't want you to be seen.'

The old bloke opened the door and Porrig squeezed into the opening. A cool breeze blew on to his face. It smelled of the sea.

It smelled of reality.

'I'll see you soon, then,' said Porrig.

'I'll keep in touch, I—' A terrible crash cut the old fellow short. 'Go on,' he said. 'I'll see what that was.'

Porrig pressed out through the opening and found himself straightening up beneath the pier. A lovely moon-bathed night it was, though nothing short of nippy.

Porrig took a deep breath of home and peace and then something scuttled past his feet.

'Rat!' cried Porrig, leaping up. 'I'll see you—' But the small door shut and now was only wall.

'Whenever I see you,' said Porrig.

He turned up the collar of his jacket, marched along the front and up the steps onto the prom. It was nearly two in the morning now and the prom was deserted. Porrig put some extra pace into his marching.

Back to the shop and up to bed was what he wanted. A cup of decaff and a read of the old bloke's book.

And then what?

Porrig shook his head. The secret? The big secret? The big secret that he was to reveal to the world?

'Got any change, mate?' The voice came out of a doorway. Porrig kept his head down and kept right on walking.

'Oi, mate! I said, got any change?'

'I haven't,' said Porrig. 'Please leave me alone.'

The beggar-for-change lurched out of the doorway. He was a fair-sized beggar and rather drunk with it. He came after Porrig at the stagger. 'Hold on, mate,' he called. 'Just a bit of small change. Enough for a cuppa.'

'I haven't,' said Porrig, increasing his speed.

'I'll bet you bloody have.' And the beggar was on him.

Caught from behind, with his arms pinned to his sides, Porrig struggled and kicked. 'Get off me. Get off me.' The beggar threw him down and Porrig rolled into the gutter. 'Get off me, I—'

The beggar put the boot in.

He kicked and he kicked at Porrig. Porrig's cries for mercy went unheard in the night. When the kicker tired of kicking, he went through Porrig's pockets, stole his wallet and the small change that he had.

And he also stole the old bloke's book.

Then he stumbled off into the darkness of an alley, leaving Porrig to bleed on his own.

Porrig lay beside the kerb, a tangled piece of wreckage. Unloved. Uncared for. All alone.

Not altogether alone.

For beneath a car parked near at hand two blue cat's eyes had seen it all. And now the owner of these eyes crept out from his hiding place and climbed to his feet. Two little grey feet on the end of two spindly grey legs, between which swung a small rubbing part.

'So this is heaven,' Rippington said. 'I can't say I'm all too impressed.'

And taking a swift sniff at Porrig, he followed the beggar-thief into the alley, his two small feet scuffling.

Just like a rat.

11

Porrig lay in a coma, all alone in a horrid little room at the Brighton General Hospital. And no-one came to visit him.

No-one.

Not a single rock star, nor a sports personality, nor even a television presenter, even though they do have it written into their contracts. Oh yes. They have to do it at least once a year, if required. And they never refuse, because if they did and people found out, it would be the end of their careers.

But they only have to do it for children. Never for adults. It wouldn't be news if they did it for adults. It wouldn't be given that nice little human interest slot at the end of the six o'clock news. And it wouldn't log up any points towards the knighthood.

So nobody famous visited Porrig. Nobody came to hold his hand and sing to him, or tell him stories while the news crews filmed them. Porrig was simply left all on his own in his coma.

There to fester and bewail his lot.

Because, as is often the case with people in comas, Porrig could hear everything that was going on around him, although he was powerless to respond. Which must be really horrible, if you think about it. Especially if you could hear what Porrig was hearing right at this very moment.

'How long has he been like this?' asked the doctor.

'Eight days,' said the nurse.

'And no response at all?'

'Absolutely none.'

'But he's otherwise in good condition?'

'Fine. His ribs are mending nicely and there's no major organ damage.'

'A prime specimen then. But identity unknown?'

'We've put the obligatory blurry photo in *The Big Issue*. But no-one has come forward to claim him.'

'Then we've fulfilled our contractual obligations. One more day and he's ours.'

'Ours, doctor?'

'For the spare parts, nurse. Eyes, heart, lungs, liver.'

'But he's still alive. He might recover.'

'I'm sure that given time and care, he would. But hospitals have to pay for themselves nowadays.'

'I suppose you're right, doctor. But it does seem a shame.'

'He's only a vagrant, nurse. A nobody. I don't think he's ever likely to do anything earth-shattering, is he?'

'I suppose not.'

'But his untimely demise will not only free up a bed, it will profit the hospital by at least fifty thousand pounds.'

'As much as that?'

'Of course. His organs will be auctioned off to private hospitals. Some part of him may well end up inside someone rich and famous and important.'

'That's comforting.'

'Of course it is. So, give him another day and if he shows no sign of recovery, switch him off.'

'Will you sign the release forms, doctor?'

'No, you sign them, nurse. I have to get up to the children's ward. Carol Vorderman is coming in to sit with a little blonde-haired comatose girl. I've got to go into make-up and rehearse my lines.'

'Break a leg, doctor.'

'Thank you, nurse. And one other thing.'

'Yes, doctor?'

'Don't forget to lock the ward door. We wouldn't want a repeat of that unfortunate business last month.'

And Porrig was left all alone to indulge in some really heavy duty lot-bewailing.

Just another vagrant, eh? Another nobody, eh? Not likely to do anything earth-shattering, eh? Cut him up for spare parts, eh? And what *was* the unfortunate business last month?

Eh?

Porrig groaned inwardly. He really had had quite enough.

On the ninth day of his hospitalization things perked up for Porrig. He didn't wake from his coma, or anything like that, but things did perk up.

At six in the morning the fire alarms went off.

Porrig sighed considerably at this. To be roasted alive was not the kind of death he might have chosen. Like most men, he favoured the 'shot by a jealous husband while caught in the arms of a page three girl, at the age of eighty-seven' kind. But life can be a bummer. And the fire alarms went off.

Nurses marched purposefully about, mostly in the direction of the children's ward. Doctors passed his door at a determined pace. The walking-wounded hobbled towards the fire exit.

Porrig lay all alone. Bloody typical, he thought. And me worth fifty grand!

But then he heard people bustling in and Porrig was dragged from his bed, trailing various important tubes and wires, bunged onto a trolley, covered with a big blanket and bumped through this door, that door and the next.

Porrig felt the chill of the car-park, then further bumpings, then a kind of folding up and a forcing into a confined space and then a lot of movement.

Porrig lay speechless, his knees up under his chin, somewhere dark and musty and on the move. Somewhat later there was some stopping, more hustling about, some carrying, some opening of doors and dragging up stairs and then a flopping onto a bed where he was left alone once more.

Oh dear, thought Porrig. I bet I'm in the dissecting room.

'I don't know what one of those is,' said a voice Porrig recognized. 'But you're not in one.'

I am *not* alone, thought Porrig.

'No, you're not,' said Rippington.

It's you!

'It's me.'

'And me,' said someone else.

Wok Boy, thought Porrig.

'That's him,' said Rippington. 'You can speak to him,' he said to Wok Boy. 'He can't reply, but he can hear and understand you. I can read his thoughts.'

'How are you doing?' Wok Boy asked.

Rippington listened. 'He says he's in a fucking coma, how do you think he's doing?'

'Ungrateful shitbag,' said Wok Boy. 'I should have left him there.'

Rippington listened. 'He says he's sorry. But how come you did get him out and how come *I'm* here.'

'I saw your photo in *The Big Issue*. I knew what they'd do to you if you didn't wake up. I busted someone out of there last month. As for this wee man, you tell him, Rippington.'

'I followed you out of ALPHA 17,' said the imp. 'And I don't like it here, I want to go home. I came in through your cat flap. I knew your address because I heard you thinking it when I first met you. Wok Boy was sleeping in your bed, I didn't half scare the breakfast out of his bottom.'

'And he got back the book the old bloke gave you from the bastard who gave you the kicking.'

'I did,' said Rippington. 'I'm such a nice fellow.'

Wok Boy leaned over Porrig. 'What's he saying now?' he asked.

'He says something about it being all too "pat" and he doesn't believe a bloody word of it.'

'Do you think if I gave him a couple of clouts around the head it might bring him out of his coma?'

'Worth a try,' said Rippington.

So Wok Boy clouted Porrig in the head.

'Any luck?' asked Wok Boy.

'None,' said Rippington. 'Although he now says that he believes everything we've told him and he wants to know whether you've read the old bloke's book.'

'Well, I did have a little peep.'

Rippington listened once more to Porrig's thoughts.

'What did he say?' asked Wok Boy.

'Nothing complimentary,' said Rippington. 'But he does want to know what's in the book.'

'Well, you tell him, you've read it too.'

Rippington now stuck his little hands over his earholes. 'Very bad language,' he said. 'Not nice at all. I'm going downstairs to read another of those comic things. You tell him all about the book.'

Rippington rat-like scuttled away. Wok Boy sat down on Porrig's bed. Porrig winced inwardly as Wok Boy settled himself, punching flat a bed lump that was caused by Porrig's foot.

'Right then,' said Wok Boy. 'Story time.' He pulled the old bloke's book from his pocket and waggled it in front of Porrig's face. 'See this,' he said. 'No, of course you don't. But it's great stuff, this book. Real top-line *X Files* conspiracy stuff. I'll tell it to you short and sweet because I've got a date over the road with this barmaid. Amazing tits, works part time at Phart-Ebum's.'

Porrig groaned internally.

'So,' continued Wok Boy. 'What you have first is your standard science fiction fare. Worlds within worlds, you know the kind of business. We are not alone on this planet. We share the same space with an almost infinite number of other realities. But they all function on different natural frequencies, so for the most part we can't see them and they can't see us. Once in a while freak conditions exist and then we get a glimpse of them. UFOs, ghosts, demons, angels, lake monsters, Bigfoot and bogy men generally.

'Frankly, I would have considered all that a pile of old pants if I hadn't met up with Rippington. So there you go. I hope you're following this.'

Porrig was and he groaned a bit more to himself.

'So, we come to magic. And I'm talking about real magic here, not stage magic. In our reality we don't have any magic, so black magicians perform elaborate rituals designed to summon entities from their own realms to perform evil deeds for them. Summon them in fact from a separate reality where magic *does* exist. Mostly it doesn't work, thank the Goddess, but sometimes, every once in a while . . . WALLOP!' Wok Boy whacked Porrig in the cobblers. 'Know what I'm saying?'

Under his eyelids Porrig's eyes crossed.

'Your uncle,' said Wok Boy. 'Apocalypso The Miraculous. Black magician. They kicked him out of the Magic Circle because he cheated, used real magic. The old bloke was working as his assistant and he tried to persuade him to turn it in. But he didn't and WALLOP!' Porrig caught it in the cobblers once again. 'Legend of Faust, mate, he paid with his very soul.'

Porrig pondered bitterly upon just how Wok Boy would pay. Heavily, he concluded.

'So,' continued Wok Boy. 'We're coming up to the last bit of the story and this is the best bit. The bit that the old bloke wants you to do the comic book about. Your uncle had managed through his rituals to access these other realities, but he was on the make and he was taking out more than he was putting back. You have to retain a balance, because everybody's on the make, no matter what reality they're in. That's what you'd call a universal truth, I suppose. So, after he got his big come-uppance, the old bloke tried to put everything right. Destroy his papers, that kind of thing. But what he didn't know was that your uncle had posted a copy of the ritual off to his sister in a letter. Your mum, Porrig.

'So, the years pass and the old bloke is living in ALPHA 17 (because he knows how to do the ritual and move from one reality to another). He's got some big problem he's trying to sort out about an angel's feather, although it's not quite clear in the book exactly what that is. So, he's there and one day he finds that someone is nicking stuff. Someone from this reality is entering that reality. He lies in wait and then he follows them and he doesn't half get a big surprise.

'He discovers that a special ministry has been set up in London. A kind of ministry of the paranormal and that the people working there are doing all kinds of deals with people and "things" from the other realities. Everyone being on the make, as I said. The old bloke is horrified, especially when he learns that this ministry is virtually running the world. And who's in charge of this ministry, eh, eh?' Wok Boy nudged Porrig painfully in his wounded ribs. 'You'll never guess if I don't tell you. So I'll tell you. The person running the ministry, the Ministry of Serendipity, it's called, is the person your mum showed the letter to. He tried out the ritual for himself, realized the potential, approached the government with it, for the good of the nation, of course, and now sits there in the ultimate seat of power running damn near everything.

'It's your dad, Porrig. It's your dad.'

Wok Boy grinned down at Porrig. 'Now what do you think about that?'

Exactly what Porrig did think about that can only be imagined. But that it was nothing altogether jolly would be a reasonable guess.

'The old bloke wants you to expose your own dad,' said Wok Boy. 'Expose him and the ministry. Tell the world who's really running everything. No publisher will touch the story, no newspaper or TV news service, the ministry controls them all. But a privately printed production, beautiful artwork, telling the whole story, could get the message across to the young. They take comics more seriously than newspapers anyway. Well, that's about it.' Wok Boy rose from the bed. 'That's the brief outline, all the details are in the book, so you can read them when you wake up. I'd read it all to you myself, but I've got other things to do, if you know what I mean.'

Wok Boy leaned over and gave Porrig's tender testicles a mirthsome tweak, then he left, leaving Porrig once more all alone.

No rock stars, no sports personalities, no television presenters.

All alone, bewailing his lot.

And cursing the name of Augustus Naseby.

Inwardly, of course.

12

Augustus Naseby, inwardly cursed but outwardly thriving,
lurked in the seat of power on the swirly-whirly-patterned
carpet that covered the floor of his little office in the Ministry
of Serendipity, beneath Mornington Crescent Underground
station.

The station itself has apparently been closed for years. In fact
the station never ever was open. Ask anyone you like. Say:
'Have you ever been to Mornington Crescent on the Tube?'
Some bugger is bound to say yes, but they will be lying.

So why exactly has the station never been open? And why is
the Ministry of Serendipity situated there?

Good questions. And ones that are relevant and so shall be
answered.

Allow me to explain.

Now, as you may well know, the London Underground
system is reckoned to be the very best of its type in the whole
wide world.

Sure, you've got the Paris Métro, with its fab Art Nouveau
fiddly bits, and Tokyo with its Sarin attacks and New York with
its muggers and junkies, but the London Underground has its
own special magic.

It's a magic that most people don't know anything of. They might travel on the Underground for all of their lives and still know nothing about the real magic. They may well know about the race of troglodytes who live down there, descendants of trapped Victorian navvies. They may know about how the government regularly tests out new strains of flu virus on the commuters there. And they may even know about the ghost of Jack the Ripper, who pushes so-called suicides to their deaths. But they don't know about the magic.

And why don't they know? Because it's a secret, that's why. Guarded by the Ministry of Serendipity.

Consider, if you will, the map of the London Underground. It's a very stylish map and has won numerous design awards. But the map conceals far more than it reveals. Certainly it shows you the order of the stations, but it does not show you their actual locations.

Allow me to explain.

The map is all straight lines – apart from the Circle Line, and the Circle Line isn't even drawn as a circle. If you take a large-scale road map of London and mark on it all the tube stations, then join these dots up, a curious pattern is revealed. A series of strange, almost cabbalistic symbols.

The reason for this is that the location for each station was carefully chosen by a group of Victorian ritual magicians skilled in the arts of geomancy and working for the government of the day. The London Underground follows the course of the major ley-line system, the stations being at node points where certain earth energies are released into the capital city. The entire system has at its very hub Mornington Crescent, and it is towards this station that the channelled energies flow like water spiralling down a plughole.

You see, once we had an empire that ruled two-thirds of the world. And how? By magic, that's how.

But then, later, what happened? Some daft twat behind a Whitehall desk decided that magic offended the British sense of fair play. And so we lost the empire.

It is not difficult to imagine how thrilled a later government was when Augustus Naseby turned up on their doorstep with a plan to restore it.

But what exactly was his plan, you may well ask, and how did he intend to put it into action?

Well, as it is Thursday and the Ministry of Serendipity always has its special meetings on Thursday, why don't we listen in and find out?

Augustus Naseby rose from the chair he was lurking in and donned the robes and fez of an Egyptian. The impersonating of Egyptians was an important part of Thursday meetings. But as its significance is a closely guarded secret, it wouldn't do to go blabbing it about here.

All donned and dandy, Augustus set out along a corridor which led him at considerable length to the big boardroom where the meetings were held.

It was a bloody big boardroom, about the size of, well, ooh, something really big, Wembley Stadium perhaps. Or if that is a bit too big, something slightly smaller. It was all panelled out in oak the way that boardrooms are and had a table so long that it dwindled away into the distance.

Augustus sat down at the head of the table. Without the aid of a telescope (something he never carried), he had no way of knowing who, or what, might be sitting at the foot.

He struck a small brass gong, which emitted a sound like a cat being put through a mangle, and called the meeting to order.

'Order,' he called.

Many faces turned towards him. Many faces of many shapes and sizes. Some very big and some really really really little. Some in between and a few it was difficult to categorize.

'Now,' said Augustus. 'Before we begin this meeting and for the benefit of anyone or thing that has not attended before, a word or two of what it's all about.'

Heads nodded thoughtfully. Big, small and otherwise.

'We at the Ministry of Serendipity take care of business. We plan next week's news, what will be in fashion next year, who will become famous and for how long and for why.

120

'Why do we do this? Because someone has to. If politicians and world leaders, who are just jumped-up politicians anyway, were allowed to do this, there is no telling where it might all end. When I took over the helm here back in the 1960s, my brief was simple. "Sort out the mess that the world's in, Augustus," the Prime Minister said to me, and that's just what I have been doing. Sorting out the mess the world's in. Or should I say, the *worlds* are in?'

There was much applause at this. Which meant that it had to mean something.

'You all have problems,' said Augustus. 'You know this and I know this. Beings from one reality want something that beings in another reality have got and so on and so forth, and I act as broker and arbitrator to see that everyone and everything gets a fair share.'

There was even more applause at this. Much clapping of hands and things that passed for hands.

'When, all those years ago, I performed the ritual that enabled me to pass from one reality to another, coming as I did in the spirit of peace, a stranger in strange lands, I did so in the hope that we would be able to co-exist in harmony. You, as chosen representatives of your separate realities, meet with me here every Thursday so that we can iron out little difficulties, trade freely and with trust.'

Even greater clapping and flapping and several cries of 'Here, here.'

An enormous maggot in a red fez rose upon its belly parts.

'Mr Chairman,' it said, in a voice that resembled the sound of two ferrets fighting in an oversized condom. 'Mr Chairman, your fairness and generosity are well known to us all. The folk of my reality, Insect World, would like to take this opportunity to thank you for all the rotten apples you unfailingly supply us with, in exchange for nothing more than their weight in useless gold.'

Augustus Naseby cleared his throat. 'Ah yes,' he said, 'useless gold.'

Hands and things went clap clap slop and soon the board-room air all but glowed with the eulogies of praise that poured from up and down the table. Praise for Augustus, the man who so selflessly plundered the riches of his own world: beer-bottle tops, used cocoa tins, horse manure and condemned veal, in exchange for the rubbish of other realities: gold, silver, platinum, diamonds . . .

Do you see a pattern beginning to emerge?

Augustus Naseby held up his hands. 'Please, please,' he said, 'enough praise.'

'More than enough,' came a voice. 'If there's any praising being done, it should be done for me.'

Augustus Naseby cast a doubtful eye towards the owner of the voice: a young and shabby-looking individual who had now risen to his feet. He was, by all accounts, human – well, humanish. His eyes were small, his mouth was large, his nose was in-between. He wore upon his unwashed head a dirty fez and a crown-of-thorns-style wreath of Christmas tree fairy lights which flashed on and off at irregular intervals. He sported an ill-fitting tweed suit, onto the shoulders of which had been glued a pair of cardboard wings. These, like his face, had been spray-painted gold.

'Ah,' said Augustus. 'Espadrille, it's you.'

'*Angel* Espadrille,' said the angel Espadrille.

He wasn't much of an angel really. In fact he wasn't really an angel at all. He hailed from a separate reality peopled by types such as himself, who had accidentally stumbled into this reality for a moment or two, been observed by some gullible sap and taken for the real McMessenger of God. And then got it into their own heads that they actually were. Sounds unlikely? Well, anything's possible. And if it's possible then it must exist in a separate reality.

The Ministry of Serendipity found the likes of Espadrille extremely useful. They were always on the lookout for bogus religions they could manipulate, the 'real church' being something that, in their opinion, held far too much power in the real world. And holding *all* the power in the world was what the Ministry was all about.

Augustus had The Twenty-third Congregation of Espadrille pencilled in as next year's big thing.

'*Angel* Espadrille,' said Augustus. 'How honoured we are that you should grace us once more with your presence.'

'I'd grace you with my presence a whole lot more if I got the chance. But my name seems to get unaccountably left off the invite list every other week.'

'I cannot imagine how that happens,' said Augustus, the lie falling from his lips with the ease of a turd falling from a passing pigeon.

'Yeah, well, I've filled out all the application forms and I want to know when I can start visiting my followers on a regular basis.'

'You wish to manifest,' said Augustus.

'He wishes to give the womenfolk a good knobbing.' A small grey head bobbed up from beneath the table. It was a small grey domed head with oval black eyes, a tiny lipless mouth and no nose whatsoever to speak of.

It was, as it were, your archetypal gray.

'Keep out of this you little weirdo,' said the angel.

'Weirdo?' said the gray. 'You're calling *me* a weirdo!'

'Yeah, well we all know what you get up to.'

'Oh yes, and what's that?'

The angel made a two-fingered gesture that is universally understood.

'And what does *that* mean?' asked the gray.

'We all know what you do with the people you abduct.'

'We have permission,' said the gray. 'In triplicate, with the Ministry's seal on the bottom. For our interbreeding process.'

'Your unlicensed shagging process you mean.'

'But it *is* licensed. Ten thousand top-class human breeding specimens a year. Kindly donated by our chairman Mr Naseby. All we have to do is go around at night and pick them up from the shop doorways where they've been left out for us.'

Augustus Naseby cleared his throat once more.

'And I'll tell you this.' The gray shook a diminutive and bony fist. 'We'll be here when you're nothing but a footnote in a book of duff twentieth-century cults.'

'I'm not duff,' huffed the angel, puffing out what little chest he had. 'I'm holy.'

'And my cock's a kipper.'

'Gentlemen, please,' said Augustus, raising his hands. 'There is no call for such undignified behaviour.'

At that moment a pig fell through the ceiling.

'Sorry I'm late,' said the pig. 'I was putting some lard on the wife's boil and you know how time flies when you're having a good time. Have I missed anything?'

'Not much,' said Augustus.

'I saw your son last week,' said the pig.

'My son?' asked Augustus.

'That's right. I recognized him from that photo you have pinned to your darts board. He was lurking around in ALPHA 17. Doesn't lurk as well as you, but I'm sure he'll get the hang of it eventually.'

'My son in ALPHA 17?' Augustus clutched at his heart. 'What was he doing there?'

'No idea at all.' The pig did sniffings with his snout. 'Any sandwiches?' he asked.

'I object to this pig,' said the angel Espadrille. 'Has he got security clearance? He's not impersonating an Egyptian.'

'What's that thing on your head?' asked the pig.

'My holy crown,' said the angel.

'No, I didn't mean the manky lights. I meant the other thing. It looks like a Kentucky Fried Chicken party bucket.'

'It's my official fez.'

'No it bloody isn't,' said the gray. 'The pig's right. It is a party bucket.'

'All right, it *is*! Some swine nicked my fez.'

'Language!' said the pig.

'This angel is an imposter,' said the gray.

Augustus shook his head. 'Of course he's an imposter.'

'No, I mean an imposter here. He's an imposter of an imposter.'

'I don't think I quite follow that,' said the pig.

'I'm the genuine article,' said the angel.

'Shut up all of you!' Augustus brought his fists down hard upon the table, flattening the maggot who was putting out a cigarette.

124

'Is it all right if I eat that?' asked the pig. 'As you've no sandwiches?'

Augustus wiped his sticky fingers down his smart Egyptian front. 'I am closing this meeting,' he said. 'I will see you all again next week. Same time, same place.'

'That's not fair,' the angel complained. 'I want my application passed.'

'And *you*' – Augustus pointed stickily at Espadrille – 'will wear a proper fez next week or you won't be allowed in.'

'L. Ron Hubbard nicked my fez.'

'Meeting adjourned!'

'You're all barking mad,' said the pig.

'And you stay here. I want a word with you.'

Augustus went off to lurk in a corner, beckoning the pig to follow him. The various representatives from the various other realities removed themselves variously. There were nearly two hundred of them, although only four had actually spoken this day and of these one had been unfortunately flattened. A small boy from a separate reality, where small boys don't have to eat their greens and are allowed to stay up as long as they like watching television, had to be persuaded to leave by asking him very nicely and giving him a big bag of sweets.

A number of chickens, who had repeatedly had their applications for temporary world domination rejected, relieved themselves on the carpet and faded into wistful imagination.

'Now,' said Augustus to the pig, 'what is all this about my beastly son being in ALPHA 17?'

A knock came at the door.

'Someone's knocking,' said the pig. 'I hope it's not that maggot's daddy.'

'About my son—'

Knock knock knock.

'Shall I answer it? I could say you were busy. Larding up your wife's boil, or something.'

Knock knock knock, went the repeated knocking at the door (repeatedly).

'I'll speak to you later,' said Augustus, ducking down behind his chair.

The door opened, the pig went out and three men walked in. They were ragged men. Ragged and woebegone, much travelled and much wearied. Their armpits sorely needed a wash and their socks smelled none too savoury.

The tallest of the three, and very tall he was, dropped down into the nearest chair and buried his face in his hands.

The youngest stood with *his* hands in his trouser pockets. 'He's hiding, I'll bet,' he said.

The one of middle years, with the white frothy barnet, pointed. 'There he is,' he said. 'He's lurking behind his big chairman's chair.'

Augustus rose with dignity. 'Thank you, madam,' he said, 'please put your bill in the post.'

'He's got a woman down there,' said the youngest, his hands at work within his trouser pockets.

'No he hasn't,' said the frothy white-haired one. 'He was just on the lurk, as per usual.'

'Gentlemen,' said Augustus. 'What a surprise. Danbury, I won't shake your hand. Dr Harney, I will shake yours.' Augustus did. 'And Sir John. Oh my God!'

Augustus stepped back. 'Your . . . your . . .'

'Don't say the word,' said Dr Harney.

'Beard,' said Augustus.

Sir John burst into a flood of tears.

The doctor comforted him. 'Have a sweetie from this bag here,' he said, patting the tall man's shoulder.

'What happened?' asked Augustus. 'The state of you all . . . the . . .'

'Monty the head man nicked his beard.' Danbury grinned as he said it.

'Shaved it off?' Augustus dropped into his chair.

'Pulled it off.' Danbury made the motions. 'It was a falsy. We never knew.'

'Nuke the island,' croaked Sir John between blubberings.

'We have discussed that.' Augustus waggled sticky digits. 'Nuking the creature is not an option.'

'I'm not talking about the creature. I'm talking about the bastard who stole my beard.'

126

Danbury clutched at his stomach with his non groin-clutching hand.

'Stop sniggering!' shouted Sir John.

'I'm sorry,' said Danbury, who wasn't.

'So, where is it?' asked Augustus.

'My beard?'

'Not *your* beard. *My* spacecraft. My seven-pointed spacecraft, which you were to retrieve for me and bring back here. Outside on a lorry, is it?'

Dr Harney shook his froth. 'Not exactly,' he said.

'What?'

'We ran into a spot of trouble,' said Danbury, offering an empty smile.

'All right,' said Augustus, 'tell me all about it.'

Danbury opened his mouth to speak.

'I'll tell him,' said Dr Harney. 'You can't do it without laughing anyway.'

Danbury tinkered once more in his trousers.

'We ran into a spot of trouble on the island,' said the doctor. 'The Americans had got there first and bribed the natives. We were captured and held prisoner while the Americans absconded in a tramp steamer with the spacecraft.'

'Oh dear,' said Augustus.

'You see, Sir John had biffed the head man of the village and the head man tried to cut off Sir John's beard and it sort of came off—'

'And I shot the head man's dog,' said Danbury.

'Yes,' said Dr Harney, 'and in the confusion we managed to escape in a canoe. We were later picked up by a rescue plane that was looking for the tramp steamer.'

'But the plane crashed,' said Danbury.

'Yes, it crashed.' Dr Harney made fists. 'Will you please shut up. I'm telling this.'

'Sorry,' said Danbury, smirking away.

'The rescue plane flew off searching for the tramp steamer. We eventually reached it. It was moored to a liner.'

'A liner?' Augustus raised his eyebrows.

'The pilot flew us in close. It was an American cruise ship

called *The Leviathan*. The creature was aboard, on deck.'

'It was horrible,' said Danbury. 'Twenty feet high, all green like a great fat sprout and—'

'Hold it!' Augustus rose from his seat. 'You mean that the alien creature is alive? That it is out of its spacecraft?'

'Afraid so,' said the doctor. 'And it *was* horrible. It was sitting there upon mounds of cushions and everyone on deck, thousands of people, were all on their knees, praying to it.'

'Dear God!'

'And it had a barbecue on the go,' said Danbury.

'Shut up!' said the doctor. 'We weren't going to mention that.'

'Tell me,' said Augustus.

'There was a barbecue and there were bits of . . .' Dr Harney hesitated.

'Bits of people,' said Danbury. 'It was cooking people on the barbecue.'

'This is terrible, terrible.'

'Agreed,' said Dr Harney. 'We were circling around, trying to take a few pictures, when the creature saw us—'

'And the pilot started clutching at his head' – Danbury now clutched at his – 'and going "aaaaagh, the pain, the pain" and the plane went out of control and we crashed into the sea.'

'Good Lord,' said Augustus.

'We were picked up by a fishing boat,' continued Dr Harney. 'But Sir John got into an argument with the captain because he wouldn't change course for us and—'

'I shot the captain's parrot.'

'Shut up! We were thrown overboard just west of Haiti. We had to swim ashore. Then we caught the plane home.'

'There was some further unpleasantness,' said Danbury.

'I doubt whether Mr Naseby wants to hear about that.'

'I bloody do!' said Augustus, who was slowly but surely reaching the boil.

'At the airport,' the doctor continued. 'They wouldn't let Sir John through passport control. Without his beard he didn't look like his photo and—'

'I shot the passport chap's goat.'

'*Goat!*'

'The airport mascot. We had to hijack the plane and—'

'Enough!' Augustus rose to his feet and brought his fists down hard once more, driving maggot smearings into the table top. 'I don't want to hear any more. You fouled it all up. I trusted you and you fouled it all up.'

'He's talking to you, doctor,' said Danbury.

'He's talking to Sir John,' said the doctor.

'I'm talking to no-one,' said Sir John. 'I shall take a vow of silence and get me to a monastery.'

'I see.' Augustus sat down and lurked in his chair. 'So no-one is going to take any responsibility for this cock-up.'

'Sir John should take full responsibility,' said Danbury.

'I should do no such thing. The blame lies with the Americans.'

'There is some truth in that,' agreed the doctor.

'And if there's any responsibility left over, Danbury should take it.'

'What a bare-faced cheek,' said Danbury.

There was a moment's silence. Then all eyes turned to the bare-faced cheeks of Sir John Rimmer.

'Oh,' said Danbury. 'I didn't mean . . .' His smirk began to grow again. 'I mean . . . it just slipped out . . .' He looked over at the doctor. 'But it's pretty good though, isn't it? Bare-faced cheek.' Then Danbury folded up. 'Bare-faced cheek,' he went as he collapsed in laughter. 'What a good'n, what a good'n!'

Dr Harney fought with a smirk of his own. 'That's not amusing,' he said through gritted teeth.

'It is.' Danbury sank to his knees, howling with laughter.

Which, as we all know, can be infectious.

Especially during times of stress.

'Bare-faced cheek,' said Augustus, pointing at Sir John.

Danbury, on the floor now, kicked his legs in the air.

Dr Harney began to titter. 'It's not funny,' he giggled. 'It isn't.'

Augustus Naseby broke into guffaws. 'It *is*,' he gasped. 'It is.'

'You're right,' and the doctor sank to the floor, clutching his stomach and laughing like the drain of yore. 'But I'll say one thing for Sir John,' he managed between convulsions. 'He takes it very well, considering all the *hair-raising* adventures he's had.'

'Oooh, that's good.' Danbury rolled about. 'And the *close shaves*. Don't forget the *close shaves*.'

'He certainly gets around,' gagged Augustus, now also on the floor. 'You could say he's *hair* today and gone tomorrow.'

'To baldly go where no man has gone before,' croaked the doctor.

'That's a quote, isn't it?' Danbury dabbed at the tears in his eyes. 'It's either Oscar Wilde, or . . . or . . .'

'Or?' gulped the doctor.

'*Hairy* Belafonte.'

'No, no.' The doctor shook his laughing head. 'It was Shakespeare. The Immortal *Beard*.'

'Shut up, you bastards!' Sir John leaped from his chair and stamped up and down on the floor. 'Shut up! Do you hear me?'

Danbury drummed his fists on the carpet. Dr Harney tried to struggle to his feet. Augustus Naseby said, 'He's right, enough is enough.'

'I want to say something,' shouted Sir John. 'Something serious.'

Augustus nodded. 'All right,' said he. 'Pull yourselves together now, lads. Sir John wants to say something serious.'

Danbury and Dr H. climbed to their respective feet and tried to look *very* serious.

'Go on then, Sir John,' said Augustus. '*Get it off your chest.*'

Another moment's silence.

Then collapse.

'You utter bastards!' Sir John Rimmer stormed about, kicking at the bellowing buffoons. 'You rotten bastards, stop!'

'All right. All right.' Augustus staggered to the table. 'Enough, and I really mean it this time. Come on now, lads, law of diminishing returns and everything. If Sir John has something to say, let's listen to what it is.'

The others nodded, pulled out chairs and placed their bums upon them.

'Go on then, Sir John.'

Sir John looked down at the three seated men. 'All right,' said he, 'you have all enjoyed a good laugh at my expense and in all truth I deserve it. The false beard was a foolish vanity. The foolish vanity of a foolish man who led a failed expedition. Who has endangered the lives of thousands now and possibly millions in the very near future. I am a failure. I am a fake. Danbury, take out your father's gun and put it to my head.'

'Sure thing,' said Danbury, reaching for his pistol.

'Don't be absurd.' Dr Harney elbowed Danbury in the ribs. 'You are not a failure, Sir John. You are a noble man. An English gentleman.'

'Then I shall take the gentleman's way out. Hand me your pistol, Danbury.'

'Sure thing,' said the lad.

'No.' The doctor elbowed him again.

'That hurts,' said Danbury.

Sir John squared his narrow shoulders. 'You are right, doctor,' he said. 'Suicide achieves nothing. It is the coward's way out. I must make amends. I will confront the creature myself.'

'Bloody hell,' said Danbury.

'Are you seriously serious?' Augustus Naseby asked.

'Seriously seriously serious.'

'That's serious all right.'

'There are at least three thousand people on that ship,' said Sir John (seriously), 'and I do not want their deaths on my conscience. The Americans have clearly hushed the whole affair up and may well be planning to nuke the ship themselves.'

'I would,' said Danbury.

'Shut up,' said Dr Harney.

'I will go,' said Sir John, 'out to the ship. We are dealing with a creature that behaves as if it is a god. I will pose as an acolyte come to praise it and welcome it back. Once I have inveigled myself into its confidence, I will kill it.'

Danbury whistled. 'That's very brave,' he said.

'Indeed it is,' said Augustus, rising from his chair to shake Sir John's hand. 'No matter the outcome, you will have my undying respect.'

'Mine also,' said Dr Harney, shaking the noble hand too.

'And mine,' said Danbury, waving the hand that nobody wants to shake. 'But . . . I suppose . . .'

'Suppose what?' asked Sir John.

'That you might . . .'

'Might not come back?'

'Well, that it could be said that you were . . .'

'Dying for my country, what?'

'No,' said Danbury. 'Going to *beard* the lion in his den.'

13

In his den of a coma and growing a beard, lay the son of Augustus Naseby.

'Well, I don't know,' said Wok Boy, pouring soup into a tube that was sticking out of Porrig. 'We'll have to do something to wake you up. You can't just lie here day after day with us waiting on you hand and foot.'

Rippington sat on Porrig's chest and nodded his little grey head.

'What's he saying?' Wok Boy asked.

'He's saying that you're pouring soup down his air pipe.'

'Oh shit!' Wok Boy tore out the funnel, spilling boiling hot soup all over Porrig's crotch.

'You'd have thought that would have stirred him.' Rippington put on a pained expression.

'He's just not responding to treatment.'

'I thought you had him going yesterday, when you put those red ants in his pyjama trousers.'

'I thought I had him going when I stuck that electric cattle prod up his—'

'He says he wants some butter on his rubbing part,' said Rippington.

'I draw the line at *that*.'

'For the excruciating pain of the boiling soup, I think.'

'Oh yeah,' Wok Boy went for the butter.

Rippington grinned down at Porrig. 'You seem to be stuffed,' he said softly. 'But I bet I could wake you up.'

Porrig's thoughts moved into hideous territory.

'No, nothing like that.' Rippington turned up the corners of his mouth, exposing his nasty little teeth. 'It's something I read in a book. One of the *Tales of Earth* series, about this woman who goes to live in a house with these seven little men and she eats this apple and falls asleep and a handsome prince kisses her and she wakes up again. And then she goes off with the handsome prince, leaving the poor little men to fend for themselves again. I think it's probably meant to be allegorical. Either that or it's intended to show what a fickle and ungracious bunch Earth women are.'

Rippington listened. 'No,' he said. 'I can understand that you don't want Wok Boy kissing you. I thought perhaps we might find a princess and she could kiss you and you might wake up. Mind you, I don't know where all the princesses live. Is there a palace nearby?'

'No,' said the vision in white. 'I won't do it.'

Wok Boy stood in The Flying Pig, his hands in his greasy jeans' pockets. 'He'll make it worth your while,' he said.

'Oh yeah? So he's worth a bit, is he?'

'He's got nearly half a million quid's worth of vintage comic books in his shop.'

'And I can have them all?'

'Well, not *all*.'

'How many, then? How much.'

'A thousand quid's worth.'

The vision in white considered this. Wok Boy considered her titties. He'd plied her with drinks all the previous evening, but she hadn't even let him have a feel yet.

'It's not enough,' said the vision.

'I might be able to push him up a bit. Mind you . . .'

'Mind you *what*?'

'You'd have to make it worth my while.'

'*What?*'

'We could both do well out of this. I can't touch any of his stock, I promised someone. But if I could persuade him to cough up a bit more, would you split the profits with me?'

'Ten grand,' said the vision. 'Ten grand for me.'

'Forget it,' said Wok Boy. 'I'll get someone else.'

'All right. Nine grand and that's my final offer.'

'Tell you what,' said Wok Boy. 'Ten grand, if you throw in a blow job.'

'I'm not giving him a blow job!'

'Who said anything about *him*!'

It would be painful to record in detail just what happened next. How Wok Boy got the blow job of a lifetime and Porrig got a bit of half-hearted lip-pecking and how Porrig confided to Rippington that he thought the kissing might just work if he had a lot more of it and how Rippington passed this on to Wok Boy who struck another deal with the vision in white and how by the end of the day Wok Boy was completely shagged out and there was not a single comic book left on the shelves of Porrig's shop.

And how Porrig still lay in a coma.

Although Wok Boy had shifted him over so he could lie down and have a rest too.

Rippington shook his little grey head. 'I think we should have another go with the electric cattle prod,' he said.

At exactly five-twenty-three and four-and-a-half-seconds-nearly the next morning, Porrig awoke with a start.

It was not the start of a cattle prod, but a natural start. A new start. A new awakening.

Porrig jumped to his feet (a jump-start?), rushed across the room, down the stairs and into his shop. Then Porrig screamed very loudly, rushed out of his shop, back up the stairs and into his bedroom and began to kick the life out of Wok Boy.

Wok Boy awoke with a start of his own. And being of a disposition given to long lies-in, he took unkindly to this treatment and dealt out some of his own.

He did not beat Porrig into unconsciousness, because that would have been unfair, what with him just having woken up and everything. But he taught the lad the error of his ways and sent him off to the kitchenette to make tea.

Porrig stirred some blue stuff in a cup. 'All my comics,' he growled and he scowled. 'All my frigging comics. And all for the frigging. I heard them outside on the landing, humping away, and her making off with my stock. Bloody woman. Rippington was right about Snow White. They're all the same. A lot of parasites out for what they can grab. I'll have to marry her now, if I ever want to see my stock again.'

'Your thinking processes are a total mystery to me,' said Rippington. 'The logic you work on is nothing less than surreal.'

Porrig turned to confront the little imp that stood grinning in the doorway. 'Oh, you know all about the Surrealist Movement, do you?'

'Nineteenth harmonic on the fish scale,' said Rippington. 'Never been there myself. But they say it's a very nice place. A bit like Penge.'

'Whatever are you going on about?'

'*Surr*ealing, where the Surrealists come from. As opposed to *South* Ealing, which is somewhere else altogether.'

'Go away,' said Porrig. 'I hold you to blame also.'

'Why, it woke you up, didn't it?'

'I woke up by myself.'

'Nonsense,' said Rippington. 'You had your last half-hearted peck on the lips at seven-twenty-seven last night, which would mean that you should have woken up this morning at precisely five-twenty-three and four-and-a-half-seconds-nearly.'

'Oh,' said Porrig. 'And aaaaaaaaaagh!' He thrust his head into the sink and turned the tap on. 'Uuuuuuuuuuurghbbbbbbrgh,' he continued as he swirled water in and out of his mouth.

'Surrealing,' said Rippington. 'That's the place for you.'

'Bastard,' said Porrig, drying his face on a tea towel.

'You've lost me again,' said the imp.

'That bloody woman. Kissing me on the mouth when she'd been giving Wok Boy a blo—'

'Still, you look well on it. Although I'd rather you didn't breathe in my direction. Are you making tea?'

'Yes.' Porrig was.

'And is that Wok Boy's?'

'It is,' said Porrig.

'Here.' Rippington climbed onto the table and . . .

'That is disgusting,' said Porrig.

'I bet you'll laugh when he drinks it, though.'

Porrig did.

And Porrig sat and looked out of the window, past the fluttering pigeons and off into a sky of deepest blue. 'All my stock,' he kept saying. 'All my beautiful stock.'

'I'll get it back for you,' said Wok Boy.

'Oh yeah?'

'Yes. All of it.'

'And how do you propose to do that?'

'I'll think of something. Although I don't know why I should. You came out of the coma. That *was* the object of the exercise.'

'I'll tell the old bloke when I see him,' said Porrig. 'He'll probably break both your legs.'

'You ungrateful bastard. I thought you might change.'

'I have changed. But you stitched me up. I heard you, don't deny it.'

'I don't know what you're so fussed about. He wasn't that good a shag.'

'*He?*' said Porrig.

'The transvestite. Very convincing tits though. Silicone.'

'*What?*' went Porrig.

'You're not telling me you thought it was a woman. I mean, I swing both ways, me. You have to sometimes, life on the streets and all that. But you didn't really think *he* was a woman . . .'

'Aaaaaaaaaaaaaaaaaagh!' went Porrig, returning once more with haste to the kitchen sink.

At precisely ten-o-two and thirty-two-seconds-almost, a free newspaper came through the door of Porrig's shop. Wok Boy

137

picked it up and brought it up. Porrig was lying on the bed reading his great-great-grandfather's book.

'This is bloody odd,' said Wok Boy.

Porrig looked up without interest.

'Look at the headline. "BEWARE THE BIG STORM".' Wok Boy went over to the window. 'What big storm? It's a beautiful day.'

'Perhaps it's a misprint,' said Porrig, still without interest.

'No, it isn't. It says that a BIG STORM is heading up the English Channel and that all ships and boats and whatever must go at once to the nearest harbour and tie up until further notice.'

'Oh good,' said Porrig. 'With my luck it will probably blow the roof off the building. Which should appeal to you.'

'Why me?'

'Well, you like a good blow, don't you?'

'Oooooh,' said Wok Boy. 'Do I smell the unsavoury twang of homophobia?'

'No, just bitterness. When are you going to get my comics back?'

'When are *you* going to start on the old bloke's comic?'

'I don't know whether I am.'

'But all the stuff in the book?'

Porrig shook his head. 'I've been giving that a lot of thought while I lay in my bed listening to you and the trannie, and I don't know how much of it I actually believe. My daft father running the world from some paranormal ministry in London? That's absurd.'

'But it's true. If the old bloke says it's true then I for one believe him. And you've been to this ALPHA 17 place yourself. Rippington told me. That's where he's from.'

'And he's going back,' said Porrig. 'I don't trust him either.'

'He wants to go back. He hates it here. Rippington reckons that this is the most stupid reality there could possibly be and he can't imagine why anyone would ever want to live in it.'

'Yeah, well, I often feel that way myself.'

'Yeah, well, now you have the chance to do something about it, don't you?'

Porrig shook his head once more. 'Why me?' he asked.

'Oh, get a grip, Porrig. Why you? Because you know, perhaps. Because it's your father, perhaps. Because you could draw the comic book, perhaps. Has it ever occurred to you why you're such an arse with people?'

'It's just the way I am. I can't help it.'

'Bollocks. You're an outsider. It's like what all this is about. Being in tune with your own. Being on the same wavelength.'

'I don't know what this has got to do with me.'

'Crap and bollocks. Have you ever really fitted in, Porrig?'

Porrig thought. 'I'm sure I have.'

'You never have. You're a genuine loner. You've got no real friends. Your family have basically disowned you. Nobody likes you.'

'Hold on,' said Porrig. 'Don't get carried away.'

'People don't like you and you don't like people.'

'I do like people.'

'You don't. You could have given that beggar some small change. But you didn't and you got kicked into a coma.'

'So that makes me a bad person, because I won't shell out money to drunks?'

'I didn't say you were a bad person. You're not a bad person. You're a different person. You're in the wrong key, Porrig.'

'I don't follow you, sorry.'

'Are you happy, Porrig?'

'No,' said Porrig.

'Have you ever been happy?'

Porrig thought once more. 'Not that I can remember,' he said sadly.

'Well, think about it and think about what's in the book. All those separate realities, all a fraction apart. An endless number of possibilities. Worlds within worlds within worlds. You're not in harmony with this world, Porrig, so perhaps you're in the wrong one.'

'What?'

'You are sure about who you are, aren't you?'

'Of course I'm sure. I mean . . .' Porrig thought back. He thought back to the last time he'd seen his parents.

'Sardine can,' said Porrig slowly.

'Pardon?' said Wok Boy.

'My father. He used to say all this stupid stuff. He was saying it the night before I left home. About how the fairies brought me, or I came free with a packet of cornflakes.'

'Or they opened a can of sardines and—'

'Stuff like that,' said Porrig.

'Makes you think,' said Wok Boy. 'Maybe you're not one of us.'

'*Us?* You're not one of *us.*'

'I never pretended I was.'

'And I've been pretending, is that what you're saying?'

'You didn't know any different. It's not your fault.'

'That's comforting.'

'Is it?'

'Not really, no. But it makes some kind of twisted sense. But if I don't belong in this particular reality, which one do I belong in?'

'What about this one?' Wok Boy fished into the waistline of his unspeakable jeans and drew out a comic book.

Porrig took it from his hands and lightly brushed the cover. '*The Silver Surfer,*' he said softly. 'The first one I saw in the shop downstairs.'

'Well, I couldn't let the trannie have that one, could I?'

'But what are you saying?'

'It's another reality, isn't it? The world of imagination. The world of comic books. Superheroes and super villains. Peter Parker's always in the shit, just like you. But he's also Spider Man. And you're much more at home in the world of comics than you are in this one. Am I right, or am I frigging right?'

'You're right,' said Porrig, leaping to his feet. 'You are right. You *are* right. I see it all now. I *am* different. I *am* an outsider and *I am* the one person who can expose the Ministry of Serendipity.'

'Eh?' said Wok Boy.

'Best the super villain. My dad, the super villain. With my awesome super powers I shall sweep down upon the Ministry and—'

'Hold on,' said Wok Boy.

'Hold on, what?'

'Super powers? What super powers?'

'The ones I'll get off Rippington as a reward for taking him back to ALPHA 17.'

'Now just hold on.'

'Everything falls into place,' said Porrig, posing before a long bedroom mirror that had somehow escaped previous mention. 'I shall be a mighty avenger for the oppressed people of the world. People like you, Wok Boy, losers, dim-wits, those kind of folk. I shall smash the mighty from their seats of power, bring justice and freedom and—'

'No!' shouted Wok Boy, flapping his hands. 'That's not what I meant. I just meant that you should draw comics because that was what you do best, I didn't mean—'

'ALPHA MAN!' cried Porrig.

'What?'

'I shall call myself ALPHA MAN, after ALPHA 17. And you shall be my companion and comedy relief partner. ALPHA MAN and WOK BOY, I can see it all now.'

Porrig snatched up the bed cover and flung it cloak-fashion about his shoulders. And then he rushed from the room shouting 'Up and away,' and, 'Rippington, where are you?'

'What a wanker,' said Wok Boy, shaking his head and putting his feet up. 'And what exactly is all this about?' He cast an eye of suspicion over the free newspaper. ' "BIG STORM",' he said thoughtfully. 'What BIG STORM?'

14

BEWARE THE BIG STORM

said the papers. And 'BEWARE THE BIG STORM', said the TV weathermen. And 'BEWARE THE BIG STORM,' said Carol Vorderman on at least four channels at once. And not to be caught napping after the last BIG STORM, folk took their washing in, tied down their dustbin lids and rushed to the shops to purchase candles and condoms.

At the Ministry of Serendipity, Porrig's dad monitored the progress of things. They have one of those operations rooms there, with the big lighting-up map of the world on the wall and lots of computer desks with smart-looking women in tight-fitting suits and black stockings, who carry clipboards around and lean over men in white coats, who study telescreens and drink coffee out of plastic cups.

The Americans do it with more style, but they copied the idea from us.

Porrig's dad had a special clipboard of his own, a black one with a light on the top, and he studied this and talked to the smart-looking women and the men in white coats and lurked about in corridors and had secret meetings and things of that nature generally.

'Progress report,' said Porrig's dad to a particularly smart-looking woman.

'All the media are carrying our bogus report of the BIG STORM, sir. Shipping has been cleared from the English Channel and the location and movement of *The Leviathan* is being monitored by satellite. It's approximately thirty miles off Land's End and travelling towards the Channel.'

'And Sir John Rimmer?'

'Sir John has been flown to Land's End. He's wired for sound, so we will be able to listen to what transpires. His companions have flown out with him.'

'Do they mean to go aboard *The Leviathan*?'

'Apparently so, sir. Things are likely to be rather unpleasant there. But Dr Harney and Danbury Collins decided to go with him. Loyalty, I suppose.'

'Loyalty?' Augustus shook his head. The word meant very little to him.

'Would you care for some coffee in a plastic cup?' asked the smart-looking woman.

'No thanks, I think I'll just go and have a lurk in the men's bog.'

The helicopter was one of those black unmarked affairs that governments deny all knowledge of owning. It rested upon the green sward (which is not to be confused with the green sword, or even the green smorgasbord) and it made that glorious CHB CHB CHB CHB CHB CHB CHB noise with its rotors that comes across so well in quadrophonic sound at the cinema.

Danbury Collins cast approving eyes in its direction. 'Do you see the armaments on that bastard?' he asked Dr Harney. 'Heat-seeking missiles, 7.62, M134 General Electric mini-guns. They've even got the loudspeakers for playing Wagner while you shoot up "Charlie".'

'Fascinating,' said Dr Harney. 'And are you still carrying your little "piece"?'

'Damn right,' said Danbury. 'I have a "certain feeling" that it might just come in handy.'

'Are you sure that you actually want to go through with this?'

Danbury shrugged. 'Come on,' he said. 'We couldn't really let Sir John do it all by himself, could we?'

'You never cease to amaze me,' said the doctor. 'You're a good lad, Danbury. Ah, see, here comes himself.'

Sir John Rimmer climbed down from the helicopter. He looked very much like himself once more. In fact he looked *just* himself. But then, as he *was* himself, this was only to be expected. Sir John was sporting a fine new beard. A blue one this time, supplied to him by the MoS amateur dramatics society. As used in their recent production of *Blue Beard*, no doubt.

And it did look dramatic, set off against the crimson robes he now wore.

He greeted his two companions. 'Greetings,' he said.

'Wotcha,' said Danbury. 'We had to come down on the train. I like the . . .'

'Careful,' said Sir John. 'You promised, no more beard gags.'

Danbury rubbed thoughtfully at the lump on his head: his reward for the one about the lion's den. 'No more beard gags,' he said. 'After all, this is a serious business. Have you planned what you mean to say to the creature?'

'It's fawning, mostly. There'll be a lot of falling to the knees and pleading. If you do as I do, we might be able to pull it off.'

'Pull it off,' said Danbury slowly. 'As in . . .'

Dr Harney raised his hand.

'Nothing,' said Danbury. 'Where's the boat?'

'Down there in the cove.'

'Then we'd best be off.'

'I think that best we had.'

And so, as best they could, they did.

The boat was one of those unmarked black affairs that governments deny all knowledge of. They are used mostly for importing drugs, as the importing of drugs has always been done by the governments of the countries concerned and not by criminal organizations as is popularly believed. There's far too much money to be made from drug importation to let criminals get their hands on it.

And if the government of this country didn't make all the money from the importation of drugs, it would never have sufficient to finance the unmarked black boats.

It all makes sense when you think about it.

Sir John climbed aboard. Danbury helped the doctor up the gang plank.

'Tasty boat,' said Danbury.

The captain sniffed them welcome. 'Hey, all right, man,' he said. 'Cool duds, Sir John, real guru. The guys and I were just doing a couple of lines before we take off. You wanna join us?'

'Yes please,' said Danbury.

'Cool.'

Sir John shook his head. 'Are you the captain?' he asked.

'Right on.'

'But you're wearing a kaftan.'

'Well, so are you, man.'

'And a beard.'

'Bigger than yours, man. But it's cool.'

'Hm,' said Sir John.

'So, do you want a couple of lines, or what?'

'Go for it,' said Danbury.

And so they went for it.

It brightens the day, does a couple of lines. And though one must never condone the taking of drugs, neither must one condemn it out of hand. Because, let's face it, if *you* were on your way to almost certain death at the hands of a mad monster, would you see the harm in doing it with a couple of snorts of angel dust up your hooter?

The unmarked boat cut through the waves, numbers were rolled and numbers were smoked, lines were cut and sniffed away and talk became merry and free. Sir John spoke untruths of his happy childhood and his dog. Dr Harney told tales of his days upon the hippy trail and Danbury did what Danbury always did. With gusto.

At a length that seemed far longer than it really was, they sighted *The Leviathan*.

The captain drew deeply on a big fat number and spoke through the smoke. 'Are you really sure about this, man?' he said. 'We could always just say we missed it and head on down to Morocco.'

Sir John took deep breaths and steadied himself against the rail. 'We have a job to do,' he said. 'For the mother country and indeed for the world.'

'If you say so, man.'

'We shall succeed,' said Sir John. 'We shall vanquish the foe.'

'Yeah,' said Danbury. 'You go for it, Johnny boy.'

'It's Sir John to you and don't forget it.'

'Rumpy pumpy poo,' said Dr Harney.

'Rumpy pumpy what?' asked Sir John.

'Poo,' said the doctor. 'I am a little red plastic truck and I go rumpy pumpy poo.'

'He's out of it,' said the captain. 'You'd better leave him here.'

'I'm not out of it.' Dr Harney made small brmming sounds.

'All for one and one for all,' said Danbury Collins. 'Cor, look at the size of that ship.'

The Leviathan loomed. In order to create an atmosphere of sufficient menace, a light mist had gathered about it and the ship presented an eerie ghost-like appearance. No sound came from the mighty vessel, which drifted upon the placid waves like a handbag on a pool table.

Well, it did if you'd been taking what Dr Harney had been taking.

'Leave all the talking to me,' said Sir John as they drew ever closer.

The captain gazed up at the great ship, which now seemed to fill half the sky. 'Can you feel it?' he asked.

'Feel what?' said Sir John.

The captain shook his head. '*It*,' he said. 'The weirdness of it. I tell you, man, I've done some stuff in my time. You know, taken some stuff, and I did some stuff in Tibet once. Special dope that the lamas do to reach the other planes. Travel into other realities, you know. And it's just like that here. This ship is giving off those vibes. It's messing with reality. Do you know what I mean?'

'I do,' said Sir John. 'I know exactly what you mean.'

'You take care, man.'

'I will,' said Sir John.

The unmarked boat pulled up alongside *The Leviathan*. The silence was palpable. The lapping of the waves made no sound at all. The liner was there, but it seemed to be removed. Separate.

Sir John took hold of a trailing cable and with no more words spoken began to climb carefully up the side. Danbury shrugged and pushed the doctor forward. 'You go next,' he whispered, 'and I'll try to catch you if you fall.'

'I won't fall,' said Dr Harney. 'I will use my caterpillar tracks and scale the mighty mountain. Goog googa jube.'

'Perfect,' said Danbury.

Mist and silence and three men climbing.

Below, the captain, muttering something.

And above . . .

Sir John reached the deck and peeped over. 'Dear God,' he said.

Beneath, the two men on the cable watched the gaunt frame haul itself beyond view.

'He's there,' whispered Danbury. 'Come on, doctor, let's get after him.'

'Chug chug chug,' replied the doctor.

And then the three of them were there. Standing breathless on the deck.

And then.

'They're dead,' said Sir John. 'Hundreds of them. It looks like they died from starvation and exposure.'

'They're . . .' Danbury held down a wave of rising vomit. 'They're naked. Why are they naked?'

'Because that's how he wished them to be.'

'You called *it* he.'

'You had better learn to call it he too,' said Sir John. 'Come on, there's nothing we can do for these people.'

The Leviathan's ballroom, lollipop lovely, was lit throughout by lilac luminescence. Floral fripperies fanned from fluted fabrications. Deco decor, cream and chrome, sunrays and swastikas, blended with bits and bobs of Bauhaus. Over all arched ormolu ornamentation in the ostentatious opulent over-the-topness of Otto Osterbrooke. It was a triumph of taste over tackiness tenderly rendered and royally realized.

Very nice indeed.

And transformed into hell.

The dance-floor was invisible beneath the naked bodies. Thousands bowed in prayer. The air was ripe and rotten with the smell of sweat and shit and vomit. And with fear, with overwhelming fear.

On the bandstand, flanked by natives, lazing on a mound of cushions, was the thing. The beast. The false god.

Dilbert Norris.

Enemy and erstwhile conquerer of man.

Buddha-big was Dilbert all about the belly regions, monstrous of head and black of eye. His skin shone with a glossy viridescence; olive, lime, myrtle and a mouldy mossy green. His great bald head was swollen like a pumpkin. The mouth, a yawning maw, turned up and leered, moist and evil. His yard-long parsnip Percy dangled detumescently.

Sir John, struck dumb by the horror that confronted him, dropped slowly to his knees. Danbury did likewise, tugging down the doctor.

Dilbert viewed his uninvited guests, repositioned his pre-posterous posterior and teased away tooth-plaque with a human thigh bone.

Sir John Rimmer raised a trembling voice. 'O Great One,' he called. 'We bring greetings from the Isles of Britannia.'

Dilbert ran a long black tongue about his teeth, each one the size of a Sainsbury's one-pint milk carton and the two in the front as big as the one-litre bargain pack. Then he spoke, in a voice that could be likened to the sound that a sink plughole makes when plunged with a plunger (only greatly amplified and three octaves deeper).

'Presents,' gurgled Dilbert.

'Presents, O Great One?' Sir John kept his head down.

'Presents,' said Dilbert, making motions with foliate fingers.

Sir John Rimmer chewed upon a length of false beard. He had indeed a present for the creature, but he wanted first to flatter and to gauge the situation. Although the situation here was very far from fab.

'The bounty of our islands is more than any single man could carry,' said Sir John. 'And all shall be yours to be taken at your whim.'

'My whim, eh?' Dilbert's mouth rose further at the corners, exposing lesser teeth that were approximately the dimensions of thirty ml Tipp-Ex correction fluid bottles.

'As it pleases you, Great One.'

'You might at least have brought me some big fat women.'

Sir John now chewed upon his bottom lip. 'We might fatten up some of the ones you have here,' he said carefully. 'In fact we might fatten them all. Have them feast upon a banquet in your honour.'

'Nah,' sink-plunger slurpy-gurgled Dilbert. 'These ones please me not.'

'They might please you better, were they plump and jolly.'

'I think not. But he' – Dilbert pointed – 'he might do.'

Sir John raised his head a mite to follow the direction of the dendriform digit. 'Dr Harney?' he whispered.

Dilbert nodded his shiny verdant bonce up and down. 'He looks very plump and jolly.'

'I hoped he might please you, Great One.'

'What?' gasped Danbury.

'Bear with me,' whispered Sir John.

'Bung him over here,' called Dilbert. 'Let's stew him up in his juices.'

Sir John's head swam, but he steeled himself enough to shout, 'He dances well.'

'He dances well?'

'A merry jig. To gladden and amuse.'

'He would amuse my innards more.'

'Dr Harney,' said Sir John. 'Will you dance for the nice god?'

'There's a bit of mosaic on this floor that looks like a poodle,' said Dr Harney.

'He's still out of it,' whispered Danbury. 'Do you want me to prance about and create a diversion, or something?'

'Dr Harney!' Sir John nudged his fellow in the ribs. 'The nice god will not be kept waiting. Dance, if you will.'

'Dance?' The doctor's head rose. 'Who wants to dance? Oh, stripe my bottom red with a razor, everybody's got their kit off.'

'Get up and dance,' said Sir John in the firmest tone he could manage.

'Absolutely,' said the doctor. 'This is what I call a party.'

At the Ministry of Serendipity the atmosphere was far from party-like. The men in white coats and the smart-looking women, the government types who were privy to top secret information, Porrig's dad and the pig sat, or in the case of the pig, stood, before the big world map on the wall. This had, through the wonders of technology, now been translated into a gigantic TV screen.

They were listening to the voice of Sir John Rimmer and watching, up on the screen, the images that were being relayed to them via the micro-camera that had been sewn into the false blue beard.

'I don't like this at all,' said Augustus. 'That horrible-looking thing behaves as if it really is a god. If Sir John can't kill it and it were to get loose in England, there's no telling what might happen.'

The pig nodded thoughtfully. 'The angel Espadrille won't be best pleased,' he said.

'Stuff the angel Espadrille. But this won't do. It's bad enough having a monster from space on the rampage. But one behaving like a god, without the Ministry's permission, that can't be tolerated.'

'Ever the humanitarian,' said the pig. 'Where are you off to now?'

'I think I'll go off for a lurk.'

'You don't think that perhaps you should apply yourself to the problem at hand? How exactly is Sir John Rimmer supposed to dispose of this thing?'

'He's got a bomb in his beard.'

'*A bomb in his beard?*' The pig made a face of amazement, which wasn't easy, but he managed it. 'But what about the people?'

Augustus Naseby shifted uneasily. 'It's not a very big bomb. Just big enough to take the creature's head off. Sir John is hoping to persuade the creature to try on the beard.'

'Wonderful,' said the pig. 'And this Ministry runs the affairs of the whole wide world!'

'At present it does.'

'Well, good luck to the man with the exploding beard.'

The man with the exploding beard was keeping his head down. Dr Harney was gambolling aimlessly about making the sounds of a big brass band.

Dilbert held up a fat finger. 'This is crap,' he said. 'This fellow can't dance. Let's have him over here and see what he tastes like.'

Several natives leaped down from the bandstand and grabbed at the dancing doc.

'No, wait,' cried Sir John.

'Wait, *what*?'

'Wait, O Great One, please, I beseech.'

'Ah,' said Dilbert. 'Beseeching. I've always loved beseeching. I'm glad to hear that beseeching still goes on in this century. What exactly are you beseeching about?'

'Don't eat the doctor,' said Sir John.

'Why not?'

'Because I *have* brought you a special gift and I'd like you to have it now.'

'Oh goody. Bring it over then.'

Sir John rose slowly to his feet and, stepping carefully between the worshippers, who still knelt naked and shivering, he approached the evil thing on the bandstand.

'It is the badge of highest office,' said Sir John. 'And I as one who has awaited your return, along with the millions of other loyal devotees on the British Isles, am honoured to present you with it.'

'Millions, did you say?' Dilbert stroked his chins.

'Many millions. Surely you did not think that you would be forgotten?'

'Naturally not,' said Dilbert, adjusting his backside once more.

'I was chosen to greet you and present you with this.' Sir John Rimmer fingered the abundant blue beard.

'You are offering me *a beard*?'

'As a token of our affection and loyalty. For you to wear as you are carried in splendour through the streets of our capital. Which is to say, *your* capital.'

'Indeed?' said Dilbert. 'Bung it over here, then.'

Sir John Rimmer removed the false beard and handed it to a native. The native bowed before Dilbert and offered it up.

Dilbert looked down upon the beard and then up at Sir John Rimmer.

'Well,' said he. 'And well well well.'

'Well?' asked Sir John.

'Well!' said Dilbert.

'Well what, exactly, O Great One?'

'Well, firstly it is a pretty crap beard. It is made from a low-quality polyester derivative and dyed with synthetic chemicals. Secondly, the wearing of such a beard could seriously harm my precious person.'

'The chemicals are in no way harmful,' said Sir John.

'No, but the fucking bomb in it is!'

'Ah,' said Sir John.

'Yes, ah, you piece of shit! Do you know why I let you on board?'

'No, O Great One.'

'Don't *O Great One* me. I let you on board because I wanted to get a look at you and *you*!' Dilbert pointed at the beard, and in the operations room at the Ministry of Serendipity his big fat finger blotted out the giant telescreen. 'You, the maggots at the Ministry of so-called Serendipity. I know you're there. I can sense your thinking. I can read all your thoughts. I did not choose to have this ship sail to your shores upon an idle whim. It's because *you* are there. *You* who rule the entire planet through your departments and your connections. I am coming to you. I am coming *for* you.'

Then the screen blanked out.

'It rather looks as if we'll have to rearrange our schedules,' said Augustus Naseby.

'That won't please the chickens,' said the pig.

15

Chickens clucked in a Brighton back yard and a rooster crowed in a new dawn. Porrig, who had been playing the night owl, was not to be found up with the larks.

The sunshine came softly through his window today and Porrig could no doubt have tripped out easy, had he wanted to. However, as he never had done so before and knew nothing of Donovan, he didn't.

Porrig stretched and wriggled. It was very crowded in his bed. Wok Boy snored away next to him and Rippington lay next to Wok Boy. And although Rippington didn't snore, he did make some very odd sounds in his sleep: snufflings and mutterings, none of them too pleasing to the ear.

Porrig put his hands behind his head and sighed towards the ceiling. Sunlight danced through pigeon shadows. No sign of any BIG STORM.

Porrig sighed once more and took to bewailing his lot.

It wasn't fair. It just wasn't fair. An empty shop below and these two buggers in his bed. And his plans for superherodom? Doomed to failure as he might have guessed.

Rippington had been all in favour. He'd offered Porrig sneak looks into the books of magic in exchange for his safe return to

ALPHA 17, and he said he'd even throw in a rather natty outfit that had once belonged to a prince of Denmark.

Porrig had flung open his bedroom door at the midnight hour, but nothing had happened. The mysterious portal to ALPHA 17 had not materialized. The gateway from this world to that remained shut.

It could only be opened by use of the magic ritual and, since Porrig didn't know it, that it seemed was that.

'Told you,' said Rippington. 'If it opened by itself every night, I'd have ducked through it last week while you were in the coma. You only got through because you disobeyed the curator's instructions. He won't let that happen again.'

Porrig climbed out of bed and took himself off to the kitchenette. Here he brewed green tea, sat down at the table and grumbled.

He'd have made a damn fine superhero. He was certainly screwed up enough. And if his daft daddy really was in charge of this ministry that damn near ran the whole world, then he did feel that it was his duty to do something about it. Something more than just drawing a comic book.

'It's as good a start as any.'

Porrig jumped from his chair and glowered at Rippington.

'Sorry,' said the imp. 'I didn't mean to startle you.'

'You lying little toad.'

'No need for insults.'

Porrig sat back down. 'I'm fed up,' said he.

'Me too, my rub-tugging friend. I want to go home. But we'll each get what fate offers us, I suppose.'

'Fate?' Porrig shrugged and his thoughts returned to his conversation on the train with the old bloke.

'I've seen that feather,' said Rippington.

'What?'

'The feather from the angel's wing that you were just thinking about. It glows in the dark and it smells really sweet.'

'He sent you, didn't he?' said Porrig.

Rippington climbed onto a chair. 'I don't know what you mean.'

'You bloody do. The old bloke let you out of ALPHA 17. You'd never have got out if he hadn't let you. Why did he let you, Rippington?'

'To keep an eye on you, of course. He has pressing business in the city of London. Secret business. I'm here to see that no harm comes to you.'

'How comforting.'

'So I wouldn't drink that tea, if I were you.'

'Why not?'

'Because that's Wok Boy's cup. The one I—'

Porrig spat green tea across the kitchenette.

'Where would you be without me?' asked Rippington.

Porrig made a bitter face. 'I'm going out,' said he.

'In your pyjamas?'

'No, I'll get dressed first. And then I'll go out.'

'I wouldn't,' said Rippington.

'And why not?'

'Because it might not be safe.'

Porrig eyed the imp. 'What exactly are you saying?'

'Well, have you looked outside this morning?'

'No.'

'You might be surprised by what you see.'

'And what might I see?'

'Nothing.'

Porrig let out a serious sigh. 'And *nothing* will surprise me, will it?'

'I think that it might. But listen, what do you hear?'

Porrig listened. 'Nothing,' he said.

'And isn't *that* surprising?'

'No.' Porrig listened again. 'I mean, yes. I should be able to hear something. Some*one*.'

'But you can't. Because there's no-one about.'

Porrig walked out of the kitchenette, across the landing and back into the bedroom. As he passed the bed he gave it a good kick. When he reached the window he looked out.

There was no-one about. No-one. Not a person. The street was deserted.

'Where is everyone?' Porrig asked.

'They're all indoors,' said Rippington. 'With their windows closed and wet towels over their heads.'

'Wet towels?'

'To avoid contamination.'

'What?'

'You'll get your notification any minute now. They did all the nice people's houses and shops first. They'll get round to you in a minute.'

'Who will?'

'The man from the Ministry.'

'What? Oh hang about, someone's coming.'

'That'll be the fellow.'

'Eh?'

The fellow approached. He was a very odd-looking fellow, all decked out in a head-to-toe one-piece radiation suit sort of affair. And he was wearing a gas mask. With a gloved hand he pulled a leaflet from a big pouch he carried and approached Porrig's shop door.

'Mailman,' said Rippington.

Porrig went downstairs to see what was what. He returned a few moments later, now knowing what was what and saying, 'What? What? What?' in a very loud voice. He gave the bed another kick.

Wok Boy awoke, going *'What?'*

'This!' shouted Porrig pointing to the leaflet. 'This!'

'What?'

'This.'

'Read it out,' said Rippington.

So Porrig did.

DANGER

[it began in big black letters]

CONTAMINATION   CONTAMINATION
CONTAMINATION   CONTAMINATION

[it continued]

Warning is hereby given to the people of Brighton and surrounding towns that a spillage of chemical toxins from a *foreign* vessel caught up in last night's BIG

157

STORM is being carried by the prevailing winds towards the southern coastline of this country. All residents of Brighton and surrounding towns are advised to remain indoors until the danger has passed. Please remain calm and sit quietly with a wet towel over your head.

Those residents who choose to ignore this warning are advised that the particular chemical toxin causes willy shrinkage in men and pronounced bottom growth in women.

Residents are further advised that martial law has been imposed and that anyone caught on the streets will be shot as a potential looter.

We thank you for your co-operation in this matter. Please await the all-clear signal.

'*What?*' said Wok Boy.

'My thoughts entirely,' said Porrig.

'Wet towels all round?' asked Rippington.

'Wet towels all round,' said Porrig's dad, lurking some way to the north. On the platform of Mornington Crescent Station, to be precise.

'Wet towels,' said a smart-looking woman. 'Pronounced bottom growth and the likelihood of being shot as a potential looter. It should do the trick for now. It was the best I could come up with at such short notice.'

Porrig's dad groaned. 'I suppose it will do. It will keep them indoors for the time being. But when *The Leviathan* docks and the creature comes ashore, what then?'

'I don't know,' said the woman. 'Why are you asking me?'

'I wasn't asking you. I was asking the pig.'

'Nuke it,' said the pig. 'Nuke it now.'

'I can't nuke it.' Porrig's dad shook his head. 'If I were to nuke it, I'd be responsible for wiping out half the population of southern England.'

'Never,' said the pig. 'Most of them will be safely inside, with their doors locked and wet towels over their heads.'

'Yes, but what about the ones who won't?'

'The unemployed ones, do you mean? The homeless ones?'

'Good point. Let's nuke the blighter.'

'Stop this at once.' The smart-looking woman raised a smart-looking hand. 'I will not be party to the wiping out of innocent people, even unemployed ones.'

'Oh, go on,' said Porrig's dad.

'Certainly not. There has to be another way.'

'We could divert *The Leviathan* to France,' said the pig. 'Nuke the monster over there.'

'Good idea,' said Augustus.

'Is it?' asked the pig.

'It is,' said Augustus.

'I certainly admire your courage.'

'It doesn't take courage to nuke France. I'd have got around to it at some point anyway.'

'No, I didn't mean nuking France. I meant the courage you'll need to go aboard *The Leviathan* and persuade the monster to change course.'

'Oh, I won't be doing that. I'll delegate. I'll send this smart-looking woman here.'

'You bloody well won't,' said the smart-looking woman. 'I may just be a two-dimensional token female, but I'm not *that* stupid.'

'I never suggested for one moment that you were. I see you as a Sigourney Weaver figure. The lone woman of strong character and resolve, standing against the alien.'

'Or that bird in *The Terminator* with the nice tits,' said the pig.

'Yes, that's right,' said Porrig's dad. 'Although Sigourney has nice tits too.'

'Very nice,' agreed the pig. 'Sigourney is the total package as far as I'm concerned.'

'So there you go then,' said Augustus. 'And actually you do look a bit like Sigourney Weaver.'

'Do I?' asked the smart-looker.

'You do,' said Augustus.

'Better,' said the pig. 'More "presence".'

'Why, thank you.'

159

'But you're probably right.' Augustus made a thoughtful face. 'It's not a job for a woman. I'd do better to call in some burly macho SAS type. A Sly Stallone figure. Huge muscles, huge ego, huge . . .'

'Todger,' said the pig.

'Huge *weapon*,' said Augustus.

'Same thing.'

'All guns blazing.' Augustus mimed the all-guns-blazing. He smiled at the smart-looking woman. 'Best leave the job to a man. Do you think you might fetch me some more coffee in a plastic cup?'

'No!'

'No?'

'No!' The smart-looking woman shook her smart-looking head. '*I* will go,' she said.

'I wouldn't hear of it.' Augustus shook his head too. 'It was a silly idea. I've been under a lot of strain lately. Not thinking clearly.'

'I will go,' said the smart-looking woman. 'There will be no all-guns-blazing. And there will be no nuking of France or anywhere else. A woman's touch is required here. This creature can read men's minds, but I'll bet he won't be able to read mine. I will find some way to stop him. You leave it to me.'

'Are you sure?'

'Absolutely sure.'

'Well . . . if you're absolutely sure.'

'I am.'

'She is,' said the pig.

'All right. Go up to the operations room. I'll phone through to tell the controller that you're to be given everything you require.'

'Thank you, sir.' The smart-looking woman saluted (smartly). Augustus saluted back. 'Take care,' he said.

'I will, sir.' And with that, the smart-looking woman turned smartly and marched away.

Augustus took out his mobile phone and pushed a few buttons. 'Hello,' he said, 'Smudger? Naseby here. The bimbo took the bait, she's on her way up to you. Make sure the bomb goes into her handbag and make sure she doesn't know it's there. Cheers then. Ta-ta for now.'

The pig looked up at Porrig's dad. 'You bastard,' said the pig. 'You treacherous, double-dealing bastard.'

16

The other bastard, green and gruesome, thought his terrible thoughts and sent them out with a smile upon his face.

The first wave of pain hit a certain coastal town of southern England at precisely ten-twenty-three and fourteen-seconds-almost that morning.

Lords and ladies, lads and lasses, the great and the good and the dull and the dreadful hollered and howled and fell fainting to their floors.

CONTAMINATION CONTAMINATION CONTAMI-NATION CONTAMINATION they thought.

Men clutched at their willies and women their behinds. But the pain was so intense that their clutching hands rushed back to their heads and stayed there.

Porrig, now dressed, had been preparing to take a quick shufti outside, having come to the not altogether surprising conclusion that *something* was going on. He was at his shop door when the pain blasted him from his feet.

Wok Boy, halfway up the stairs, screamed loudly and tumbled down.

Rippington stood looking puzzled.

From *The Leviathan*, now lying half a sea mile off Brighton, the pain arced out. Dilbert grinned and thought more horrible thoughts and his thoughts took flight and hurt like hell.

Folk were rising now and, driven by a compulsion they were powerless to resist, were taking to the streets. They flooded into the thoroughfares in wave after wave, human flotsam borne upon a tide of pain. '*Come and greet your God,*' called the thoughts of Dilbert, '*Come and greet me now.*'

Forward, forward, at the double they came, tumbling and treading down the weak, scrambling and clawing into the main roads and onward to the sea.

In their thousands.

Onto the promenade, that Victorian prom where elegant gentlemen and ladies in lace had strolled arm in arm to the bandstand refrains, came the folk of this age in a staggering horde. In a crush of confusion, in agonized terror, herded and driven, forced ever onwards over the railings and down to the beach.

And onwards.

Into the sea.

Knee-deep now, the old ones sagging, children parted from their mothers, lover torn apart from lover, all apart but all together, thousands, thousands, fear and horror.

Then the silence, dry mouths open, frightened eyes all staring forward . . .

For *He* comes.

The God comes now.

White ship splendour.

Wave-crest bow-break.

Lifeboats lowering.

And His seven-pointed star.

> *And I stood upon the sand*
> *of the sea and saw a beast*
> *rise up out of the sea . . .*
> Revelation 13.1

And so they fell, one upon another, forced down to give homage. To worship their new God. He who was their old God. Come once more among them.

Man bow down before your master.

Porrig fought to keep his face above the waves, but the pain forced him down, down. *You will worship. You will kneel.*

And Porrig's face went down into the waves and the pain drove into his head and his breath was gone and the water flooded into his lungs and Porrig floated lifeless in the sea.

'This is bad. So very bad.' Augustus Naseby gazed up at the big world map that had once more been translated into a giant TV screen and now projected images received from Brighton's street surveillance cameras.

'He's driven them into the sea.' A man in a white coat crossed himself. 'The entire population of the town, they were helpless to resist him.'

'He's making his point.' Augustus Naseby turned away. 'He'll come to us. *For* us. We must leave now, enter the escape pod, travel north. Stay beyond the range of his influence.'

The man in the white coat turned a cold eye upon Augustus. 'No, sir,' he said.

'No? What do you mean, no?'

'Sir, I mean: no. We cannot just run away.'

'It is called a strategic withdrawal.'

'I don't give a fuck what it's called. We can't do it.'

'We can and we will. The Ministry of Serendipity must remain in control. We must co-ordinate. This situation can be contained.'

'It cannot be contained, sir. The creature is too powerful. He treats people like dirt. They are nothing to him. He'll cut a swathe across the country, killing thousands. We must stand and fight and we must do it now.'

'Where is the woman with the handbag?'

'Agent Artemis?'

'Agent *who*?'

'Artemis, sir. In Greek mythology she was the virgin goddess of the hunt and the moon. The twin sister of Apollo. The Romans called her Diana and she—'

'Yes, all right. Agent *Artemis*. Where is she?'

'I called her a cab, sir.'

'Called her a cab! Why didn't you send her off in one of the unmarked helicopters with the big guns all over it?'

'She said she'd prefer to take a cab.'

'All right. Forget her. Get me the Ministry of Defence on the blower. Patch me through to the Commander-in-Chief of the armed forces.'

'So we are going to stand and fight, sir?'

'There will be standing and there will be fighting. I shall lurk and *you* will fetch me some coffee in a plastic cup. Agent bloody Artemis indeed!'

Agent Bloody-Artemis-indeed sat in the back of a London black cab. The driver, who 'recently had that Chris Evans sitting just where you're sitting, ginger git that he is, but you have to like him, don't ya, because he's a laugh and having a laugh is what it's all about, ain't it, and what line of trade are you in if you don't mind me asking, rag trade, is it, because I had that Versace in here once, well, not *had him* if you know what I mean, but had him in this cab, before he was gunned down, "shoot you, sir" eh? ha ha ha', viewed her in the driving mirror.

Agent Artemis, without the bloody, ignored the driver. She studied her reflection in her make-up mirror and, finding it pleasing to behold, smiled secretively, recrossed her impossibly long legs and gazed through the window at London and its life. Knowing well, as most women do, the wicked ways of maledom, she had taken the greatest care to check through her belongings. It hadn't taken all that long to find the hidden bomb. She had stored it in a secret place that was *not* a euphemism, and had tooled herself up with certain pieces of restricted hardware that she was totally unauthorized to carry.

Agent Artemis smiled once more, said, 'Drive me to Brighton,' and settled back upon the seat which had known the bums of famous folk.

The infamous one sat on His fat bum and waved a limp green hand at His subjects. They were up from the beach now, those who still lived; they lined the way and they cheered through their tears and they hated and feared and they hurt.

165

His Nubians carried Him on His cushions in His seven-pointed star. Others, too, jostled to lift Him. And three men walked before, wearing nought but their Y-fronts, strewing rose petals and singing Him praise.

Sir John Rimmer sang through gritted teeth. He lurched along upon buckling legs, all thousand-yard-stare and no stiff-upper-lip. Danbury dawdled and swore when he could, the doctor just marched and recited His words as a robot.

Praise be unto Him. Praise be unto Him.

The crowds took up the chant, for it hurt less to do so, and followed after Him as His obscene parade moved on towards the railway station.

And praise be unto Him.

And praise be unto Him.

And . . . 'Aaaaaghooooohuuuuurgh . . . urgh urgh urgh.'

From somewhere far away and long ago and god knows where and how, came Porrig. 'Aaaaaaaaaaghoooooh,' and, 'urgh urgh urgh.'

'Cough it up, you rub-tugger, it might be a gold watch.'

'Urgh, urgh, urgh,' and 'Get the fuck off me!'

'You're showing some definite signs of improvement.'

'Get off my face, you . . . urgh urgh urgh.'

'Spit it out, it's only water. Though not mine this time.'

Porrig sat up. He coughed some more and then he was sick all over the place.

'Look out where you're chucking up. Oh dear me.' Rippington scuttled for cover.

Porrig blinked seawater from his eyes. He was beneath the pier. Evidently still in the land of the living.

And the dead.

For the dead lay all along the beach, tossed by the tide, broken dolls alive only in memory.

Porrig was violently sick again.

'Mostly green tea,' said Rippington, peering down at the puddles of puke. 'You really should eat a good breakfast. Most important meal of the day, breakfast—'

'Shut up,' Porrig spluttered. 'What happened here? These people, all these dead people!'

'It was Dilbert Norris,' said Rippington. 'He's a vegetable.'

'This is no time to take the piss, you little—'

'I'm not taking the piss. It *was* Dilbert Norris.'

'Dilbert who?' Porrig coughed some more. 'How did I . . . How did I . . .'

'How did you survive? I pulled you out of the sea. It was a right struggle, I can tell you. And I had to stick my foot right down your throat to clear your windpipe. And then, funny you should mention taking the piss, because when you still wouldn't wake up I—'

'Urgh urgh urgh, you bastard!'

'Some thanks,' said Rippington, folding his spindly arms. 'Perhaps I should have left you to feed the little fishes like . . .' His voice trailed off.

'Like who?' Porrig's red-rimmed eyes fixed on the small grey fellow.

'I couldn't find Wok Boy,' said Rippington. 'And I can't hear his thoughts any more. I think he might be . . .'

Porrig buried his face in his hands. 'Oh no,' he wept. 'Oh no.'

'Sorry,' said Rippington. 'But he did take up a lot of room in the bed. And those jeans of his smelled really bad and—'

'Shut up.' Porrig staggered to his feet. 'This is madness. What happened here? Why? Who?'

'Dilbert. I told you.'

'I don't understand.' Porrig stumbled back and nearly stepped on the corpse of a woman. 'All these people. This is Brighton beach, for God's sake. Is this the end of the world? Are we at war, or what?'

'He came off that ship out there.' Rippington pointed towards *The Leviathan*. 'He isn't human, he comes from another world far far away. And he isn't made of flesh and blood, he's a vegetable.'

'How do you know what he is?'

'Because I can hear his thoughts, Porrig. He's got the loudest thoughts on the whole planet. And the biggest rubbing part by the looks of him. His thoughts are so strong that he can control people with them. And he doesn't like people at all, because he's a vegetable. On his planet it was vegetables that evolved, not mammals. He has as much concern for people as you would for the welfare of a carrot.'

'I quite like carrots.'

'Cooked is how you like carrots. Which is just how Dilbert likes people.'

'No!' Porrig's greeny-grey face became more greeny-greysome. 'He eats people? Is that what you're saying?'

'He intends to farm them. Once he's taken over.'

'No.' Porrig shook his head violently, making himself feel sicker. 'This is a fucking nightmare. I'm dreaming this. Tell me I'm dreaming this.'

'You're not.' Rippington shook his own head. 'But if you'd like to be absolutely certain, I wouldn't mind sticking my little wand right up your bu—'

'No!' Porrig tore at the hair on his head. 'Stop, just stop. This thing. This Dilbert thing. It has to be stopped.'

'So how do you intend to stop it?'

'Me?' Porrig looked down in horror at the imp. '*Me?* How do *I* intend to stop it?'

'I give up. How *do* you intend to stop it?'

'I don't! I'm off out of it. Off to foreign parts. I'll go to ALPHA 17 with you.'

'But we can't go, can we? We don't know the magic ritual.'

'Where is the old bloke?'

'I give up,' said Rippington. 'Where *is* the old bloke?'

Porrig, who had given up on the hair-tearing owing to the pain, threw up his hands in despair. 'Someone has to do something. Someone. I know. I know!' He shook his hands about in an I-know kind of fashion. 'I know who can do something.'

'Do you want me to make a guess? Or would it be easier if I just gave up again?'

'The one person,' said Porrig. 'The man in charge.'

'God?' said Rippington. 'That's a bit of a long-shot, asking God.'

'Not God. My dad.'

'Ah . . .' said Rippington. 'Your dad. Ah . . .'

'What do you mean, ah . . . ? What are you saying ah like that for?'

Rippington shifted from one small foot to the other. 'Well, I wasn't going to mention it to you just yet, what with all this nastiness and everything. I thought perhaps I'd wait until you had gathered your wits together. Maybe over a nice cup of tea.'

'Spit it out, Rippington.'

'Well, it's about your dad. You see, Dilbert Norris knows all about your dad. He sent out his thoughts all over the world to see who was really in charge and your dad's name came up top of the list and . . .'

'And?'

'And so Dilbert is now on his way to London. To the Ministry of Serendipity. To meet your dad for lunch.'

'You mean that my dad is going to collaborate with him?'

'Er, no. When I said that he's going to meet your dad for lunch, what I meant was that your dad will . . . er . . .'

'Will what?'

'Be lunch,' said Rippington.

'Aaaaaaaaaaaaaaaaaaaagh!' went Porrig. 'Call out the army!'

17

The Commander-in-Chief of the armed forces. The Supreme Commander of the allied forces. The Acting Head of allied forces and network high command forces supreme chief of forces forces allied armed forces forces forces chief commander commander commander, King of Denmark and Lord of the entire universe and handsomest soldier in the whole of the world and good at games and captain of the cricket team and lkjdlqierflxr23p.

'Stop that!' A fellow with the title of adjutant, which means an officer who acts as an administrative assistant to a superior officer, slapped the wrist of the Commander-in-Chief. 'That's my type-writer and I won't have you using it without my permission.'

'I want a typewriter of my own,' whinged the Commander-in-Chief. 'To type up my memoirs.'

'Paper costs money,' said the adjutant. 'And who's going to pay for it? Not me out of my salary.'

'I could put it all on a floppy disc.'

'Oh, could you now? And what exactly *is* a floppy disc? Do you know?'

The Commander-in-Chief made a puzzled face. Out of Plasticine.

'That doesn't help,' said the adjutant. 'You don't know what a floppy disc is, do you?'

'I know what a tank is and if you're waging war on four fronts and the enemy is chucking everything it has in your direction, where's your floppy disc then? Tell me, sir, tell me.'

'I do believe that computers play a large part in the sophisticated weaponry of today.'

'Ptah!' said the Commander-in-Chief.

'The Egyptian god?'

'The very same fellow. Hell's bollocks, I'm bored.'

'We're all bored,' said the adjutant. 'But some of us have work to do.'

'I never have any work to do.'

'Well, of course you don't. You're the Commander-in-Chief.'

'So why don't I ever have any work to do?'

'Because you *are* the Commander-in-Chief. You give orders; you delegate. That's what the army is all about. You order me to do something and I pass that order down the chain of command.'

'Do you want to play I-Spy again?'

'No, because you cheat.'

'I don't cheat. You're the one who cheats.'

A telephone began to ring.

'I'll answer it,' said the Commander-in-Chief.

'I'll answer it,' said the adjutant, snatching up the receiver.

The Commander-in-Chief twiddled his thumbs. Then, tiring of this, he put his thumbs back in their special carrying case and twiddled his tie instead.

The adjutant replaced the receiver. 'Mother Mary's holy handbag,' said he.

'Was that my friend the Pope?'

'No, it was my friend Augustus Naseby from the Ministry of Serendipity.'

'And what did he want?'

'He says we are to go to Green Alert.'

'*Green Alert?*' The Commander-in-Chief stiffened in his breeches. '*Green Alert?*'

'That's what he said.'

'State of the Nation threatened? That Green Alert?'

'That very one.'

'By Jumbo's jockstrap!' The Commander-in-Chief fell back in his big posh leather-backed chair with a cough and a wheeze and a whistle. This was the big one he'd been waiting for. His call to arms once more. His call to further honours.

He'd had honours before, of course. Lots of the blighters. Big honours in brass with ribbons attached, when he'd served his King and his country. He'd bravely fought and bravely won and returned to a land fit for heroes.

But what he'd done, and when, and how, you'll hear no word of here. For although many pages could be spent chronicling his long and noble career, it would all be so much guff and timewasting. Because, as may well be realized already, the Commander-in-Chief of the armed forces was a character with less depth to him than a coat of paint and so utterly two-dimensional that should he turn sideways he would surely cease to exist.

Of the looks of him it might be said that he was passing six feet in an upwards direction and nearing three across ways. He had one good eye, a gun-metal thigh, a heart of oak and the constitution of an Egyptian. And one with a proper fez too.

Of the habits of him it might be said that he enjoyed shunamitism, algolagnia and frottage. But who doesn't, eh?

'Green Alert, eh?' said the Commander-in-Chief. 'Well, if it's Green Alert you'd better get on the blower and call up some of me top brass chums to give us a hand. Get me Chunky Wilberforce, Tubby Molesworth, Snake-hips Henderson, Frog-bottom Battersby—'

'Shagger Shanks-Greebly?'

'Him too.'

'Saddle-sniffer Snapdragon?'

'And him.'

'What about Poo-nudger MacArse-Trumpet?'

'Oh yes, best call up old MacArse-Trumpet.'

'And what about Sheep-fondler Bill Muff-Wrestler?'

The Commander-in-Chief looked at the adjutant.

The adjutant looked at the Commander-in-Chief.

'You're making these up now, aren't you?' said the Commander-in-Chief.

'So are you!'

'But I'm the Commander-in-Chief and if I want to make up a few campaign chums to take with me on a Green Alert, that's my privilege.'

'All right,' said the adjutant. 'I suppose it is allowed. So which ones *do* you want me to call up?'

'Just the last two.'

'But I made them—'

'But me no buts, sir. But me no buts. Saddle up me horse and break out the brandy. And, adjutant?'

'Yes sir?'

'Tell Muff-Wrestler to bring an extra sheep.'

'I'll tell him to bring two,' said the adjutant.

'I brought two coffees,' said the man in the white coat. 'How did you get on with the Ministry of Defence?'

Augustus Naseby took one of the coffees. 'I spoke with the office of the Commander-in-Chief.'

'Knob-gobbler Nackershaw?'

'Knob-gobbler took an early retirement. This is a new bod. Major-General Sir Stanley Burke-Hampshire.'

'What a very strange name. I trust the fellow's not some kind of pervert.'

'Any progress to report?'

'The coffees are still hot. But that's about all.'

'And what news of the monster?'

'Well, I assume that the monster will be all sorted out, now that the cream of the nation's military minds are being applied to the problem.'

'Yes indeed,' said Augustus, without too much conviction. 'So where exactly is the monster now?'

'The surveillance cameras are keeping an eye on it. It seems to be making its way towards Brighton Station. Didn't you say something about your son Porrig moving to Brighton?'

Augustus Naseby made a bitter face. 'My son Porrig,' he said. 'In all the excitement I'd quite forgotten about Porrig.'

But Porrig hadn't forgotten his dad. And Porrig didn't want his dad to end his days in a monster's guts. Certainly Porrig's dad was what you'd call a dodgy customer. Certainly he could not be trusted. Certainly he was treacherous and downright unspeakable. But he *was* Porrig's dad. And your dad is your dad, no matter how he behaves. You still go on loving him. Oh yes you do. He's your dad.

'I really hate my dad,' said Porrig as he trudged through the deserted streets.

'You don't,' said Rippington. 'You love him really.'

'Maybe.'

Porrig tried ringing for help, to alert the army or contact his dad, but the phones didn't work. None of them.

'What are all these postcards of big-fronted ladies?' asked Rippington as Porrig flung down the phone in the umpteenth phonebox.

'Never you bloody mind. Let's go back to the shop.'

'Why the shop?'

'So I can get some dry clothes on and my head together. And telephone for help.'

They returned to the shop.

The phone there didn't work either. No phone in Brighton worked. The Ministry of Serendipity had cut the lines.

Porrig took to some big time lot-bewailing.

'Come on,' said Rippington. 'Have a cup of tea.'

Porrig put the kettle on. 'What are we going to do?' he asked the small grey fellow.

'Since when have you taken to employing the royal "we"?'

'*We* have to do something. This is a major disaster here.'

'See what's on the wireless set.'

Porrig shook his head and rubbed it with a towel. 'Why the wireless set?'

Rippington tapped at his near noseless nose. 'You never know,' said he. 'Perhaps something quite as big as this might get a mention on the news.'

Porrig switched on the radio that stood on the kitchenette table. It was Wok Boy's radio. Porrig felt sick inside.

The radio crackled, then issued the news.

It was general news and first reports. First reports are always worth listening to. They may be a bit sketchy and vague, but real news *is* sketchy and vague. Real news is messy stuff, red in tooth and claw and things of that nature. And first reports *are* real news, because first reports have not been tidied up and sanitized and given a spin by the men who pull the strings.

'The first reports coming in about a major incident in the Brighton area,' said a voice on Porrig's radio, 'are a bit sketchy and vague, but we are awaiting official reports of what has occurred and will be bringing these to you as quickly as we can. On the world front the new Pope, Gregory the Chicken-worrier, has declared television presenter Carol Vorderman a living saint, while here at home Porrig is drying his armpits on a tea towel and wondering just what he should do next.'

'What?' said Porrig.

'However,' the voice on the radio continued, 'it is expected that he will soon reach a decision.'

'Who's saying this?' Porrig asked.

'You are, aren't you?' Rippington scratched at his little grey head.

'No. On the radio. Someone is talking to me.'

'That's what radios do, isn't it?'

'To *me* personally.'

'Ah,' said Rippington. 'To *you* personally. And you get these voices often, do you? The voice of God is it? Or Elvis? Does Elvis speak to you?'

'*Elvis?* How come you know about Elvis?'

'Porrig, everybody, *everywhere* knows about Elvis.'

'Yeah, well, you just listen to me, you little sod. I'm not losing my mind. Someone is speaking to me on this radio. *Personally* to me. So shut up and listen.'

Rippington shutted up and listened.

'—accused of impersonating an Egyptian while under the influence of alcohol and found in possession of pamphlets which claimed that chickens were planning to take over the world, pleaded guilty to—'

'It's stopped now,' said Porrig.

'Make sure you dry between your toes,' said the voice on the radio, 'and put on a vest. You don't want to catch a cold.'

'I know that voice,' said Rippington. 'It's—'

'The curator,' said the voice of the old bloke. 'And just what are *you* doing there?'

'Ah,' said Rippington. 'Porrig kidnapped me from ALPHA 17.'

'You lying little sod,' said Porrig. 'And *you* know why he's here. *You* sent him.'

'Just pay attention, both of you,' said the voice on the radio. 'There really isn't much time. You have to stop the monster, Porrig.'

'Me? Stop that thing? Get real, please.'

'It can be done, Porrig, and I will instruct you on how you will do it.'

'No,' said Porrig firmly. 'No no no. I nearly died down there in the sea. That thing can force thousands of people to kill themselves by doing nothing more than thinking it. I'll draw your comic book, but . . .'

'But?'

'But I'm no superhero. Never could be.'

'I'm not asking you to be a superhero. I will tell you the words of the ritual that enables one to move from this reality to others. You will take it down on paper and learn it by heart. I will be with you shortly and then I will instruct you how to use it.'

'Why don't you do it yourself?' Porrig asked. 'You're the big magician.'

'Do you wish to save your father's life or not?'

'Of course I do.'

'Then get yourself a pencil and paper.'

Porrig did as he was bid and then took down the seeming gibberish the old bloke dictated to him.

'Is that it?' Porrig asked, when he seemed to have finished.

'That's it. Now learn it by heart and I'll be with you soon.'

'But what if—'

'—and speaking from his hospital bed Sir David Attenborough said that he bore no ill will to the islanders of Gwa-tan

176

Qua Cest'l Potobo and would soon be up and hopping about on his one remaining leg.'

'Hang on!' shouted Porrig, 'Speak to me!'

'That is the end of the news.'

'Hang about!'

'He's gone,' said Rippington. 'Which is nice for him.'

Porrig sighed a big and heartfelt one. 'And so it's going to be up to me, is it? Slay the beast and save the country? Ludicrous. Madness.'

Rippington sauntered across the table and sat himself down on the kettle. 'Ouch,' he cried, rising again.

Porrig examined the words he had written; they still seemed like gibberish. 'This is all nonsense,' he said.

Rippington peeped at the paper. 'Ah,' said he. 'I think you'll find that it's all in the way that you read it.'

'Go on?'

'Each of these words represents a note. A musical tone. But they're not notes you've ever heard of. These are the notes that exist in the cracks between the piano keys.'

'So I'm supposed to sing out these words in the correct tones to make the magic work?'

'That's it. Remember when you came to ALPHA 17 and I asked you what key you were in and you didn't know?' Porrig nodded. 'Well, each of the realities is in a different key. A different frequency. You sing out these words and you can tune from one frequency to another.'

'Singing has never been my strong point.'

'It has mine,' said Rippington. 'And I know all these notes.'

'Then do it.'

'What?'

'Sing out the notes.'

'No way.' Rippington shook his little head. 'I don't have the authority.'

'But you want to go home, don't you? We could go to ALPHA 17.'

'We could and it is tempting. But the curator would be furious. He'd have my rubbing part for a pipe cleaner.'

'All right. Forget ALPHA 17. There's another way of doing

this. A way to get everything sorted really quickly. And I do mean everything. The monster, the Ministry of Serendipity, my dad. Everybody and everything.'

Rippington looked up at Porrig. 'Are you really thinking what I think I hear you thinking?'

'I give up. Am I?'

'Search me,' said Rippington. 'I was only bluffing that time. Your thoughts are so confusing I can't make a hog's head or a pig's tail out of them.'

'Then you'll just have to trust me. And if you do, we'll get the whole thing sewn up before the old bloke gets here and you can go back to ALPHA 17 a hero.'

'A hero, eh?'

'You'll be a hero and I'll be a hero and all the world will be happy and everything will be well and all before the old bloke gets back.'

'Now that,' said Rippington, 'would be what I'd call a most remarkable feat.'

18

It *was* a most remarkable feat. Remarkably achieved. Single-handedly achieved. Remarkable.

The President of the United States, in his speech, said just how remarkable he thought it was. The Prime Minister of England, who always agreed with anything the President said, agreed that it was indeed remarkable. Various crowned heads of Europe, who hadn't said anything much for a very long time, said that they too considered it remarkable. And the new Pope Peter the Pigeon-fancier said that even he found it remarkable.

The motor cavalcade that progressed slowly through the streets of London, carrying Porrig to Buckingham Palace, where he received his knighthood, was cheered for every inch of the way by crowds that were thrilled to their hearts and souls by the utter remarkability of just what Porrig had achieved.

To have single-handedly defeated the monster, which had by this time taken control of all the known world, but for the island of Gwa'tan Qua Cest'l Potobo, was indeed remarkable.

In his speech, Porrig, displaying the modesty and self-restraint and also the caring kindly manner for which he had always been so loved, said that anyone in his position would have done the same. He did not wish to take all the credit for himself. He thanked his parents for the love and thoughtfulness they had shown him over the years and hoped that now the world had experienced something so awful as the monster's reign of terror, that nation would speak peace unto nation.

All the proceeds from the film and TV rights of his life story would, he said, be donated to the needy, to help house the homeless.

Porrig bowed, had his hand shaken by the Prime Minister and received a kiss on the cheek from the Queen.

The slap-up nosh at Windsor Castle was attended by many celebrities; Arnold Schwarzenegger, who had been picked to play Porrig in the forthcoming Hollywood movie, gave him pats on the back; Sigourney Weaver offered him 'the eye'. Porrig sat beside Elton John, whose tribute record about him was currently topping the pop charts.

The toast was proposed by a small grey figure with a little baldy head and blue cat's eyes.

'To Porrig,' said Rippington, for it was he. 'To Porrig for being such an unmitigated rub-tugger.'

'What?' said Porrig.

'You pig's behind,' said Rippington. 'Did you really think you could just shift yourself into an alternative reality where you had already defeated the monster and were now getting all the rewards?'

Porrig nodded with enthusiasm.

Rippington shook his little head.

'No?' said Porrig.

'No!' said Rippington.

'Oh,' said Porrig. 'Damn!'

Porrig sat in the kitchenette drinking a cup of mauve tea.

It was raining outside and the radio, although on, had nothing whatever to say. The last news to come out of it was an official report which said that the centre of London had been sealed off owing to traffic-light failure.

Porrig sipped his tea and sighed to himself. Perhaps he'd make a start on that comic book. Or perhaps he wouldn't.

Wok Boy appeared at the kitchenette door. 'Check this out,' he said.

Porrig turned and took what he was handed. It was a free paper. Its headline read: 'CREATURE DEAD'.

And under this were the words: 'MONSTER KILLED BY COMMON COLD.'

'Yes!' went Porrig, raising a fist.

'No!' said Rippington, shaking his head. 'Though it was a nice touch bringing Wok Boy back to life.'

The Silver Surfer sped down from the sky and—

'No!' said Rippington.

The Earth's crust cracked open and swallowed the creature and—

'No!'

'No?' said Porrig.

'No!'

'Then what about if—'

'No!'

'I don't get it.' Porrig threw up his hands. 'Why do you keep saying no?'

'Because you *don't* get it. You can't do it this way. These are alternative realities.'

'But I thought that was the point of having them and visiting them and being in them. Because they *were* alternative. It doesn't matter how the creature is destroyed, does it?'

'No. It doesn't matter at all. As long as it *is* destroyed. In *this* reality. The one it's really in.'

'Oh,' said Porrig. 'So how am I expected to do that?'

'You have to find a way of altering *this* reality.'

'But how?'

'I think what the curator has in mind is that you visit one of the existing separate realities and acquire something there to help you here.'

'Acquire something? You mean steal something.'

'Borrow something.'

'What sort of something?'

Rippington waved his little magic wand. 'Something like this, perhaps.'

'A magic wand. Why can't we use yours?'

'Because mine doesn't do very much. You'll need something much more powerful.'

'And where am I going to find it?'

'I know a place,' said Rippington. 'I read about it in one of the big books.'

'Then let's go there.'

'There isn't time. The curator may be back at any minute. And I'll get in big trouble and my rubbing part will end up as a pipe cleaner and I'll—'

'Look,' said Porrig. 'I will take *all* the blame. You can say to the curator that I forced you to take me. Tell him anything you like.'

'Well, I don't know.'

Porrig mimed vicious pinchings of a small rubbing part. 'About this place,' he said.

'Well,' Rippington hesitated. 'It's not a very nice place and it's rather dangerous.'

'Oh yes?'

'Oh yes. It's one of the less desirable versions of this place. In fact it's probably the very least desirable version of this place.'

'I don't want to go there,' said Porrig.

'I think it's probably the only place where you'll get what you need.'

'And what is this place called?'

Rippington stroked his pointy little chin. 'Well,' he said. 'I'm from ALPHA 17, which isn't such a bad place. And this here is BETA 23, which probably isn't such a bad place either, most of the time, but probably isn't quite as nice as ALPHA 17. This other place, the one you have to go to, is somewhat down the other end of the niceness scale. Down at the not-at-all-nice-at-all end.'

'And what is it called?'

'Well, I can't remember exactly what it's called, but I do recall the frequency.'

'Which is?'

182

'OMEGA,' said Rippington. 'OMEGA 666.'

'OMEGA 666!' said Porrig. 'Oh hell!'

'Oh yeah,' said Rippington. *'That's* what it's called.'

'War is hell,' said Major-General Sir Stanley Burke-Hampshire. 'MacArthur said that, doncha know?'

'What, old Minge-worrier MacArthur?' asked Billy Muff-Wrestler.

'Don't be a damn fool,' said Poo-nudger MacArse-Trumpet. 'He's talking about old Mattress-muncher MacArthur, pride of the Cameroon Highlanders.'

'I'm talking about General MacArthur,' said Sir Stanley. 'American chappy. I think George C. Scott played him in the film. Damn good film too, if I recall. Lots of tanks.'[1]

'If you top brass chaps are ready,' said the adjutant, 'I have the big board laid out. Perhaps you'd care to discuss strategy.'

'Who's this cove?' asked Poo-nudger.

'My adjutant,' said Sir Stanley.

'I had an adjutant once. Got involved in some ghastly business in Hamburg. Impersonating an Egyptian.'

'Impregnating an erection,' said Sir Stanley. 'He was making love to a traffic cone. All covered in lard. He gave the policemen the slip.'

'Haven't had one since,' said Poo-nudger. 'Can't be bothered with them.'

'If we might get on?' said the adjutant.

'See what I mean?'

'So,' said Sir Stanley to his adjutant. 'Big board out, you say? Lots of tanks on the big board?'

'Lots of tanks, sir.'

'Let's have a look at it then.'

The adjutant led Sir Stanley and his two campaign chums to the Ministry of Defence operations room. It was not quite as large as the Ministry of Serendipity operations room, but it was more elegantly lit.

---

[1]The movie was actually *Patton: Lust for Glory*. And it was Sherman who said 'War is hell' anyway.

'Nice lighting,' said Poo-nudger.

'Big board,' said Sir Stanley.

And it was a very big board. It was a big map on a big board. A big map of southern England. There were lots of little English flags sticking in it: some in London; others in Sussex and Kent. In Brighton there was another flag: a German flag with a swastika on it.

'Good God!' said MacArse-Trumpet. 'Not the bloody Boche again?'

'Damned monster from outer space, apparently,' said Sir Stanley. 'Didn't have any monster flags though. Lots of German ones going spare. Used one of those.'

Poo-nudger studied the map. 'How many regiments you got?'

'Six,' said Sir Stanley. 'All tanks.'

'Got any planes?'

'Can't be having with planes, go too fast. Know where you are with a tank.'

'This space chap got any planes?'

'Got a flying saucer, apparently. Hasn't been flying it though. Got some native chappies carting him about.'

'Odd bod,' said Poo-nudger.

Billy Muff-Wrestler glanced all about. 'Need sticks,' he said.

'Tanks a lot better than sticks,' said Sir Stanley.

'No no. Sticks for here. To push the little flags about.'

'Good point. Adjutant, fetch sticks.'

The adjutant fetched sticks.

'Right,' said Sir Stanley, waving his stick in the air and nearly putting Poo-nudger's eye out. 'Where *exactly* is the monster now?'

'Right here,' said the adjutant, flourishing a stick of his own. 'At the rear of a procession that is approaching Brighton Station.'

Brighton Station: still as beautiful as ever, graceful curving roof of glass, cathedral to the god of steam. Empty now of passengers, but not deserted altogether.

For lo. And indeed, behold.

Who is this we see?

Who is this sitting behind the ticket window, all on his own and reading a copy of *Bogie World*?

Russell The Railwayman. It is he.

Russell munched upon a sandwich that his mum had made for him and chuckled through the spam at a cartoon in his magazine. It was a drawing of two railwaymen looking down at a coupling. One said, 'That's supposed to be a 8134/7.' The other replied, 'Looks more like an 8137/4.'

Russell The Railwayman chuckled once more. 'That's a good'n,' he said.

The sound of chanting drifted to his ears. Russell raised the wet towel from his head and listened. The chanting grew louder. The chanting sounded frantic.

'Chanting,' said Russell. 'And sounding rather frantic.'

A naked chest lurched into his eye-line. Russell stared hard at the chest. It was a male chest. It had hairs on it. Chanting and a naked chest. Russell put aside his magazine.

The chest began to lower and a head became visible. The face on this head was not happy. It was a haunted face. A grave and fearful face. It was the face of Sir John Rimmer.

'When does the next train to London go?' asked this face.

Russell smiled at the face. 'You've missed it,' he said.

'Missed the next train? How can we have missed the next train?'

'Only joking,' said Russell. 'Graham Moffat said it in the 1937 film classic *Oh Mr Porter*, starring Will Hay. One of the few comedy films ever made about the railways. They never did a *Carry on*, you know. Apparently they had one planned, but Bernard Breslaw had taken a Shakespearean part with Sir Peter Hall at the National and Jim Dale had emigrated to America. Although I can't say I ever rated Jim Dale, what do you think?'

'I . . .' Sir John's mouth opened and shut and then opened again. 'The next train, when is the next train?'

'Hold on just a moment, sir.' Russell peered past Sir John towards the chanters who were pouring onto the concourse. 'You'll have to stop that chanting,' he shouted. 'And go home at once.'

Sir John's mouth flapped. 'The next train, the next train,' he said.

'I'm only here for a couple of days,' said Russell. 'Just arrived. I put in for some relief work because of the clubs and the pubs. I do stand-up comedy, you see, hoping to make the big breakthrough any time now. You'll get contaminated, you know, standing there without your shirt.'

'The next train,' went Sir John.

'Keep the noise down out there,' shouted Russell. 'You can't do that without a licence. Go home, please.'

'The next—'

'Excuse me,' said a lady in a straw hat, with wet towel veil attachment.

Russell smiled at his mum. 'How can I help you, madam?' he asked.

'*Me*,' said Sir John. 'Help *me*.'

'One at a time now, sir. I think this lady was here before you.'

'Buffet cars,' said the lady in the straw hat. 'I want to enquire about buffet cars in the Norfolk area.'

'And what exactly is the nature of your enquiry?'

'I want to buy one.'

'Tickets,' went Sir John. 'Many tickets. All tickets. Now. London. Beware. He comes.'

'*He* comes? Who comes?' Russell asked.

'Obey with haste. Beware the pain.'

'Have you been drinking?' Russell asked. 'Or are you con- taminated?'

'Obey. Now. Train. London.'

'Keep it down out there!'

'Since privatization,' said the lady, 'I thought I might open a macrobiotic restaurant.'

'Just excuse me for a minute, madam.' Russell waved Sir John aside and yelled through his microphone: 'Just listen to me! You can't chant on station property and you must form an orderly queue.'

'They're not listening,' said the lady. 'Put it out over the tannoy.'

'Right,' said Russell. 'I will.' He flicked the necessary switch and a big burst of feedback screamed about the station.

'Attention,' shouted Russell. 'Your attention please. The mmmmphphn mmmmpphmmm mmmm regulations require mmmmph no chanting mmmph hmmmmnh orderly line at the ticket-office window and mmmmphm mmph . . . wet towels . . . mmph.'

'He's mumbling.' Sir John waved his hands in the air. 'About the train? Is he talking about the train?'

'He has lovely diction,' said the lady. 'He doesn't really mumble, he's just softly spoken.'

'Aaaaaaaaaagh!' went Sir John Rimmer.

Chant chant chant, went the chanting chanters. Hump hump hump, went the humping strugglers. Yawn wave and blow-upon-the-fingernails-in-a-distracted-Noël-Coward-sort-of-a-way went Dilbert Norris, most impressively.

For most impressive did he look, all things considered. Carried in his shining, spotless, buffed and burnished silver seven-pointed spacecraft,[2] on the shoulders of his Nubians and many others. Big and bad and bulbous, he was borne aloft through the great iron arch into the booking hall. Sunlight, angling down through the high glass roof, caught him to perfect imperfection. He was wrong, all wrong, this monstrous sprouty bastard, sunrays dancing on his huge and horrid head. The eyes as big as basket balls and black as new-mined coal. The glistening skin; the upturned mouth all drippy wet. The bulging belly full with folk; the three-foot parsnip wanger still no joke at all.

The chanters chanted hymns of praise, their eyes rolled up in agony, their muscles knotted by the pain. Praise unto He who had returned to rule them once again.

Dilbert cast his swarthy peepers all about the place. This wasn't bad, this gaff, most high about the roofy regions, as might be appreciated by one such as He. Most High Himself. He waved a bloated hand to urge His minions on and settled down upon his cushions, feeling mighty fine.

[2]Try saying that with your teeth out.

He'd triumph here, would Dilbert. They would know His power; they would feel the pain that went with disobedience, that, in fact, went with the vaguest hint, the smallest flicker of wilfulness. For He was God to these small mammals, God as they were gods to creatures smaller than themselves. This race that thought itself so powerful, so assured, He'd show them real power. They would know their master, they would worship, they would show Him the reverence that was His due. Respect, allegiance, loyalty and—

'What the fuck is that great green ugly-looking object?' came the voice of Russell at three hundred decibels.

And with that, silence fell.

19

Is it silent in hell, do you think?
For is silence more horrid than noise?

Does hell echo forever with the screams of the tormented, or is there no sound at all? Imagine that, no sound at all. Screaming and screaming and screaming, but not a sound, just utter silence, for ever and ever and ever.

Horrible.

'It's horrible here,' whispered Porrig, 'but it doesn't look like hell.'

Rippington flicked the tip of his little magic wand and held it close to his earhole. 'OMEGA 666,' he whispered back. 'The frequency's correct. What should hell really look like, then?'

Porrig made wild and unpleasant gestures. 'Fire and brimstone and the gnashing of teeth. But this looks like a—'

'Theatre,' said Rippington. 'That's just what it looks like.'

And it did, because it was a theatre. An old-fashioned music hall theatre and one sorely gone to seed and dust and damage and decay. They stood in the foyer, gilt-cracked walls about them. Above a ceiling domed and done with cherubs. Pinkly bummed and jolly boys they'd been, but now the paint was flaked and the plumpsome cheeks and dimpled knees were

189

pocked with leprous-looking scabs. The foyer smelled of damp
and mould and misery. A chair or two of once royal stuff sagged
in wormy ruination. A carpet, bare to threads and direly stained,
moved obscenely as a rat went questing underneath.

Porrig shivered. 'It's bloody cold too. Shouldn't hell be hot?'

Rippington shrugged his skinny little shoulders. 'I read in one
of the big books all about how witches had congress with the
devil—'

'Congress?' Porrig asked.

'Shagging.'

'Oh.'

'And when they had congress, they said that the devil's
rubbing part was cold as ice.'

Porrig sighed. His first sigh in hell. 'How is it,' he asked, 'that
no matter what the conversation is about, you always manage to
bring rubbing parts into it?'

'You started it.'

'I never did.'

'Let's go in and see the show.'

'There's going to be a show? In *here*?'

'That's what we came to see. Dress circle, do you think, or
royal box?'

'Stalls,' said Porrig. 'I'm not going upstairs and falling to my
death through rotten floorboards.'

'Can you fall to your death in hell, if you're not already dead?'

'Stalls,' said Porrig. 'Follow me.'

The door to the stalls hung off its hinge, but the house lights
were up and the auditorium looked almost welcoming.

But almost is the same as 'not quite' and not quite is the same
as 'not'.

Porrig peeped in. 'It's empty,' he said. 'No it's not.'

'Who's there?' Rippington peeped in also, from between
Porrig's legs.

'Over there.' Porrig pointed. 'And there and there too.'

'Can't see,' said Rippington. 'Give us an up on your shoulders.'

Porrig stooped and lifted the imp. Again he felt the cold grey
flesh. Again he didn't like it.

'I don't like yours either,' said Rippington. 'What's there to be seen?'

What was there to be seen was a Victorian music hall, with a sagging proscenium arch, lacking its mask of comedy, but with its mask of tragedy still intact. Red velvet curtains, moth-gnawed and manky, were swagged by dust-blurred golden cords. The high-domed ceiling was lost in shadows; the seats ranked out in widening arcs. And seated here and there and no two together, was the audience. Of six.

'Hardly a full house,' whispered Rippington. 'Let's sit down the front.'

Porrig hesitated. 'I don't like this. It's all wrong.'

'It's hell. You're not supposed to like it.'

'But it's not my idea of hell.'

'Because it's not *your* hell.'

'Whose is it then?'

'You'll see.'

Porrig sighed another sigh and—

'Don't even think about it,' Rippington said. 'Bewailing your lot. Not *here*.'

Porrig shrugged and Rippington fell off his shoulder.

'Ow!' went the imp.

'Sorry,' said Porrig.

They wandered down to the front row seats and took two close by the aisle.

Porrig opened his mouth to complain that his seat was damp, but the house lights suddenly dimmed.

Curtains creaked apart and footlights flickered. On the bare-board stage stood an odd-legged table and on this stood many strange things. A brass megaphone with an ivory handle. Two pairs of specs and a fat lady's sandal. One round of sandwiches, cheese by the look. The skull of a fish and a queer-looking book. Rings made of pewter and balls made of wood. A saw and a hammer, a large Christmas pud. A gaudy collection, though far from aesthetic. Was more than eclectic and very poetic.

Behind all this was a backdrop painted to resemble an Egyptian market scene: stalls and bundles, terracotta pots and camels and so on and so forth and suchlike.

From stage left came a grunt or two, followed by a crank-ing sound, a hissing sound and a crackling sound. And then another sound: the sound of music played through an old horn gramophone. The tune was 'In a Monastery Garden'.

Further sounds of grunting and cranking. The sound of Silence. More crackling and 'In a Persian Market' (flip-side of 'In a Monastery Garden').

'Are you sure we've come to the right place?' whispered Porrig.

'Ladies and gentle*men*,' came a voice from off stage. A strident voice, a forceful one. 'Ladies and gentle*men*. For the first time here at The Omega Theatre. An act so wired and weird and wondrous strange, so oddball odd and damned deranged, so pinky pink and blackly grey, that ne'er before has seen the light of day. Put hands together, raise your voices, cheer. The one, the only one is here. Amazing and incredible, spectaculous . . .

'Apocalypso The Miraculous!'

'Whoa!' went Porrig.

'Clap the man,' said Rippington.

And they did. Porrig clapped and Rippington clapped. They clapped and clapped, but their clapping didn't make a single sound.

Porrig gaped at his silent palms. 'What is *this*?' he mumbled.

Rippington shrugged.

A fellow walked onto the stage. He did not so much walk, as shamble. He was pushed and then he shambled. One foot dragging, then the other. Dragging sandalled feet. Ankles bare, veined blue as Stilton cheese[1] and above, a long striped night-shirt kind of jobbie, big, loose-sleeved and collarless. Turkey neck, gaunt face, deep-lined. Eyes sunk dark, cadaver-ous. Narrow nose too long and mouth too small and head topped off by a battered red fez.

Apocalypso The Miraculous looked very far from being that.

'He looks wretched,' Porrig whispered.

'He looks dead,' the small grey fellow whispered in reply.

Apocalypso folded his scrawny arms then flung them wide.

[1]Or is it Gorgonzola?

Withered flowers in withered fists appeared as if from nowhere. Then two more fell out of his sleeves.

'Boo,' went someone.

Porrig turned around in his seat. 'Shut up,' he shouted. 'Give the man a chance.'

'Thank you.' Apocalypso bowed.

Porrig tried to clap once more, but once more no sound came.

'For my first trick,' said Apocalypso, in a wheezing distant voice, 'I shall require the services of a member of the audience.'

Porrig rose.

'Don't do it,' Rippington said.

'Why not?'

'Just a hunch. Trust me on this one.'

Porrig sat back down and made a grumpy face.

A lady in a straw hat stood up. It was not Russell's mum, but it looked a lot like her.

'Madam,' called Apocalypso. 'Madam, thank you. If you would be so kind as to come up onto the stage.'

Porrig craned round in his seat to view the volunteer. 'She looks familiar,' he said, and, 'Oh.'

'Oh what?' asked Rippington.

'Well, oh, the auditorium is full now. I never heard them all come in.'

Rippington climbed onto his seat to have a good look round.

'Sit down, you little turd,' said the man sitting behind him.

Rippington sat down and edged a bit closer to Porrig.

Porrig glanced over his head and all along the front row. It was also full. Which was reasonably impossible, as the folk who sat there would have had to step past him to sit there.

The lady in the straw hat was now on the stage.

'And what is your name, madam?' asked Apocalypso.

'And what is your name, madam?' said the lady.

'Please tell the audience your name.'

'Please tell the audience your name.'

'Madam, if you would not repeat what I say. Just please tell us your name.'

'Madam, if you would not repeat what—'

'Give him a chance,' called Porrig.

'Shut your face,' called the lady.

'Yeah, shut your face,' shouted the man behind Rippington.

'Madam,' said Apocalypso.

'Madam,' said the lady.

'Give him a chance,' called Porrig.

'Shut your face,' shouted the man.

'Best stay out of it, Porrig,' said Rippington.

'Best stay out of it, Porrig,' said the lady.

'Don't start on me,' said Rippington.

'Don't start on me,' shouted the man.

'Please,' begged Apocalypso. 'Please, not again.'

'Please,' said the lady.

'Please, not again,' chimed in the shouting man.

'One trick,' sobbed Apocalypso. 'Let me do one trick.'

'One trick,' said the lady. 'Let me—'

'Boo,' shouted Porrig. 'Get that woman off the stage.'

'Boo!' shouted someone else. And 'Boo' and 'Boo' and 'Boo'.

The curtains fell. The house lights came on.

'You pack of bastards,' cried Porrig, turning in his seat. 'And – Oh . . .'

'And oh once more?' asked Rippington.

'They've gone. All gone.'

Rippington climbed once more onto his seat. The house lights went down once more and the stage lit up again.

Same table, same props, same backdrop. Same noises off.

Same introduction.

Apocalypso pulled withered flowers from his sleeves.

The lady in the straw hat went up once again.

She mimicked Apocalypso again.

Porrig protested again.

The curtains closed again.

Footlights off.

House lights on.

Audience there.

Audience not there.

Flowers. Mimic. Protest.

'See a pattern beginning to emerge?' asked Rippington. 'Get the picture about just whose hell we're in?'

'Again and again,' said Porrig in a voice full of fear. 'He goes through this again and again and again.'

'And he suffers again and again. He's the only one thinking. I can hear him. There's nobody else. The audience doesn't really exist.'

'They're just an illusion?'

'His illusion. His pain. His punishment.'

'But for thirty years? He's been going through this for thirty years, ever since he died?' Porrig felt breathless. Stifled. The sheer horror of it, the torture, it was all too much.

'I think that's what hell must be,' said Rippington. 'I don't think it's that fire and brimstone and the devil and all. I read in one of the big books about dharma, have you ever heard of that?'

'I've heard of it, but I don't know what it means.'

'It's the essential principle of the cosmos, the natural law. You get out of life what you put into it. That kind of thing. Apocalypso is paying his dues.'

'Well, he's paid enough,' said Porrig. 'I've never felt such sadness before, it's terrible. I can't let it go on.'

'Let's just get what we came for.' Rippington pointed to the stage. 'See that book?'

'Book?'

'The one on the table. It's Apocalypso's book of magic.'

'And you want me to nick *that*? That's what got him here in the first place.'

'No no no,' said Rippington, shaking his little baldy head. 'This isn't the "demons speaking at his ear" kind of magic book. This is the "now you see it, now you don't, it's all done with mirrors" kind of magic. He was the real bee's bollocks, with or without the demons.'

'You seem to know a lot about him.'

'I read your book. *Beyond Doubtable Reason* by Sir John Rimmer.'

'So I should go up on stage and compound his misery by stealing his book?'

'Well, he doesn't have much use for it here, does he?'

'No. But I can't leave him here. Not like this.'

'We can't take him back with us, Porrig. He's dead, he'd fall to pieces. And I'd get in all kinds of trouble. More than I'm in already.'

'All right.' Porrig made a thoughtful face. 'Maybe we can't take him back to our reality. But what about if . . .' and he whispered to Rippington.

Rippington listened, then Rippington grinned. 'I suppose we could,' he said. 'I mean, who else would know, if we didn't tell them?'

'Sing the magic words,' said Porrig.

Rippington sang the magic words.

The curtains creaked apart once more to reveal the same stage, the same table, the same backdrop. From stage left came the grunting sounds, the cranking sounds, the hissings and the crackles. And then the sound of music.

'It's a kind of magic,' sang Freddie the Mercury.

Porrig settled back in his seat. Rippington sat up in his.

'Ladies and gentle*men*,' came the strident off-stage voice. 'For the last time here, or anywhere. Long in the tooth, but brave as a bear. Marvel, mystic and manipulator. Pre-eminent prestidigitator. Lord of legerdemain. Came by bus and not by train . . .'

'You get far better poetry in ALPHA 17,' whispered Rippington.

'The one, the only, and he still rhymes with spectaculous. Apocalypso The Miraculous!'

There was a puff of smoke.

And he was there.

Black top hat and tails and cape all lined with crimson silk. Patent pumps and, in his white-gloved fingers, twirling canes. Crisp white shirt with matching dicky bow. And underneath, red ladies' underwear (a private peccadillo).

'I can't stop him being a perv,' said Rippington.

'What do you mean?'

'Nothing, Porrig. Just enjoy the show.'

196

Apocalypso grinned from ear to ear and back again. His face was young and fit and tanned. He wore a black moustache and an Imperial upon his chin.[2] He looked as he had while still in his prime, which once again he was.

'He looks good,' said Porrig.

'Don't he just.'

Apocalypso's twirling whirling canes became a blur and then became two sprays of fresh red roses. The magician bowed, then flung them to the crowd and they became a flock of doves that circled overhead.

'How did he do that?' Porrig asked.

'Without the aid of demons. Watch this bit.'

Apocalypso raised his hat, the circling doves flew back to the stage and, spiralling down like water into a plughole, they vanished one after another into the upraised hat.

Apocalypso bowed once more, turned the top hat upside down and patted the crown. A foot appeared, a lady's foot, followed by a fish-net-stockinged leg, another leg, then a torso, head and arms and all.

'Ladies and gentlemen,' cried Apocalypso, his voice going boom about the auditorium. 'Ladies and gentlemen, I give you my lovely assistant, Myra.'

'Myra?' said Porrig. 'But Myra's my . . .' He paused.

'Your what?' asked Rippington.

'My mum,' said Porrig. 'And it *is* my mum. I've seen pictures of her when she was very young. This *is* her.'

'The rubbing part thickens,' said Rippington.

'It's *the plot* thickens, actually.'

'No it's not,' said Rippington. 'I've always gone for fish-net stockings.'

'Don't be so disgusting, that's my mum!'

Porrig's mum did that stage assistant curtsy that Debbie Magee does with such grace, then the open-palmed point to the magician, which indicates to the crowd that they have just witnessed something well deserving of their stingy praise.

[2]The little Bonsai beard, as favoured by the late and legendary Frank Zappa.

The crowd clapped. And the claps sounded. Sounded loud. Rippled and crashed and sea-washed over the theatre, rising and rising and rising.

Porrig joined in and Rippington did too. The great magician bowed and Porrig's mum curtsied, did some more open-palming, then clapped a bit herself.

'It's going brilliantly,' Porrig shouted through the wild applause. 'But I never knew that my mum had been his assistant,' he whispered to Rippington.

'Your family has got more secrets than the CIA.'

'Ladies and gentlemen.' Apocalypso raised his gloved hands and the audience stilled to silence. 'This is to be my final performance and you will witness sights that you have never witnessed before. You will tell your grandchildren that you were here this night. That you *saw* Apocalypso The Miraculous.'

'Top man,' shouted Porrig.

Apocalypso gazed down upon him. 'Did somebody speak?' he asked.

'I just said, "Top man," ' said Porrig. 'Sorry to interrupt your flow.'

'Not at all, young man. Would you care to step onto the stage and take part in the performance?'

'No, not really. I'll just watch, if you don't mind.'

'But I do, I do.' Apocalypso beckoned. 'Come onto the stage. Come onto the stage.'

'No, really, I . . .'

Apocalypso pointed and stared a most unsettling stare.

'I would this time,' said Rippington.

Porrig rose from his seat and scrambled onto the stage.

'And what is your name?' Apocalypso asked.

'Padraig,' said Porrig. 'But it's pronounced Porrig, so that's what everyone calls me.'

'What a nice name,' said the lovely Myra. 'If I ever have a son, I think I might call him that.'

'Er . . .' said Porrig.

'So,' said Apocalypso, 'do you believe in magic, Porrig?'

'Oh yes,' said Porrig. 'I certainly do. And fate. And dharma too.'

'So much belief for one so young.'

'I'm learning how to learn.'

'Then top man too. Let the show begin.' Apocalypso threw wide his arms and the show began. Oh yes!

Rippington looked on in awe as Porrig was first levitated, then made to climb up a rope that hovered of its own accord, before vanishing at the top to appear a moment later at the back of the auditorium. Then thrust into a suitcase that was pierced through with spears, lifted out unharmed, rammed into a cannon and fired through a hoop of fire, collected up in pieces from the stage floor, jammed into Apocalypso's top hat, then poured out wearing Myra's clothes while she clapped loud from Porrig's seat, all dressed up in his.

'For my finale,' cried Apocalypso. 'The terrible electronic wasp-filled torture box, that will be lowered into the pit of flames, whilst simultaneously—'

'No,' begged Porrig.

'No?' said Apocalypso.

'No. I'm definitely stealing all your thunder. Go into the box yourself.'

'No fear,' said Apocalypso. 'I put my last assistant in there. We haven't found all of her yet.'

'Go on, Porrig,' called Rippington. 'Wasp-filled torture box. It'll be a doddle.'

'A friend of yours?' asked Apocalypso.

'Another volunteer,' said Porrig, wiping sweat from all manner of places. 'I'm sure he'd rather do it than me.'

'Well, let's have him up on the stage. It is a *him*, isn't it?'

Rippington waggled his small rubbing part.

'You had to say *that*,' Porrig said.

Rippington scuttled onto the stage. 'Pleased to meet you,' he said, extending a slim grey hand.

Apocalypso shook it gently. 'And where are you from?' he enquired.

'ALPHA 17. The place where you're *not* going to go.'

Apocalypso's smiling face became a face of fear. 'You've come for me,' he whispered.

Rippington shook his little grey head. 'On the contrary. As

this *will* be your last performance, and you will *only* be using stage magic, and not *any other kind ever*, no-one or thing is going to come for you. Porrig is giving you a second chance. So don't foul it up.'

'But I don't understand.'

'Boo' and 'Hiss' went the audience, and 'Get on with it' also.

'Your public awaits,' said Rippington. 'Can the wasp box trick be done without help from . . . how shall I put this? Help from other quarters?'

Apocalypso shook his head. 'I don't think so,' he said. 'It was because of the tragedy that befell my last assistant that I invoked the help of those from other quarters. In the hope of getting her back.'

'It's all beginning to make sense now, isn't it?' said Porrig to Rippington. 'Why he, you know, went over to the Dark Side of The Force, as it were.'

'Boo boo' and further 'Hiss' went the audience, who could not hear the conversation. Someone threw an apple and another threw a fish.

'Must be a party in from Surrealing,' said Rippington. 'Better do the trick yourself, Mr Miraculous.'

Apocalypso took deep breaths and his smile returned. 'All right,' said he.

'Hold on,' said Porrig. 'I mean, he might get killed doing this.'

'Dharma,' said Rippington. 'We've entered a reality in the past, where Apocalypso has not yet got fully involved with the demon-ear-whispering. You chose it, Porrig. It was your idea. To save him from the thirty years of torture.'

'Yes, but if he gets killed, what have I saved him from?'

'He might not die. Might you not, Apocalypso?'

The magician's smile had a forced look about it. 'Certainly not,' he said in a voice that was none too convincing.

Members of the audience were standing now and a large selection of fruit and veg, socks and shoes, teabags and tambourines, chimney-pots and carrycots, condoms full of semolina and pork pies fashioned into the shape of battleships and hedgehogs were being hurled at the stage.

200

'We could just bring down the curtain,' said Porrig. 'Leave'm wanting more, eh?'

Rippington shook his little grey head.

Apocalypso shook his larger and tanned one.

'God's cods,' said Porrig.

'Ladies and gentlemen,' cried Apocalypso, throwing wide his hands once more and beaming at the audience. A tube of Dr Doveston's Patent Pile Ointment and Strawberry-flavoured Mouthwash sailed through the air, missed Apocalypso and caught Porrig full in the face.

'Ouch,' went Porrig, falling to the stage.

'Ladies and gentlemen. My apologies to you for the slight delay in the performance. I was simply dictating my will to my colleague here.'

Porrig climbed to his feet and curtsied.

'You look a right rub-tugger in those fish-net tights,' said Rippington.

Porrig's mum shouted from the stalls: 'Get on with it.'

'The act I am about to perform,' continued the magician, dodging falls of spanner sandwiches and cheesecake, 'has never been successfully attempted before. No-one has ever survived going into the electronic wasp-filled torture box and being lowered into the pit of flames whilst being simultaneously scorned by an Anglican Bishop for impersonating an Egyptian.'

'Don't like the sound of that last bit,' said Rippington. 'Give us a kiss.'

'Piss off,' said Porrig.

'If I might just ask my lovely assistant Myra to assist me in a lovely manner?'

Porrig's mum returned to the stage. 'I rather like this cross-dressed look,' she said to Porrig. 'I might suggest it to my friend Marlene Dietrich, she's looking for a new gimmick to use in her next movie.'

'Myra,' said Apocalypso. Myra bowed, displaying much cleavage and some hint of nipple to the audience. All throwing ceased and much cheering began.

'Oi!' went Porrig. 'That's my m—'

'Best keep a few secrets for yourself,' suggested Rippington.

The lovely Myra did some more open-palm work and Apocalypso clapped his hands. Down from somewhere or other on high came a large glass case of telephone-box proportions. It descended slowly towards the stage, lowered upon sturdy chains.

'The terrible electronic torture box,' cried Apocalypso.

'Oooooooooooooooooooh,' went the audience.

'As you can see,' Apocalypso said, 'the torture box is constructed of glass, but for the top and the bottom, which are formed from high conductivity steel. I will enter the box from the door in the front. Taking with me these.' He gestured stage right, and from stage right a chap appeared. He was clad in the full bee-keeper's get-up: mask, white suit, the whole bit. And he carried before him, held at arm's length, a small glass cabinet. From within came a mad mad buzzing, for within were many wasps.

'Amazonian killer wasps,' said Apocalypso.

'Oooooooooooooooooooh,' went the audience.

'One sting will drive a man insane with pain, two stings and . . .' Here he drew a gloved finger across his throat. 'Two stings are fatal. And here, in this cabinet, are one thousand wasps. Would anyone care to count them? You, perhaps, madam?' He pointed to a lady in a straw hat.

'No thanks,' called the lady. 'I'll trust your arithmetic.'

'Just so. And should one thousand killer wasps not do the trick, then how about this?'

The lights suddenly dimmed and the world went black. And then with a pop and a crackle and a shock, great sparkings of electricity flashed about.

The lights went up to reveal another figure on the stage: chap in a white coat this time, holding two very large cables. He brought them within two feet of each other and sparks flew like special effects in a Frankenstein movie.

'Oooooooooooooooooooh,' went the audience once more.

'Fifty thousand volts,' said Apocalypso. 'One cable will be attached to the top of the box and one to the bottom. I shall be standing between the two when the switch is thrown to complete the circuit and receive the full force of the shock.'

'Ooooooooooooooooooh,' went the audience.

'Madness,' said Porrig.

'Now,' said Apocalypso. 'Should the wasps not sting me to death and the voltage not turn me to jelly, how about *this*?'

He clapped his hands and, beneath the still dangling torture box, a trapdoor opened in the stage. From this belched fire and smoke. A regular Moloch of a blaze.

'Ooooooooooooooooooh,' went the audience one more time.

'Down,' cried Apocalypso. 'Down the torture box will be lowered. Into the fiery furnace.'

'Hold on there,' shouted Porrig, shielding his face from the heat of the flames. 'This is all too much. Call this off.'

'Boo,' went the audience. 'Throw that trannie off the stage.'

'How dare you!'

Someone threw another fish. A diamond-finned loonbelly, this time. Or possibly a splay-jawed grum-doodler. Porrig ducked it, whatever it was.

'This must be done,' said Apocalypso to Porrig.

'No it mustn't.'

'Yes it must,' said Rippington.

'Box into furnace,' cried Apocalypso. 'That indeed should finish the job.'

Audience heads bobbed up and down. That indeed *should* finish anybody's job.

'And one more thing.' Apocalypso held high a hand as the trapdoor closed upon the flames. 'If all this isn't bad enough, I shall perform this feat in this fashion.' He drew his cape about himself, turned around in a circle, then flung his cape aside to reveal that he now was dressed in the costume of an Egyptian.

'Oooooooooooooooooooooooooooooooooooooooooooooooooo ooooooooooooooooooooooooooooooooooooh,' went the audience, *very* impressed.

'This Egyptian stuff is quite lost on me,' said Porrig.

Apocalypso adjusted his fez. 'Ladies and gentlemen, the bishop.'

Wild applause from the audience. Bewildered looks from Porrig.

The bishop swept onto the stage, robes all flying, mitre

cocked at a more than jaunty angle. He bowed to the audience, blew kisses, winked and grinned, performed a double somersault and came to rest upon one leg with his crook held high in the air.

'Nice crook,' said Rippington.

'Lost on me,' said Porrig.

'All right,' Apocalypso cried. 'I shall be mocked by the bishop, shamed by the bishop and I will enter the torture box with the killer wasps. The box will be locked, the electric cables will be attached top and bottom. At my signal the power will be switched on. I will release the wasps, the box will be lowered into the fiery furnace. And if I survive all *that*, I would ask that you favour me with a small round of applause.'

The audience responded with a very large round.

'Thank you.' Apocalypso bowed, produced a key from nowhere and handed it to Myra. Myra unlocked the door of the torture box and swung it open. The bishop camped about the stage, hoisting up his vestments and baring his bottom. 'What a wanker!' he called at the magician. 'What a useless wanker!' Apocalypso took the cabinet of killer wasps from the wasp man and entered the torture box. Myra closed and locked the door upon him.

'On my word,' cried Apocalypso, 'hook up the cables. *Hook.*' The chap in the white coat stepped forward. The power had been switched off and he attached the cables top and bottom to the torture box with giant jump-lead clamps: most impressive.

'On my word, raise the torture box. *Raise.*'

Chains clanked and the torture box, now trailing its mighty cables and containing Apocalypso and the cabinet of killer wasps, rose to a height some ten feet above the stage.

As the audience hadn't ooooooooooooooooooohed in a while, it had another ooooooooooooooooooh now.

'Stop this!' shouted Porrig and was felled by a well-aimed flounder.

'On my word, open the furnace doors. *Open.*'

The trapdoor in the stage opened, belching fire and smoke.

'Ooooooooooooooooooh!'

'On the count of three I will open the wasp cabinet, the

power will be switched on and the torture box lowered into the flames. I will remain there for thirty seconds – you may count them with the lovely Myra. Then the box will be raised, and you, perhaps, will applaud.'

The audience now did not oooooooooooooooooh or applaud. This looked terribly serious, terribly dangerous. This looked like suicide, really.

Porrig floundered with the flounder. 'Somebody stop him,' he shouted as he floundered.

Myra did open palms and showed a bit more cleavage.

The bishop waggled his bum about and called abuse in Latin.

Rippington shook his little grey head as the bee-keeping man and the white-coat chap retired to the sides of the stage.

'On the count of three,' shouted Apocalypso, taking a grip on the cabinet handle. 'One . . .'

'No,' said Porrig.

'Two . . .'

'Don't do it,' begged Porrig.

'Three!' Apocalypso tore the lid from the wasp cabinet and the insects whirled up about him in a buzzing murderous storm. Off stage the switch was thrown and the electricity tore through the torture box from top to bottom, arcing from one pole to the other. Down and slowly down went the torture box, down into the fiery pit.

Porrig covered his eyes, the crowd held its collective breath and Myra began to count.

She hadn't got to three before it happened. There was a creak and a terrible splintering sound. Somewhere above, the winch that lowered the chains was faltering.

The fifty thousand volts that crackled through the torture box were flying also up the chains, igniting the engine that held them.

The engine graunched and one chain snapped. The torture box swung crazily, sparks flying from it, all hell and mayhem within. And then the other chain gave and the box plunged down, snapping the cables too as it fell.

Down into the fiery pit beneath.

Down into the mouth of Moloch.

Down into hell fire and damnation.

Porrig tried to leap forward, but the heat drove him back. Myra screamed and her screams were taken up by the audience. Men with fire extinguishers rushed forward from the sides of the stage to fight the flames.

'Bring down the curtains,' shouted someone and the curtains fell.

The auditorium was in riot. Folk fought to flee the horror, tripping and tumbling over one another.

The bishop appeared from between the curtains. 'Please,' he shouted. 'Calm yourselves, please. Return to your seats. Return to your seats.'

They really should have stoned him for that. Return to your seats indeed! But they didn't, they stopped. Became calm. They trusted this bishop; they knew him, they loved him. Which was probably why he was there.

'There has been a slight technical problem,' said the bishop, making calming gestures with his crook, 'but do not panic. All will be well. Return quietly to your seats. Please.'

Behind the curtains, the fire extinguishers worked at their extinguishing. The flames were dying down and then the trapdoor closed.

'We have to get down there.' Porrig flapped his hands foolishly. 'Try to get him out. See if he can be revived.'

'Porrig,' said Rippington. 'Porrig.'

'Which way?' dithered Porrig. 'Which way?'

'There's no way, Porrig, there's no way at all.'

'But we must do something.'

'He's dead, Porrig. He could never have survived.'

'No . . . no . . .'

Rippington patted Porrig's stockinged leg. 'Let it go. Get the book and let us go too. We've been here much too long.'

'I can't just leave. He's dead. My God, he's dead.'

'I think he's paid his dues. I don't think he's gone to the bad place again.'

'No,' said Porrig. 'No.'

And then a great cheer went up from the auditorium.

'What the fu—'

'I think it's the bishop,' said Rippington. 'Telling jokes, probably.'

'Bastard!' Porrig rushed to the curtains and pushed his way between them.

The audience went, 'Oooooooooooooooooh' at his appearance.

'Hello, darling,' said the bishop.

'What?' went Porrig.

'Would you care to waltz with a man of the cloth?'

The audience laughed.

Porrig gaped.

The bishop waggled his bum once more. 'Give us a kiss,' he said.

'I'll punch your fucking lights out.'

'OOOOOOOOOOOOOOOOOOOH!' went the audience.

'Hold hard,' said the bishop. 'No need for bad language.'

'No need for . . .' Porrig coughed and sputtered. 'No need for bad language? He's dead, you shithead. He's dead and you say—'

'*Who's* dead?' asked the bishop.

'Apocalypso. Apocalypso The—'

'Miraculous!' cried the bishop. And he tore off his mask and he threw off his robes and then, bishop no more, it was *he*. Apocalypso The Miraculous!

'Oooooooooooooooooooooooooooooh,' went the audience.

'Oooooooooooooooooooooooooooooh,' went Porrig.

20

Porrig was all ooooooooooooooooohed out by the time Apocalypso The Miraculous had taken his twenty-third curtain call and retired at last to his dressing room.

Porrig and Rippington joined him there, accepted the glasses of champagne that were offered and, along with the bee-keeping man, the chap in the white coat, the lovely Myra and the unlovely bishop, they toasted the health and skill of the great magician.

'A raging stonker of a show,' said the bishop, his arm about the lovely Myra's shoulder. 'Your best performance ever.'

'Thank you,' said Apocalypso. 'My best and also my last.'

'Come, come,' the bishop said, his arm now round the lovely Myra's waist. 'You're on your way to the very top, my boy. You could make the impossible possible. All you have to do is take that little extra step.'

Apocalypso shook his fezless head. 'That little extra step, as you call it, is one that I shall never take.' He smiled in the direction of Porrig. 'You and your little friend there know exactly what I'm talking about, don't you?'

'We do,' said Porrig. 'And you're making the right decision. So how exactly do you plan to spend your retirement?'

'I shall open a little bookshop. In Brighton, I think. I have always been a great admirer of comic-book art. I will specialize in that kind of thing.'

'Top man.' Porrig raised his glass. 'Well, we have to go now,' he said. 'But it has been amazing to meet you. Quite amazing.'

Rippington tugged at Porrig's trouser leg. 'Not without the book,' he whispered.

Apocalypso viewed the imp. 'What did that small fellow say?'

Porrig cleared his throat. 'We need something. Something of yours. It's very important in the time we come from.'

'Time?'

'It would take far too long to explain. But we're in big trouble where we come from and Rippington here thinks that if I were to *borrow* your book . . .'

'What book?'

'Your book of magic.'

'The ritual?' Apocalypso stiffened.

'No, not that. Destroy the ritual, throw it away. Your book of *stage* magic. How you do your tricks.'

'That is a great deal to ask.'

'I suppose it is. But please tell me this: how exactly did you escape from the torture box without the aid of the ritual?'

'Trade secret,' said Apocalypso.

'You *are* retiring,' said Rippington. 'We'd keep it a secret.'

'All right then. And as you're the only ones in the room who don't know how it was done. But you'll be disappointed. It was only a trick.'

Rippington climbed onto Porrig's lap, much to Porrig's distaste. 'I'm sitting comfortably,' Rippington said.

'Then I will begin.' Apocalypso sipped champagne and spoke through the bubbles. 'Firstly, the absurd outfit – the fez and the sandals. Heavily insulated with rubber to spare me from electrocution. The "killer wasps" were ordinary hover flies, sprayed with iron filings to conduct the electrical charge, which instantly killed them when they were released. Now, had I actually been lowered slowly into the flames I would surely have cooked. So an accident was contrived to add an extra thrill for the audience and ensure my safety. The chains snapped by remote control, as did the cables, cutting off the power. The box plunged down between the roaring gas jets and dropped onto cushioned pads beneath the stage. I stepped out, donned bishop's garb and a mask and returned to the stage.'

'Incredible,' said Porrig.

'Thank you,' said Apocalypso.

'No,' said Porrig. 'I meant in-credible as in not credible at all. I was there, I saw it close up. I don't believe a word of that.'

'The quickness of the hand deceives the eye.' Apocalypso reached forward and produced a parsnip from Porrig's right ear.

'We know something with a rubbing part like that,' said Rippington. 'We really should be going now.'

'Can I borrow your book?' asked Porrig. 'I'll let you have it back when I've finished with it.'

'All right,' Apocalypso smiled. 'I can see by the look in your eyes how important it is.' He took the parsnip between his hands, gave it a squeeze and a rub and lo and behold . . .

'The book,' said Porrig. 'Thank you very much. And I *will* return it. Law of dharma and all that kind of thing.'

'If you're ever in Brighton you can drop it into my shop. I'll have to think of a name for it, won't I?'

'How about ALPHA 17?' said Rippington.

Apocalypso smiled once more, champagne glasses clinked and a further toast was raised.

'We must go,' said Porrig. 'But just one thing before we do.'

Porrig chinned the bishop.

Back at the shop in the kitchenette, Rippington asked him why.

'Because he was touching up my mum.' Porrig sought tea to brew, but all the tea was Wok Boy's and this made Porrig sad.

'Perk up though,' said Rippington, scaling the leg of the table. 'We got the job jobbed and we did it with style.'

'It was certainly some adventure.' Porrig sat down at the table and helped the imp onto it. 'Travelling back to the past. Saving Apocalypso from thirty years of hell and even meeting my mum when she was young. That was quite something, wasn't it?'

'And you got the book. And you didn't have to steal it.'

Porrig picked up the book and gave it a brief leafing through. 'Do you really think we can stop that horrible monster with this?'

'The quickness of the hand deceives the eye. And talking of quickness, we got back here before the curator's even arrived. We couldn't do better than that, could we?'

'I suppose not.' Porrig put down the book and took up Wok Boy's cup. 'But I only wish—'

'What do you wish?' asked Wok Boy, appearing at the open door.

'What?' went Porrig.

'What?' went Wok Boy.

'But you're—'

'But you're—'

'*Alive!* But you're *alive!*'

'But you're . . .' Wok Boy paused.

'But I'm *what*?'

'But you're wearing a woman's corset and fish-net stockings.'

'Forget about that. You're alive! *You're alive!*'

'Of course I'm bloody alive. Why wouldn't I be? But let's talk about you. How long have you led this double life? Why didn't you tell me? It's nothing to be ashamed of, I'm wearing ladies red underwear myself.'

'You pervert,' said Porrig. 'But you *are* alive. How did you survive? How come you didn't drown?'

'Are you on something, Porrig? I got a pain in my head and fell down the stairs. I must have rolled under the shop shelves, I've only just come to. Any tea on the go?'

Porrig made a very doubtful face.

'Let it go,' said Rippington. 'He's alive, which is something, I suppose.'

'Incredible.'

'Don't start that again. Just brew him some tea and explain to him what's on the go.'

'So,' said the Commander-in-Chief, of whom little had been heard for a while. 'What's on the go?'

'We're in Croydon, sir,' said the adjutant. 'We've just driven down here in convoy from London.'

'Croydon, eh? Must have dozed off. What are we doing in Croydon?'

'You and your chums pushed all the little flags on the big board towards Croydon. To stop the train with the monster on board reaching London.'

'You think little flags will stop the blighter, then?'

'When each flag represents a regiment of tanks and the tanks have all been assembled here, yes, I think it might do the trick.'

'So are the tanks all here?'

'Yes, sir, they are.'

'Even my special one?'

'Even your special one with your name on the side and the fitted cocktail bar.'

'Let battle commence then. Which way's the railway line?'

The adjutant pointed through the windscreen of the staff car. 'Up ahead, where all the tanks are parked. But the train is packed with hostages.'

'Military personnel?'

'Civilians.'

'Casualties of war, you mean.'

'Sir, you cannot open fire on civilians. Especially *our* civilians. It's against the Geneva Convention.'

'Never go to conventions meself. Always that damned Simo and his chums from SFX propping up the bar. A chap can never get served.'

'Stupid bastard.'

'What did you say?'

'I said the train will be passing through in a matter of minutes. We've been trying to contact the driver. Get him to slow it down enough so that we can derail the train gently, with the minimum loss of life.'

'Any luck?'

'None at all. We've been unable to get through. We don't even know who's driving the train.'

★　　★　　★

The driver's name was Russell. Russell The Railwayman.

Russell had never actually driven a train before, although it had long been one of his ambitions. He'd applied to take the course, but his mum hadn't been keen. She'd put him off; it was dangerous, she told him.

Russell had explained that there was more chance of winning the National Lottery than of being killed in a train crash. But his mum, who had already won the National Lottery three times, but was keeping quiet about it, was adamant. And a boy's best friend *is* his mother. At least it was for Norman Bates.

Russell was enjoying himself. He hadn't enjoyed the terrible pain that Dilbert had thought upon him, that had driven him into the cab of the train and demanded that he do the driving. He had no idea quite how he'd started the train and no idea whatever about how to stop it. But he *was* enjoying himself now: rushing through the red lights and taking the corners at dangerous speed. He'd learned early that the faster he went, the less the pain the monster inflicted upon him. He'd soon got the message.

And so Russell whistled a brisk Abba medley and pushed his foot nearer to the floor.

Ahead of him lay trouble with a capital T.

This time the T stood for Tanks.

'Tanks is what you need,' said Wok Boy, having heard Porrig's breathless tale. 'Tanks or – failing tanks – nukes.'

'Porrig's got a book,' said Rippington.

'Porrig always has a book,' said Wok Boy. 'He should start putting his books downstairs in the shop. There's plenty of space on the shelves now.'

Porrig arose to take issue regarding the matter of his empty shelves, but painfully recalling the previous beatings he'd received at the fists of Wok Boy, he sat down again. 'I want my comics back from that trannie,' he said in a sulky tone.

'Perhaps you should ask him yourself. You and he being of the same persuasion, as it were.'

Porrig kept his rage in check, he had more important things on his mind. 'The old bloke will be here soon,' he said. 'He'll know what to do.' And as an afterthought he added, 'You can explain to him how you mean to get the comics back.'

'I'll make the tea while you get changed,' said Wok Boy.

Porrig went off to the bedroom to rummage about for clean clothes. There weren't any. His best trousers and shirt were somewhere in the past being worn by his own mother before he was even born. Porrig sat down on the bed and sighed. It was all too much really. Much too much.

A couple of weeks ago he had been an engaged-to-be-married cleaner of cars in Brentford. Now what was he? Interdimensional time-traveller and potential saviour of mankind? *Him?*

Absurd.

Porrig removed his mother's stage-wear and rooted out a pair of jeans and a T-shirt with tolerable armpits. He slipped his unsocked feet into a pair of plimsolls and examined his reflection in the mirror.

And sighed again.

He'd have taken once more to bewailing his lot, but the sound of a car drawing up outside caused him instead to drag himself over to the window.

A black cab was parked in the street below and stepping from it was a rather smart young woman in a tight-fitting suit. She slammed shut the cab's rear door and strode towards the shop.

'What *now*?' Porrig asked himself. 'More trouble?'

The smart-looking woman entered the shop and marched up the stairs. 'Porrig,' she shouted. 'Porrig, where are you?'

Porrig hastened from the bedroom. 'I'm here,' he said. 'Who are you and what do you want?'

'Hurry up, come on.' The smart-looking woman hustled him into the kitchenette.

'Who's this?' asked Wok Boy. 'What's going on?'

'Agent Artemis,' said Agent Artemis. 'From the Ministry of Serendipity.'

'One of your dad's minions,' said Wok Boy to Porrig.

'Never mind about minions. Where's the book?'

'What book?' said Porrig.

'Don't waste my time with what book. The one you just stole. Apocalypso's book.'

'Now see here,' said Porrig. 'I never stole it, I was given it. And how do you know about *that*?'

'There's no time to waste with explanations.'

'I've got time,' said Porrig. 'I'm waiting for someone.'

'There isn't time. This is the book, isn't it?' Agent Artemis snatched up the queer-looking book from the table.

'That's mine, give it back.' Porrig made a grab at the book, but Agent Artemis stepped nimbly aside, took his left wrist and twisted it violently, nearly wrenching his arm from the socket.

'Hang about,' said Wok Boy.

'Shut it, Wok Boy, or you'll get the same.'

'How do you know my na—'

Agent Artemis elbowed Wok Boy in the stomach. Wok Boy doubled up and fell upon Porrig who was now taking up much of the floor space.

'Before you hit me,' said Rippington, 'I'm not with these people. I'm an Avon lady.'

'Shut it, Rippington.'

'Ah, you know me as well.'

'Of course I know you and you know me.'

'You look a bit like Carol Vorderman.'

'No I don't.'

'Sigourney Weaver?'

Agent Artemis leaned forward and gave Rippington's rubbing part a tweak.

'EEEEEEEEK!' went Rippington, falling from the table onto the strugglers beneath.

'You bloody useless bunch.' The boot went in: a stylish high-heeled shoe. 'You Wok Boy!' Boot. 'All those comic books!' Boot. 'You, Porrig!' Boot. 'Using the ritual without permission!' Boot. 'And you, Rippington!' Tweak. 'Letting him do it!' General booting and tweaking.

'Get off us!' howled Porrig. 'Leave us alone, you bloody madwoman.'

'Woman?' The boot went in once more. But this time it really was a boot.

Porrig looked up and did blinkings.

'Had you fooled there, didn't I?' said the old bloke, for it was he.

'What?' Porrig gaped and gasped.

'Had those wankers at the Ministry of Serendipity fooled too. The old quick-change routine, Apocalypso taught it to me when I was his assistant.'

'Hang about.' Porrig struggled unsteadily to his feet, rubbing his wounded wrist. 'I know you told me that you were his assistant. But when you went on stage, were you dressed as a woman?'

'Of course. Every stage magician has to have a beautiful woman as an assistant. It's a tradition, or an old charter, or something.'

'Hang about, hang about. This is all falling into place now. Were you the assistant that went into the electronic wasp-filled torture box and didn't come out again?'

'The bloody trick went wrong. If I hadn't used the ritual I would have been roasted.'

'You would have been killed.'

'Not killed, Porrig. I cannot die until I have returned the angel's feather. But I didn't intend to be roasted.'

'Has the kicking stopped?' asked Wok Boy, uncovering his head. 'Oh shit!' he continued, seeing the old bloke.

'The kicking's stopped,' said Porrig. 'But my confusion continues. How come, if you weren't killed—'

'There's no time now,' said the old bloke. 'Have you had time to read this book?'

'Not really, and I still don't see how—'

'Then you'd best study it on the way. We're going after the creature. We have to try and stop it before it reaches London.'

'Er, excuse me,' said Wok Boy.

'What do *you* want?' asked the old bloke.

'Well . . . just . . . er . . . you don't want me to come, do you?'

'No I bloody well don't. You can stay here and get my comic books back.'

'*My* comic books,' said Porrig.

'Porrig's comic books.'

'I'll stay and help him,' said Rippington.

'Oh no,' said the old bloke. 'You'll come with us. I have a use for you.'

'Oh dear.'

'Oh dear,' said Russell as the first tank shell burst overhead. The train was going flat out now and Russell had been singing 'Waterloo'.

'Stop this,' shouted the adjutant. 'You cannot fire upon unarmed civilians.'

The Commander-in-Chief made circular finger-movements to the gunner. 'Right a bit, stop, up a bit, stop.'

'Sir,' said the adjutant, trying to stand up in the special tank (the one with the Commander-in-Chief's name on the side and the fitted cocktail cabinet) and striking his head on the little trapdoor thingy. 'Sir, with all respect, I must insist that—'

'Fire!' said the Commander-in-Chief.

Bang and recoil and Doppler effect whistle and WHAM!

Russell ducked in the cab. 'That was bloody close,' he mumbled. 'Why are they shooting at *me*?'

'Sir, please, there are thousands of people on that train.'

'Adjutant, if you're going to fuss around like a silly big girl, then I'll have to have you chucked out of me tank.'

'But, sir—'

'Down a bit, left a bit.'

'Sir—'

'Fire!'

A signal box exploded, spewing flaming wreckage onto the track. Russell shielded his face as the train tore through the mayhem. 'Mum!' screamed Russell. 'I want my mum!'

The gap was less than two miles and was closing very fast.

Inside the special tank a special telephone rang. The adjutant snatched up the handset. 'Yes,' he shouted into it. 'Yes . . . What? . . . Yes I understand. Cease firing, sir.'

'That's it, you great Nellie, out of me damned tank.'

'But, sir, that was a communication from the train, patched through to us from GHQ. Sir John Rimmer is on the train. He's called to say stop firing, the monster is *not* on the train, repeat, the monster is *not* on the train.'

'It's a damned trick. Get out of that seat, gunner, I'll take this next shot meself.'

'Sir, please. Sir John Rimmer says that the creature was in the last carriage and that it had the last carriage detached from the train ten minutes ago.'

'Can't take any chances. Could be a damned trick.'

'Sir, it's no trick and we're in the path of the train. Back the tank out of the way.'

'Here it comes, by crikey.' The Commander-in-Chief pointed through the forward port. 'No time for namby- pambying about now. If you can't take the meat, stay out of the butcher's trousers, what. And where do you think you're off to, gunner?'

'I can't take the meat, sir.'

'Damned nancy boy. And you too, adjutant? Come back, you poltroon.'

'Back!' shouted Russell, fleeing the cab and rushing into the first carriage. 'Everyone to the back of the train. We're going to crash. We're going to crash.'

A tall man in underpants stepped past Russell.

'Not *that* way, sir. Move to the back.'

'You move and hurry,' said Sir John Rimmer. 'I will try to stop the train.'

Thunder and rattle and now blowing whistle, the train hurtled forwards. Less than a mile in it and that gap closing fast as before.

Sir John Rimmer sat in the driver's seat, all firm jaw and stiff upper lip, one hand on the whistle, two bare feet upon the brake. He took a deep deep breath and held it and he didn't close his eyes. If this was to be his death, he'd stare it full in the face and meet it like a man.

No false beard, no bloated pride, near-naked and alone.

'So be it,' said Sir John.

So be it.

And as these things do when they happen, *this* thing did as *it* happened. All in slow motion and just like a dream. Or an art house movie montage.

The eyes of Sir John staring ever ahead become the skidding train wheels, then become the crescent of a thumbnail as the thumb goes pushing down upon the blood red FIRE button in the tank, become the eye now of a dog, Sir John's dog, fetching sticks for him in boyhood; running legs now the running legs of passengers, the passengers falling, tripping, stumbling; a face now fills the screen, expands, the mouth becomes a pit, then a tunnel and the train screams through the tunnel; whistles, screams and people scream and eyes and wheels and eyes and wheels and—

Cut by the producer, who cares bugger all for art, and wants some action.

So, cut to the eyes of Sir John.

Cut to overhead shot of train rushing forward.

Cut to overhead shot of tank, someone climbing in.

Cut to skidding train wheels.

Cut to passengers tripping and falling.

Cut to interior of tank, thumb about to press FIRE button.

Cut to eyes of Commander-in-Chief, looking up.

Cut to eyes of Sir John, sweat dripping, knuckle rubbing across.

Overhead shot, gap closing fast.

Interior of tank, special telephone handset being snatched up.

Train wheels.

Passengers.

Handset smashing into Commander-in-Chief's temple.

Tank's POV[1] of approaching train.

Train's POV of tank.

Eyes of Sir John.

Eyes of adjutant. Oh!

[1]Point-of-view, as if you didn't know already.

219

Sir John's feet on brake.
Adjutant's hands gripping tank controls.
Train wheels skidding.
Tank tracks whirling.
Eyes of Sir John.
Eyes of adjutant.
People falling.
Sir John's hand going up to face.
Skidding wheels.
Whirling tracks.
Falling people.
Subliminal cut of Danbury Collins playing with himself in carriage toilet.

And medium shot as train tears past tank, missing it by inches and grinds and grinds and grinds and grinds to a halt.

And cut!

And print.

21

Printouts spewed from computer machines, telephones rang and smart-looking women in tight-fitting suits marched up and down. Men in white coats drank coffee from plastic cups and Augustus Naseby lurked in a corner.

It was all go at the Ministry of Serendipity.

A man in a white coat named Albert (he had named the coat himself, after Queen Victoria's beloved husband), poked Augustus with a stick.

'Oi!' said that man, 'who do you think you're poking?'

'Damn thing doesn't work,' said the man with the coat called Albert.

'What is it, anyway?'

'Divining rod, sir. I got it out of the stores.'

Augustus Naseby sighed in a manner much favoured by his son. 'Why?' he asked.

'Trying to locate the escape pod, sir. You know, the emergency escape pod that was built into the underground system by the Victorian magicians we deny all knowledge of. The escape pod you sent me to find and prepare.'

'Sssh,' went Augustus, with finger at his lips. 'We don't want to go causing panic, now do we?'

'Absolutely not, sir.'

'Let's have a look at the thing.' Augustus snatched the stick and gave it an all-over peering. 'Didn't it come with any instructions?'

'Just this little booklet, sir.' The man pulled this from a pocket in Albert; Augustus pulled it from him.

' "Thank you for buying *The H. G. Wells 1900 Emergency Escape Pod*," ' he read. ' "*The HGW 1900* supercedes all previous escape pods, having the full brass fittings of *The Verne* and the black Gothic leather interior of *The Poe*. Blah blah blah blah—" '

' "Blah"?' asked the man.

' "Blah",' said Augustus. 'Look, man, there's a map here of how to get to the pod and there are full instructions for firing it up and getting it launched.'

'I would assume so, yes, sir.'

'So why didn't you just read the booklet?'

'Not authorized to, sir. Ouch!'

Augustus Naseby raised the stick and struck the man once more.

'Ouch!' cried the man once more. And, 'Ouch!' he cried once more once more as Augustus hit him once more.

'The stick works all right,' said Augustus, 'You just weren't using it properly.'

'Sir,' said another man in a white coat called Brian (the man's name was Brian, the coat was called Phil). 'Sir, there's a lot of news coming in from Croydon.'

'Tell me the worst,' said Augustus.

'Well,' said the man, 'the worst was when I got my willy stuck in the tube of the vacuum cleaner. I was hoovering naked because it was a very hot day and, as I said to the nurse at the hospital, I . . . Why are you looking at me like that, sir? Ouch!'

'Croydon,' said Augustus. 'Just tell us about Croydon.'

'This was in Croydon. Ouch!'

'It does work well, doesn't it?' said the man with the coat called Albert. 'Can I have a go?'

Augustus handed him the stick.

'Just you bloody dare,' said Brian.

'Tell me the news from Croydon or I will shoot you dead,' said Augustus, drawing out a pistol.

'Well, sir, it was really exciting. The train was rushing along and the tanks were lined up on the track and the Commander-in-Chief was parked on the actual track in his special tank and he was firing and the train was rushing forward and he was firing and the train was rushing forward and ouch!'

'Nice shot,' said Augustus.

Brian rubbed his head. 'Sir John Rimmer was on the train and he managed to stop it safely.'

'Bravo, Sir John.'

'But the monster wasn't on the train. It was in the last carriage and that was detached from the train somewhat earlier. The monster got off at a village called Bramfield.'

'And how do you know that?'

'Street surveillance cameras, sir. Most towns and villages are now fitted with them. Crime prevention, we like to call it. Sounds a bit better than "Big Brother is watching you", but it amounts to the same thing.'

'Go on then.'

'Right sir. The monster had itself installed in a furniture van and continued its journey towards London up the A24.'

Augustus made heart-clutching movements with his non-gun-toting hand. 'It's coming to get me. Prepare the pod, we're going to escape.'

'Can I come too?' asked Brian.

Augustus made a thoughtful face and then shot Brian dead. 'No,' he said, 'there won't be room for three.'

'Three for London, cabbie,' said the old bloke.

The cabbie leaned out of his window and looked the old bloke up and down. 'Sorry, mate,' he said, 'but this cab's taken. Tart from London, actually. Nice legs and cracking Charlies; gagging for it, she is. I reckon I'm onto a promise there.'

The old bloke leaned down to the cabbie and whispered certain words into his ear: explicit details regarding the punishments that would be dealt out in the event of non-compliance.

'Hop in,' said the cabbie.

The three hopped in and the cabbie drove off at a breakneck speed. Porrig settled down to read Apocalypso's book of magic. The old bloke spoke sternly to Rippington. 'What have you been up to?' he asked.

'Porrig made me take him to Omega 666. He said he'd torture me.'

The old bloke shook his head. 'You took him to help him. I knew you would. But this is *not* the same reality that I left you in. I can sense that it's different.'

'It's only a slightly different one.'

'How slightly different?'

Rippington beckoned and whispered at the old bloke's ear. 'Well, in *this* reality Wok Boy didn't drown in the sea.'

The old bloke shook his head. 'Fair enough. But what else is different?'

'Only Porrig.'

'*Porrig?* How?'

Porrig closed Apocalypso's book. 'Finished,' he said, 'what an interesting book.'

'Well, he can read a lot faster now,' said Rippington.

'This gives me an idea,' said Porrig. 'We must stop off on the way and pick up a few things.'

'And improvise.'

'Get a bloody move on, cabbie,' said Porrig.

'And he's more assertive.'

Porrig sighed.

'And that's about all, really.'

The cabbie glanced into his driving mirror. 'So,' said he. 'What have you got there, then? Ventriloquist's dummy, is it?'

'I'll stick my wand up your fudge-tunnel, mush!'

'Very droll,' said the cabbie. 'And very convincing. Dying art, ventriloquism. Like snuffing.'

'Like *what*?' asked Porrig.

'Snuff taking. Gone right out of fashion, it has, but it'll be back, you mark my words. Smokers are fed up with being discriminated against. You can't smoke here, you can't smoke there. They'll revive snuff taking, you wait and see. No laws about not taking snuff. There'll be snuff shops back in the high street before the turn of the century, or my name's not Sebastopol Van Meer de la Pine Gwa-tan Qua Cest'l Potobo. Or is it Kevin Smith?'

'Kevin,' said the old bloke.

'Yep?' said Kevin.

'Shut up and drive the cab or I'll . . .' And he leaned forward and whispered once more.

Kevin hunched low at the wheel and shuddered. 'You've got a serious attitude problem,' he said.

If Dilbert Norris had a serious attitude problem, and many would probably say that he had, he was unaware of it himself. Does the man who stamps on a cockroach or swats a wasp have a serious attitude problem? No. Does the man who eats vegetables for dinner have a serious attitude problem? No. Does the man who considers that the human species is superior to the animal kingdom have a serious attitude problem? No. Does the man who eats wasps, sticks cucumbers up his backside and hobbles around Safeways howling that chickens should rule the world, have a serious attitude problem? No.

Well, not as such.

Dilbert did *not* have a serious attitude problem. Certainly he stamped upon people rather than insects. Certainly he ate people rather than vegetables. Certainly he considered that his species was superior to the human species. But if judged by the standards of his own race – and by what other standards could he be judged? – he did not have a serious attitude problem.

Well, not as such.

Dilbert's entry into London was a very swank affair. He wanted it 'showy', he wanted it 'big'. Something that his subjects would tell their grandchildren about. Not that he wouldn't be there to tell them himself. He would. And then some. But today was special. Today he would make himself known. To everyone.

He dispensed with the furniture van and had himself installed once more in his seven-pointed spacecraft with its top open and plenty of cushions. And plenty of carriers too: he was putting on weight. But it suited him. Made him more majestic. More transcendent. Peerless, unparalleled, dominant, paramount, *nulli secundus* and top of the tree.

He liked that, did Dilbert, top of the tree. Vegetative connotations, but so much more. Top of the tree. Top of the tree of life, perhaps?

Dilbert nodded a great many chins. Top of the Tree of Life.

His bands marched before him. Big bands and showy. He'd gathered them up on the way. Sought out the minds of musicians, hurled his pain into them, forced them to collect their instruments, forced them to march and to play.

And fine-looking women, men and children he'd gathered as well. He'd sorted the wheat from the chaff, the good seed from the god-awful, the rose from the thorn and the Sumatran dogwort from the Cambodian marsh lily.

He had become a connoisseur of humans. And as a man might strive to breed the perfect rose or racehorse, so would he, in turn, breed the perfect man, pleasing both to eye and palate, serving his taste.

For Dilbert did have taste. And while there are many who claim that taste is purely subjective, there are a few, better informed, who understand that some things are better than others and that some people are capable of making the distinction.

At the present, Dilbert's tastes *were* subjective. Him being the only creature on the planet to hold them. But, if Dilbert got his way, and Dilbert *would* get his way at any cost, this situation would rapidly change.

But more of this from Dilbert, during his forthcoming speech to the world.

For now let us wave our knickers in the air, cheer his arrival and bow at his passing. Thrill to the curious inhuman rhythms of his many bands. Gaze in awe at the thousands of nudists and buy a silver-coloured helium-filled balloon with the words *I ♥ Dilbert* printed on the side from one of the many stalls that have sprung up along the way. And sing an anthem to his praise.

> Oh glorious and green thou art
> Most high and wide and mighty.

How wonderful thy rubbing part
We welcome you to Blighty.[1]

'What a bloody awful song,' said the cabbie, fiddling with his radio. 'It seems to be on all the stations.'

Porrig glanced at the old bloke, who in turn glanced at Rippington, who glanced back at Porrig.

'Why all this glancing?' Rippington asked.

The cabbie glanced into his driving mirror. 'I didn't start it,' he said.

'So where exactly are we now?' the old bloke asked.

'Croydon,' said the cabbie. 'Twin town with Sarajevo.'

'Is it?' Porrig asked.

'Nah, only joking. Although I do think it has a suicide pact with Grimsby.'

The old bloke duffed the cabbie on the head. 'Can't you go any faster?'

'Ouch!' said the cabbie. 'No I can't. There seems to be some kind of military parade going on. Look at all these tanks.'

'Smart tanks,' said Rippington. 'Look at that special-looking one with the name on the side, there's a bloke being lifted out of it and put on a stretcher.'

'Go up on the pavement,' said the old bloke. 'Just get a move on.'

The cabbie drummed his fists upon the wheel. 'Look,' he said, 'the road's blocked with tanks. I can't get through. You'll just have to be patient.'

'Patient?'

'Be like me,' said the cabbie. 'I'm a Buddhist. All black-cab drivers are Buddhists now, you have to be to get the job. We practise inner calm. Meditation, at-oneness, that's why we never lose our tempers or behave badly in traffic. You could learn a lot from me. Would you like me to give you a mantra?'

The old bloke leaned forward and gave the cabbie something.

It wasn't a mantra.

[1]Copyright. All rights reserved by Dilbert Norris World Publishing Inc.

'Who's going to drive now?' asked Rippington.

'I will,' said Porrig.

'No,' said the old bloke. 'We'll never get through this traffic. We need something faster.'

Porrig peered through the windscreen. 'What about that?' he asked. 'I bet that goes fast.'

'What?' asked the old bloke.

'That big black secret unmarked government helicopter with the armaments all over it, parked in the school playground over there.'

'We'll take it,' said the old bloke.

The cabbie didn't get a tip. Neither did he get his fare. Which was two fares really, considering that he had driven the old bloke down from London. Sometimes life can be a bitch, even for a Buddhist.

Porrig dashed towards the playground, followed by the old bloke and the ever-scuttling imp.

A parking warden, observing the cab on double yellow lines, began to write out a ticket. And spying the driver unconscious at the wheel said, 'Dead drunk too, I'll report you for that.'

Porrig entered the playground and looked up at the helicopter. It really was impressive right up close: the guns and missile tubes and the big loudspeakers for playing Wagner.

The old bloke puffed to a standstill at Porrig's side. 'Ministry of Serendipity gunship,' he said. 'Probably brought some top brass militaries down from London. They sent the tanks to stop the train. By the sound of the hymn-singing on the radio, they evidently didn't succeed.'

'But who can we get to fly it for us?'

'Oh, I can fly it. In my guise as Agent Artemis I got all kinds of training.'

Porrig stared at the shaky old man. His wrinkled fingers were trembling and his ancient knees seemed ready to give out at any moment.

'Piece of cake,' said the old bloke. 'Knock on the hatch door and see if there's anyone at home.'

Porrig shinned up the three-runged ladder and knocked upon the said hatch door.

'Piss off,' called a voice from within.

'Someone's home,' said Porrig.

'Well, bluff it, boy, get them to open up.'

Porrig cleared his throat. 'Commander Naseby of the MoD here,' he said in the voice of his father. 'Open up this door at once.'

'Oh shit!' said the voice from within. 'It's him.'

Porrig gave a thumbs up to the old bloke. 'They think I'm my dad,' he whispered.

The hatch door slid open a couple of inches. Porrig smiled in, but a fist flew out and knocked him from the ladder.

'Ouch!' said Porrig, which was appropriate and currently quite fashionable.

'Leave this to me.' The old bloke turned away and then turned back as Agent Artemis once more.

Porrig rubbed his aching parts (which happily didn't include his rubbing one) and shook his head in amazement. 'That really is most impressive,' he said.

Agent Artemis now drew a large gun from her handbag.

'That too,' said Rippington.

'Let us in.' Agent Artemis fired shots into the air.

'God's knob,' said Porrig, covering his head.

The hatch door opened a tad further. 'Madam,' called another voice from within. 'This is an armoured helicopter. You are wasting your time.'

Agent Artemis, already halfway up the ladder, rammed the barrel of her gun halfway up the speaker's nose. 'Open the Goddamn door,' she said.

The helicopter's door slid fully open. 'You might as well come in,' said the man with the gun barrel up his hooter. 'None of us know how to fly this thing anyway.'

Agent Artemis climbed fully aboard. Porrig helped Rippington up the ladder.

'Now,' said Agent Artemis, surveying the interior of the helicopter and the exteriors of three men. 'Hands up.'

'Rub-a-dub-rub,' said Rippington, observing that the three men wore nothing but their underpants. 'Gay orgy, is it? Do you mind if I watch and take notes?'

'What the fuck is *that*?' asked the youngest of the three men, raising his hands as he did so.

'Who are you?' asked Agent Artemis. 'And what are you up to?'

The tallest of the three men, whose hands couldn't go up at all as his head was already touching the roof, said, 'My name is Sir John Rimmer and these are my two companions, Dr Harney and Danbury Collins. We are trying to steal this helicopter.'

'Pleased to meet you,' said the doctor.

'Get out of the helicopter,' said Agent Artemis.

'No, hang about,' said Porrig. 'Sir John Rimmer? Not *the* Sir John Rimmer, who wrote *Beyond Doubtable Reason: The Biography of Apocalypso The Miraculous*?'

'Among many other books,' said Sir John.

'What a small world it is,' said Rippington.

'What the fuck *is* that?' said Danbury Collins.

'Out of the helicopter,' said Agent Artemis.

'But, madam, please.' Sir John fluttered his fingers. 'My colleagues and I are bound upon what amounts to a sacred mission. We must destroy a monster from outer space that seeks to dominate the entire planet.'

'What a small world it is,' said Rippington.

'What the fuck *is that*?' said Danbury.

Agent Artemis cocked her pistol. 'I really should shoot the three of you,' she said. 'I know all about you and what you've done.'

'What have they done?' asked Porrig.

'They're to blame for all this. They brought up the monster from under the sea.'

'Ah, now,' said Sir John, 'that's not strictly true. The Americans brought it up and—'

'Get off or I shoot you dead.'

'Oh come on,' said Porrig. 'We're wasting time. If they want to help, let them help. We need all the help we can get.'

Agent Artemis tucked away her pistol. 'All right,' she said. 'You can take responsibility for them, Porrig. Everybody strap up tight and I will fly the helicopter.'

'Oh dear,' said Sir John. 'I don't know about that.'

'And why not?'

'Well,' said Sir John. 'And no offence meant. But you're a . . . you know . . . girlie.'

'*What?*'

'Well, it's just that we never have much to do with girlies. I am strictly celibate, due to being bitten in the cobblers by my pet spaniel when I was a child. Dr Harney is past that sort of thing and Danbury just plays with himself.'

'I'm doing it now,' said the youth.

'Urgh,' said Porrig. 'So you are. But as I've spent so much time lately being called a wanker, it's quite a pleasure to find myself in the company of the genuine article.'

'I'm Britain's champion,' said Danbury. 'Everybody knows my name, but nobody wants to shake my hand.'

'The old ones are always the best,' said Rippington.

'Will somebody please tell me what the fuck that is?'

'I'm Rippington,' said Rippington. 'I am a dvergar and I work as a librarian in ALPHA 17, which is an alternate reality where all the ancient books of magic are stored. My hobbies include reading and making small animals out of paperclips. My ambition is to have a larger ouch!'

'Shut it,' said Agent Artemis. 'And those paperclips will come out of your wages. Now, gentlemen. We have wasted more than enough time. You are all wankers in my opinion and I am going to fly this helicopter. Are you coming with us, or getting off?'

'Depends where you're going,' said Danbury. 'You haven't told us yet.'

'Women,' said Sir John. 'Typical.'

Porrig covered his eyes to spare them the sight of the violence.

When the violence was finished he opened them again.

Three men lay unconscious on the floor, their knickered bums in the air. Agent Artemis sat up front, her bum on the pilot's seat.

'Right,' she said, in the voice of the old bloke. 'London it is, to do battle with the monster.'

231

Porrig went up front, settled himself onto the co-pilot's seat, strapped himself in, perched Rippington upon one knee and Apocalypso's book upon the other.

'All right,' said Porrig. 'Let's go for it.'

22

Dilbert Norris went for it. Big time.

His procession moved in regal splendour through the streets of London. At the vanguard, some five hundred or more big strong men pushed forward like a human battering ram, overturning parked cars and thrusting aside anything that blocked the progress of The Great Green One. Then came the bands and the beautiful people, then The Great Green One himself, waving a limp green hand and smiling a terrible smile.

At the Ministry of Serendipity, Augustus Naseby lurked at a desk before the big wall screen, viewing the image of Dilbert, beamed to him via London's many street surveillance cameras.

'Unstoppable,' he said with a sigh. 'He's unstoppable.'

The man in the white coat called Albert nodded. 'His ability to project pain telepathically is without precedent. People are powerless to resist. He has absolute control over them. He is a singular and most remarkable being.'

'Yes, all right.' Augustus made fists. 'I'm sure he's a triumph of evolution. But he has to be destroyed. I wonder over how great a distance he can project his power.'

'About a mile, I'd say.'

'Then we'll soon be in range. We have to get out. What news of the escape pod?'

'Well, sir. Following the instructions in the handbook, I located it all right. It's a two-man jobbie, lovely Victorian craftsmanship, powered by a sophisticated steam turbine system, which, had the government of the day not chosen to keep to themselves, would have made the internal combustion engine a non-starter. Don't you sometimes feel, sir, that we could do so much good for the world if we didn't just greedily hoard stuff like that?'

Augustus Naseby gave the man a certain look.

'Sorry, sir,' said the man. 'I don't know what came over me there.'

'So where exactly is this escape pod?'

'You'd never guess in a thousand years.'

'Nor do I intend to try,' said Augustus. 'Because if you don't tell me right this minute, I will hit you with this stick again.'

'Well, sir, it is cleverly disguised as a famous London monument. It's—'

'Sir! Sir!' went another man in a white coat, bustling up. 'The monster's reached Trafalgar Square. I think something big's about to happen.'

And indeed it was.

Dilbert had built himself a mountain on the raised plaza that surrounds Nelson's Column. It wasn't a very large mountain, more of a hillock really, but it was impressive. Thirty feet in height it was, and built from living men.

Dilbert had been conveyed to the very top and he lazed there, soaking up the sun and being moistened here and there by attentive naked women bearing little plant sprays.

The human hillock squirmed beneath him. Those at the top groaned dismally. Those at the bottom were already dead.

Trafalgar Square was carpeted with people wall to wall, down on their knees, their faces to the paving slabs. Television news crews that Dilbert had gathered on the way angled up their cameras and checked their furry mics. This *was* news, and although they really didn't want to be here recording it, they had no choice. They were Dilbert's people now, controlled by his thoughts, utterly without wills of their own, his to do with as he pleased.

Dilbert turned his big bad head from side to side. Green and glistening, broad-smiled and glossy-black-eyed, he examined his reflections caught (to perfection, he considered) in the long mirrors looted at his command from department stores and held by his Nubian favourites, who balanced about him on his hill of death.

'How do I look?' he asked.

'Big God-fala tasty-good,' said a finely muscled fellow.

'Picking all this up all right?' called Dilbert to the news crews below.

'Fine,' said a CNN man, giving the thumbs up.

'Then do it from down on your knees.' Dilbert flung down mental pain and the news man sank to his knees.

'Still fine?'

'Perfect, O great one.'

'Then I shall begin.' Dilbert waved away the sprayers and holders of mirrors and comfied his big bad bottom. 'People of Earth,' he began. '*My* people. Oh, and yes, hello.' Dilbert waggled his fingers towards a street surveillance camera high atop a not-too-distant lamp-post. 'Hello to the boys from the Ministry watching too.'

'He sees us,' whispered a man in a nameless white coat. 'He knows we're watching him.'

'Of course I know,' said Dilbert. 'I know all and see all and hear all too. But all of you will learn this in time. So, now, let me begin. People of Earth – *my* people – many of you will not remember me. Most, in fact, will not remember me. It is so very long since I was last among you. But, praise be unto me, I am back.

'Now, I know what you're asking yourselves. You are asking yourselves, who is this handsome fellow broadcasting live to us. Well, I will answer that. I am your God. Some big surprise, eh? Last thing you expected today was to have God appearing live on your television. But, glory be to myself, it is now something that you will be enjoying each and every day.

'Because, each and every day from now on, I will be appearing on your television and you will be watching me and listening to me and I will be telling you what you can do to please me and you will be doing it. Do I make myself clear?'

Dilbert smiled his terrible smile and stared with his terrible black eyes towards the cameras.

'Oh,' said Dilbert. 'Apparently I do not make myself clear. Apparently not all of you out there are convinced of my Godly credentials. I think perhaps that now would be the time for a demonstration of my powers.'

'Switch it off!' shouted Augustus.

'Sir?'

'Switch the big wall screen off *now*.'

The man in the nameless white coat switched it off.

And not a moment too soon. Because WHAM, ZAP and no doubt POWEE too, from Trafalgar Square, through the ether and over the airways and out of every television set that was tuned to Dilbert's broadcast—

WHAM, ZAP, POWEE and a big time OUCH!

Pain flung from Dilbert's mind tore into every viewer. Folk fell from their chairs and couches, sucking in their breath and clutching at their heads as the message reached them, forced in and rammed home, destroying every other thought.

I AM GOD AND YOU WILL WORSHIP ME.

And in Downing Street and in the White House and in palaces and mansions and rooms of state and shops and homes and houses and hovels, all who watched Him felt His power and sank before to worship.

I AM GOD AND YOU WILL WORSHIP ME.

'Well,' said Augustus. 'If we had any doubts about his capability of controlling everything, I think we should dismiss it from our minds while we still have minds to dismiss it from.'

'Two-way TV,' marvelled the man in the nameless coat. 'We know he can see whoever sees him. You think he can hurt them too?'

Augustus nodded. 'I have absolutely no doubts at all.'

'We're in the shit here, sir, aren't we?'

'Get me some more coffee in a plastic cup,' said Augustus,

lurking ever lower in his chair. 'And make sure that every TV set in the ministry is switched off.'

'It's going to make it rather difficult to keep tabs on what the monster's up to, sir.'

Augustus waved the man away. 'I'm sure he'll let us know.'

'I am currently, as you can see, in London,' said Dilbert. 'Beside' – he gestured – 'Nelson's Column. What a big column that Nelson had! I've a very big one myself. But enough of humour. I shall soon be arranging a world tour, so that I can get to know you all personally. You will find me an easy God to please. All you have to do is obey. What could be simpler than that?

'There will naturally be some changes in lifestyle. Total world disarmament, a single world economy and a single world language. I will teach you mine. Regular hours of worship, and I will, of course, frown upon the worshipping of any gods other than myself. And there are rather too many of you at the present and the standard is somewhat low. It will be necessary to cull about a third. I will let you know who is to cull whom.

'So, it's all good news, really. No more wars, no more religious strife, everything in order and jolly times ahead. For some of you, at least. I'll bet you're really glad I came back, aren't you?'

Dilbert smiled once more into the cameras and the viewers caught once more his power.

And their heads bobbed up and down. They were really glad that he was back. Really, yes, really, they were, yes they were.

'I'm really pleased that you know how to fly this helicopter,' said Porrig to the old bloke, who was the old bloke once more.

'Do you have your plan all worked out?'

'Well, I would have liked to have stopped off to pick up some stage props, but I think I can manage without them.'

'You seem very confident, Porrig.'

'Yes I do,' said Porrig. 'Although I can't imagine why.'

'Oh look,' said Rippington, peeping over Porrig's shoulder. 'The Chippendales are waking up.'

The old bloke shook his ancient head, his dog-eared crests of hair a-wagging as he did so. 'Go and help the buggers, Porrig,' said he. 'Check that I didn't break any bones.'

Porrig unstrapped himself and lifted Rippington down. The two of them edged back through the helicopter, which was now moving across the sky at a fair old kind of a lick.

'How are you doing?' said Porrig to Danbury.

The callow youth rubbed at his head. 'People keep hitting me,' he said.

'I know the feeling. Sir John?'

'Fine,' said the long man, who didn't look fine. 'But you see what I mean about women? Whatever brought on such violence? PMT would be my guess.'

'I think you'd better keep your misogynist remarks to yourself from now on.'

'Listen to you,' said Rippington. 'What is this, the new Porrig, or something?'

'Or something. You all right, doctor?'

'Neck's a bit stiff,' said Dr Harney, sitting up. 'The girlie used Dimac, didn't she?'

Porrig nodded. 'But you're quite safe. The, er, girlie has gone. We have a chap flying the helicopter now.'

'Good thing too,' said Sir John.

'Easy,' said Porrig.

'Quite so.'

'Porrig has a plan to destroy the monster,' said Rippington.

'Sir John has a plan too,' said Danbury. 'Although I do have a "certain feeling" about it.'

'Not surprised,' said Rippington. 'I can hear him thinking it and it's a really crap plan.'

'It is not.' Sir John climbed slowly to his feet.

'It's as bad as the bomb in the beard.'

'The what?' asked Porrig.

'Bomb in a beard,' said Rippington. 'Sir John's previous failed plan to destroy the monster. Brave attempt though.'

'Thank you,' said Sir John. 'And I do take responsibility for what's happened. If only the Americans had not reached the monster first.'

'They would never have reached it first,' said Rippington. 'If Dr Harney hadn't tipped them off.'

'Outrageous,' said the doctor, jumping to his feet. 'I did no such thing. Which way is this helicopter flying?'

'He did too,' said Rippington. 'I can hear him thinking it.'

'The creature's mad.' The doctor fiddled at his underpants.

'Dr Harney is a CIA agent, planted in the Ministry of Serendipity,' said Rippington. 'And it was he who bribed the head man of the island village to duff up Sir John and nick his beard.'

'You bastard,' said Sir John, taking a swing at the doctor.

'Back off,' said Dr Harney, drawing out a pistol.

'Blimey!' said Danbury. 'Where did he keep that pistol hidden?'

'Hands up all of you.' Dr Harney motioned with his pistol. 'It's true, Sir John. It's all true.'

'But why?' the long man asked. 'I thought we were friends.'

'Ptah!' went Dr Harney, in the manner much favoured by villains. 'I was sick of playing second fiddle to you. Watching you poncing about and getting all the credit for everything we did together.'

Sir John hung his high head. 'I have failed everyone,' he said dismally.

Dr Harney turned his pistol upon Porrig. 'Tell the pilot to change course,' he said. 'Any nearer to London and we will be caught in the blast.'

'Er, excuse me,' said Porrig. 'But, blast, did you say? What blast is this?'

'The five megaton nuclear blast. The Americans are preparing to—'

'Nuke the creature,' said Danbury. 'No wonder I had a "certain feeling". What did I tell you right from the start? It will end in nuking, I said. But did anybody listen? Oh no, take no notice of Danbury. When I said nuke it now, what did you say? There will be no nuking, you said. And what's going to happen now? Nuking, that's what's going to happen, and I OUCH!'

Danbury fell fainting to the floor.

Rippington examined the tip of his magic wand. 'Works a treat up the old chocolate speedway, doesn't it?'

'What is going on?' Porrig made fists with his upraised hands. 'What is all this about nuking?'

'The only way to be sure,' said Dr Harney. 'I radioed back to my base in America after we got off the train.'

'Where do you keep your radio?' asked Sir John.

'Same place that I keep my pistol.'

'He does have a very big arse,' said Rippington.

'I do not!'

'Oh yes you do.' Rippington waggled his small one about.

Dr Harney brought his gun to bear upon the imp.

Sir John kicked it out of his hand and floored him with a mighty blow.

'Nice one, Sir John,' said Rippington. 'I thought you might do that if I distracted his attention.'

'What are we going to do?' Porrig asked.

'Well,' said Rippington. 'You could get the doctor's radio, call his base in America and get them to call off the nuking.'

'What are we going to do?' Porrig asked.

'Well,' said Rippington. 'You could get the doctor's radio and . . . Oh, you heard me the first time, didn't you?'

Porrig nodded.

'And you don't fancy . . . er . . .'

Porrig nodded again.

'Oooooooooooooooooh, my bum,' moaned Danbury, coming round.

'Bum jokes,' said Rippington. 'Makes a change from knob gags, I suppose.'

'But what are we going to do?'

Porrig's dad knew exactly what *he* was going to do.

He was going to escape in the *HGW 1900* escape pod. Just as soon as the man in the white coat called Albert returned to tell him that all was prepared.

The man in the nameless coat came sauntering up. 'Sir,' said he. 'You know you told me to make sure all the TVs were switched off?'

Augustus nodded and lurked a bit lower.

'Well, I did that, sir. But while I was in the communications room, I happened to overhear a message being sent on the Americans' top secret waveband.'

'The one that they don't know that we know about?'

'Yes, that very one. And you'll never guess in a thousand years what they were saying on it.'

'No,' Augustus sighed. 'You're quite right there. Because I don't give a toss.'

'Oh you should, sir. You really should.'

'All right.' Augustus sighed once more. 'I've a minute or two to kill before I—'

'Before you what, sir?'

'Never mind. So you want me to guess, do you? Is it anything to do with Egyptians, or chickens?'

'No, sir. And I must say that the chaps from the other realities we deal with are keeping a bit of a low profile.'

'Hardly surprising that, is it? So, not Egyptians or chickens. Penises?'

'No, sir.'

'Bottoms then?'

'Not even close.'

'Give me a clue then.'

'Right. It's something that flies through the air.'

'Ah,' said Augustus. 'Is it one of those big black secret unmarked government helicopters that we deny all knowledge of having?'

'No, sir. Although one of them has gone missing.'

'An aeroplane then.'

'No.'

'A rocket?'

'Close.'

'Oh, I'm bored with this. Tell me what it is.'

'The Americans have launched a nuclear warhead from one of their secret satellites that they don't know that we know about.'

'I was pretty close, then, when I said rocket, wasn't I?'

'Very close. Would you care to guess at the target?'

'That's easy,' said Augustus. 'I'll just bet they've targeted London, to wipe out the monster.'

'Well done, sir. And, for three in a row, would you like to guess how long it will be before the warhead arrives?'

'Easy too, I can work that out in my head. About thirty minutes I'd say.'

'Close enough, well done.'

'Now it's my turn,' said Augustus. 'I spy with my little eye, something beginning with . . . Hold on . . . Would you care to run all that by me again?'

'Hold on. Hold on,' said Porrig in the helicopter. 'Whatever are we worrying about?'

'The nuke, I think,' said Rippington.

'No, I mean, think about it. If the Ministry of Serendipity controls just about everything, then they're perfectly capable of knocking an approaching missile out of the sky.'

'Of course they are,' said Sir John.

'Of course they are,' said Rippington.

'Of course they are,' said Porrig.

'Are you quite certain?' Danbury asked, 'Because I have a "certain—"'

'Are you quite certain of this?' asked Augustus Naseby, growing quite white in the face.

'Quite certain, sir. The warhead will reach ground zero in a little less than fifteen minutes.'

'Then only one course of action lies open.'

'Engage the nuclear defence network that the Americans don't know we have?'

'The very same.' Augustus delved into his shirt and brought out one of those special keys on a chain that very very top brass always carry with them for unlocking and arming the nuclear capability.

He flipped up a section of desk top to reveal one of those special units with the flashing lights and the big red button with keyhole arrangement that goes with the special key in question.

Augustus Naseby inserted the special key and gave it a twist. The word ARMED sprung up on a little screen.

'It's a jolly good job the Americans don't know we have this,' said the man in the white coat, which, although nameless, was growing a little sweaty at the armpits.

'Why?' asked Augustus.

'Well, sir, if the Americans knew, then they would have encoded a scrambler into their warhead that would cut all our power.'

'You're not wrong there, I suppose.'

'Better push the button, sir.'

'Right then, I will.'

Augustus reached to push the button.

But all the lights went out.

23

'Bugger me,' said Augustus in the dark.
  'Was that an order, sir?'
  'Who said that?'
  'I did, sir. Man in a white coat called Julian.'
  'Have you got a big torch?'
  'No, sir, it's just the way my trousers hang. Ouch!'
  'Well at least I've found the stick.'
  'I've got a torch, sir,' said another voice.
  'Who's that?'
  'Man in the white coat called Albert, sir. If you'd care to follow me, I think we should be heading for the top secret steam-turbine-driven Victorian escape pod that is cunningly disguised as a well-known London landmark. Sir.'
  'What escape pod?'
  'Who said that?'
  'Who said "who said that"?'
  'I did.'
  'Who are you?'
  'Who's asking?'
  'Sir, I really think you should follow me now.'
  'Well switch your torch on then, you twat.'

'I haven't got a torch.'

'But I thought you said—'

'*I'm* the one with the torch, sir.' The man in the white coat called Albert switched on his torch. Its name was Trevelyan.

'Nice torch,' said Augustus.

'Thanks,' said Trevelyan.

'Who said that?'

'Just follow me, sir.'

'Who said *that*?'

'That was me,' said the pig. 'It's fun this, isn't it? Does anybody have a plan?'

'So that's my plan,' said Porrig, who had been outlining his plan in the cockpit area of the long black secret unmarked Ministry of Serendipity helicopter. 'What do you think of it then?'

Above the rotor blades CHB CHB CHBed.

In the cockpit area there was silence.

Porrig glanced at his watch. It was twenty past four.

'Have you ever noticed that?' said Porrig. 'The way if there's ever a lull in the conversation and it all goes quiet, it's always either twenty to, or twenty past the hour. I wonder why that is.'

'It's a tradition, or an old charter, or something,' said Sir John. 'Although on this occasion I feel it is something else entirely.'

'Oh?' said Porrig. 'What?'

'Sheer bloody horror!' screamed Sir John. 'You cannot be serious, you just cannot.'

'Why?' asked Porrig.

'Because . . . because . . .'

'I think,' said the old bloke, adjusting the throttle and fiddling with the gears, 'that Sir John is just a little concerned about the scale of your plan.'

'It will take a *big* plan to stop a *big* monster.'

'Yes, I've no doubt of that. But what you're suggesting is a tad ambitious.'

'Nah,' said Porrig. 'Piece of poo. It's all here in Apocalypso's book. I can do it all by myself. Easy peasy.'

'No no no.' Sir John waved his long hands about. 'You don't grasp the complexity. A trick like this—'

'*Illusion*,' said Porrig. 'Call it an illusion. It sounds much better than trick.'

'*Illusion*, then. An illusion like that would take days to set up. It would require a team of skilled technicians. Cost thousands of pounds. Need to be—'

'Nah,' said Porrig once more. 'There's no need for all that fuss and bother. I can probably find all the bits and bobs I need right here in the helicopter. And Rippington will help me.'

The imp bobbed up and down on Porrig's knee. 'I certainly will,' he said.

'Tell him,' Sir John implored the old bloke. 'Tell him it can never work.'

The old bloke double-declutched and changed down. 'I don't think he'd listen,' he said. 'And Rippington's keen, aren't you, Rippington?'

Rippington nodded his little grey head. 'I think Porrig's plan is the polecat's purple plonker.'

'And that's good?' Porrig asked.

'The very best. It outshines the bee's bollocks and the tom cat's testes and ranks alongside the lion's lingam and the elephant's cloakroom ticket. It is an inspired plan.'

'He likes it,' said Porrig.

'I do,' said Rippington. 'But it's all somewhat academic really, isn't it?'

'Why?' Porrig asked.

'Well,' said Rippington. 'Do you see that little telescreen jobbie on the instrument panel there?'

'I do,' said Porrig.

'And you notice it has the nuclear symbol above it?'

'I do,' said Porrig.

'And the words INCOMING MISSILE in capital letters flashing on and off?'

'Yes,' said Porrig, 'I do.'

'And the little digital clock counting down? Do you see the little clock?'

'I *do* see the little clock,' said Porrig.

'Well, *that's* why it's somewhat academic.'

'Academies of learning,' said Dilbert Norris, who hadn't finished speaking; who, in fact, was only warming up. 'Great seats of higher education. And when I talk about great seats' – he waggled his bottom – 'I know just what I'm talking about.'

Dilbert paused. 'I didn't hear laughter,' he said. 'I made a funny and I didn't hear laughter.' He folded his brow and thought very bad thoughts and the whole world that was watching laughed out loud.

'That's better,' said Dilbert. 'Try to keep up, it's less painful. You'll soon get the knack. Yes, indeed, academies of learning. We will do away with those. Mankind has become over-sophisticated, which, considering how stupid you all remain, is perhaps somewhat oxymoronic. But you've lost your roots. And when I talk about roots, I know what I'm talking about.'

Gales of laughter blew in Dilbert's direction.

Dilbert sighed. '*That* wasn't a joke, you dimmos. That was a statement of fact. You have entered the computer age. You could be moving outward to the stars. But what have you done with your computers? Turned them into mindless games and weaponry. I despair, I truly do. But we'll have no more of it. Back to the land with you, I say. But for a few. A chosen few, who will work on a little project of my own.'

Dilbert grinned greenly into the nearest camera. 'I am going to have myself cloned,' said Dilbert. 'Produce a crop of little Dilberts and Dilbertas. Seed the planet with my kind. You lot will be farmed the way that you farm chickens. He who is top of the food chain is top of the tree of life.'

'We're all gonna die!' Danbury flapped his hands about, and Sir John Rimmer flapped *his* hands about. The old bloke did not flap his hands about, because he was holding the joystick. Rippington didn't flap his hands about, because he was afraid he'd fall off Porrig's knee. And Porrig didn't flap his hands about because he thought it was really uncool.

And Dr Harney didn't flap his hands about because he was unconscious.

'Stop flapping!' ordered Porrig.

'I wasn't,' said Rippington.

'Nor me,' said the old bloke.

'Danbury, wake up Dr Harney,' ordered Porrig. 'Make him fish out his radio from its . . . er . . . hiding place and call up his American base. Have him tell them that the situation is under control and they must disarm the missile.'

'Okey-doke,' said Danbury.

'Bravo, Porrig,' said the old bloke. 'So are you still going ahead with your inspired plan?'

'Absolutely. If we can stop the nuke, we'll still have to deal with the monster. And if we can't stop the nuke, and it's all academic, we'll still have had a bloody good try.'

'Bravo once more. I am proud to call you my great-great-grandson. So what would you like me to do?'

'Land the helicopter, so that I can make all the necessary adjustments. Then on to . . .' Porrig paused. 'Where exactly is the monster now, Rippington?'

'Somewhere called Trafalgar Square,' said the imp. 'I can hear his thoughts and they're very very noisy.'

It was very very quiet in London. Very quiet. Deathly so. No traffic moved and no hooters honked. No hawkers hawked and no pedlars peddled. No gits with mobile phones stood in shop doorways showing off. And no rich bastards minced out of their chauffeur-driven motor cars parked on double yellow lines and swanned about in Harrods. Streets and pavements were deserted. Shops and businesses abandoned.

The rich and the poor, the great and the good and the godless, moved and weaved and meshed together no more.

Those who could flee, had long since fled.

Those who could not, now knelt.

The sun shone down upon Trafalgar Square. A light breeze ruffled some pigeon feathers. And the great fat green and sprouty sod lounged upon his human hillock, farting mightily.

'Must be someone I ate,' said he. And the silence broke to huge cries of mirth, though none with a trace of amusement.

'Well,' said Dilbert. 'I really would like to sit about chatting with you people for the rest of the day, but I regret that I must leave you for a while. You see, being the kind of God that I am, the all-seeing and all-listening kind of a God, I am ever alert to potential danger. And you will never guess what is heading this way. Nuclear missile, that's what.'

A terrible moan rose up from the kneelers. The terrible moan of the damned.

Dilbert nodded his big bulbous head. 'It's true. Launched by the Americans from one of their secret satellites. Can't trust anyone, can you? Except for me, of course. Yes, the Americans. I heard it from the Ministry of Serendipity, you know. That's the secret organization that really runs your planet. I can hear their tiny minds at work. They're scurrying about beneath the ground like little rats, trying to escape, even as I speak.

'I wonder if they'll make it. I know that I will.' Dilbert reached down into his human hillock and tore off an arm with a wrist-watch on it. 'Let's see,' he continued. 'Yes, I have a ten-minute margin of safety. Kindly convey me to my spacecraft and I'll prepare for the off.'

He cast out his terrible mental pain and the kneelers rose and gushed towards him, sweeping up over the human hillock, bearing his enormous weight upon their straining shoulders, lowering him gently down to his waiting spacecraft. And Dilbert gazed up into the clear blue sky and smiled and then said, 'Hang about.'

The strainers and lifters and carriers and shifters halted and hung about. And gazed up also.

Dilbert pointed and all the people stared.

Because something was coming. Something quite wonderful.

It was coming in low from out of the sun and it glittered and twinkled and twirled as it came. It didn't look like a nuke and it didn't look like a fighter aircraft or a long black secret Ministry of Serendipity helicopter. It looked like a silver seven-pointed spacecraft.

Just like Dilbert's in fact.

Dilbert rubbed his eyes and Dilbert squinted. And Dilbert

sent out thoughts and thoughts came back to him. Then Dilbert shouted, 'Clear the decks, make room, make room,' and he fluttered his fingers and sent people running and he gazed on as the craft gently settled.

And Dilbert said, 'Mum, is that you?'

24

Dilbert's mum was smaller than her son. Much smaller. But then mums so often are. Because with mums it really is the case that size doesn't matter. The smallest mother can have the largest son. In fact the smallest mother often seems to. And no matter how large that son may be, he grows really small in the presence of his mum.

And as the dome of her spacecraft opened and Dilbert's little mum climbed carefully down, you could almost feel Dilbert shrinking.

You could almost see it as well.

Dilbert's mum was a sproutish little body. She wore a little pinny, as mums used to do. She had mean little arms and mean little shoulders, a mean little mouth and mean little eyes too. She walked with a shuffle, on mean little feet. And she fretted as she shuffled; in the way that mums still do.

Dilbert gazed down upon his mum, and his face took on that anguished expression that big sons' faces always take on when confronted by their mums at quite the wrong moment.

'Well,' said Dilbert's mum. 'Aren't you going to give your mum a kiss?'

Dilbert's big mouth opened to emit a strangled croak. His big fat fingers fluttered and he waved away his people.

'Go on,' he muttered, between clenched teeth. 'Go on, bugger off.' He flung his pain this way, that way and the other and people took to hurrying away. At considerable speed.

'Come on then,' said Dilbert's mum. 'What are you doing there?'

'Just . . . er . . . just . . . er . . .'

'And what is all *this* about?' Dilbert's mum pointed a mean little finger and Dilbert knew just where it was pointing.

'Dead things,' said Dilbert's mum. 'A big pile of dead things. You've done this, haven't you?'

'I . . . er . . . I . . . er . . .'

'Speak up, speak up. I let you out of my sight for a couple of hundred thousand years and this is what happens. You just wait till your father gets here.'

'My father . . .'

'You're in big trouble, my lad.'

'Big trouble?' Dilbert's mouth fell horribly open. 'Big trouble,' he said once more, then he held up the arm with the wrist-watch on it. 'Mum, you have to go. You have to go *now*.'

'Go now?' Dilbert's mum folded her mean little arms. 'Go now? I've only just arrived and I haven't even had time to stretch my old legs.'

'Mum, this is very important. You are in great danger.'

'Stop it at once, you silly boy, and give your mother a kiss.'

'No, Mum, really. You really shouldn't be here.'

And it was quite true, wasn't it? Dilbert's mum really shouldn't have been there. She really wasn't part of the equation. Dilbert did have a lot on his plate. Things to do, people to conquer. And there was that nuke approaching.

'Mum, you have to go. You really do.'

'I'll go when I'm good and ready and not till I've had a kiss.'

'But, Mum . . . I . . .'

'Kiss,' said Dilbert's mum, indicating her mean little cheek with her mean little finger.

'Then you'll go? You promise you'll go?'

'I promise.'

252

'All right. But just one. And no tongues.'

'Urgh!' said Dilbert's mum. 'You revolting boy.'

Dilbert leaned down to his mum and puckered up.

'*And* your breath smells.'

'Yes, Mum,' Dilbert puckered up some more.

'*And* you're not wearing any trousers.'

'No, Mum, I'm sorry.' Dilbert did further puckerings up. 'I'm very sorry indeed.'

'And so you should be. That ruddy great rubbing part is scaring Jack shit out of everybody.'

'Yes, Mum, I . . .' Dilbert ceased with the puckering up. He drew his big face back from his mum's little one and stared most deeply into it. 'What did you say?' Dilbert asked.

'Give your mother a kiss.'

'No, not that. About a rubbing part. You said something about a rubbing part.'

'Don't argue with your mother. You're not too big for a smack.'

'Hold hard,' cried Dilbert, peering. 'Something smells here and it isn't my breath.'

Dilbert's mum turned away as if in disgust.

And then she turned back.

Of a sudden.

To reveal that she was not really Dilbert's mum at all.

But really Porrig.

Ta-rah!

With Rippington on his shoulders.

Ta-rah! Ta-rah!

And Porrig held in his hands an axe.

A big fire axe from the emergency kit on the helicopter.

And as Dilbert stared down in horrified awe, Porrig swung this axe.

And what a swing it was. The kind of swing that the Mighty Thor might have taken. Or even the Wolf of Kabul. Had it struck home in Dilbert's head, it would damn near have cleaved it in two.

But Dilbert's head was out of reach.

His wanger wasn't though.

The axe head caught the three-foot parsnip of a pecker and pinned it to the pavement.

And then there was a silence.

It wasn't your twenty-past or twenty-to kind of silence.

It was more your calm-before-the-storm kind of silence.

Your calm before the apocalyptic holocaust.

And then Dilbert screamed and the silence was over.

Dilbert screamed and screamed.

It was a sound like no other ever heard upon the Earth. A sound so terrible and loud and awful that it rattled the chimney-pots three miles off and turned the milk sour on the steps. It made babies fill their nappies and strong men weep into their beer. And it just got worse and worse.

Dilbert screamed and threw out pain and he tore the axe from his wounded willy and flung it high in the air. And he yelled and he howled and he hollered and he sought the most hideous vengeance.

He turned his great head to the right and the left in search of his tormentor. His great head raged with pain and fury. With disbelief at this atrocity. This attempt at deicide. This blasphemy. This abomination.

Dilbert stooped painfully and clawed up the bundle of rags and the mask of screwed-up newspaper that had somehow fooled him. Fooled *him*! And the spacecraft! Dilbert stared at the spacecraft. It wasn't a spacecraft at all, it was just an old parachute, draped around an inflatable dingy. And suspended from . . .

Suspended from? Dilbert's awful pain-filled eyes turned upwards. A cable dangled from a tiny cloud. A tiny cloud not fifty feet above.

Dilbert snatched at the cable and gave it a tug. A vicious one. And out of the cloud came a helicopter. A long black secret unmarked Ministry of Serendipity helicopter, that had been silently hovering in stealth mode. (The way they often do, which is why you rarely see them.)

Dilbert flung up terrible pain and those in the helicopter caught it.

The old bloke clawed at his head and Danbury clawed at *his* head and Sir John Rimmer clawed at *his* head. And Dr Harney, who had been shouting into a sticky radio, clawed at his head also.

Down came the helicopter, CHB CHB CHBing, shaking and rocking and turning about in a circle. And the forward rotor nearly took the head from Dilbert Norris. In fact, had not a second and sudden and most excruciating pain, this time in his backside, caused him to leap up and somewhat sideways, he would surely have been done for.

Dilbert's face took on an agonized expression and his hands did some clawing of their own. He screamed once more as his clawing hands came quickly to the cause of his latest torment: the shaft of the big fire axe, protruding from between the cheeks of his very big behind.

Dilbert swung around, howling and moaning. The old bloke yanked back on the joystick and the helicopter rose once more, went into stealth mode and vanished.

Dilbert floundered around, green fingers fumbling, black eyes crossed.

'I'll bet that smarts,' said Porrig.

Dilbert's eyes uncrossed. He drew in breath and held it. He gazed down upon the defiler of his holy bum and a great roar rose from his mouth.

'Keep it down,' said Porrig. 'What a fuss you make.'

Dilbert turned his pain upon Porrig. Every ounce of it; every pound. Every hundredweight and every ton too.

But Porrig just stood there and grinned up at him. 'You can't hurt me,' he said.

Dilbert's jaw went drop drop drop. His brain went hate hate kill. He knotted his fists and folded his brow, he hunched up his shoulders and screwed up his eyes and squeezed pain from places there'd never been pain and he hurled the lot upon Porrig.

Porrig just laughed. 'You're losing it, fat boy,' he said.

'Maggot!' slurpy-gurgled Dilbert. 'Worm! And filth! And vermin!'

'Who ate all the pies?' sang Porrig. 'Who ate all the pies?'

'What . . . I . . . what?' Dilbert's mouth flapped up and

down, his ghastly eyes bulging from his ghastly head. 'I am your God,' his voice gulped and gargled. 'Kneel before your God.'

'God?' Porrig laughed again and offered the use of two fingers. '*That* to you, you fat bastard.'

Dilbert rocked and shuddered. He took a step forward, paused and winced. Then, with much moaning and groaning, he wormed the axe out of his arse.

'You're dripping your juices,' said Porrig.

Dilbert viewed him from on high. 'Who are you?' he demanded. '*What* are you?'

'It doesn't really matter who I am,' said Porrig. 'But as to *what* I am, I am this. I am your Nemesis, Norris. I have come to kill you.'

'Me?' Dilbert broke sweat from many strange places. '*You* kill *me*?'

Porrig nodded. 'I have already tricked and ridiculed you. I've punctured your pranger and rammed an axe up your old fudge tunnel. Your followers have gone and there's just you and me. Do you want to beg for mercy?'

Dilbert shook from baldy head to big and horny toe. He was genuinely lost for words. This was unthinkable. Impossible. Preposterous.

'Yes,' said Porrig. 'It is, isn't it? But nevertheless it is true.'

'You . . . you . . .' Dilbert made great pump-house pantings. 'You can read *my* mind.'

'Correct,' said Porrig. 'And it's in a bit of a state at present. You'd really like to stamp me flat, but time is running rather short and if you don't get to your spaceship in the next couple of minutes, you are one cooked sprout.'

Dilbert glanced towards his seven-pointed spacecraft. It stood upon the raised plaza next to Nelson's Column.

'So near, but yet so far,' said Porrig, who stood between Dilbert and his means of escape. 'You'll have to get past me.'

'You think that you can stop *me*?'

'I can do anything I like.' Porrig danced a little jig. 'I am the miracle worker. I am your god now, Norris.

'Out of my way, little man.' Dilbert took a giant step, but

256

Porrig cast wide his arms and Dilbert's giant step stayed hovering in the air. Dilbert gaped down in horror.

Before him a chasm now yawned with a wide open mouth. It was deep, it was dark, it was wide, it was there.

'Don't fall down the hole,' called Porrig from the other side. 'And watch out for the killer wasps.'

The wasps came down from nowhere and engulfed Dilbert in a wild and buzzing storm. He floundered and swatted, shrieked, swore and staggered. And Porrig just stood there and laughed.

'What are you laughing at?' asked Augustus Naseby, climbing into the pod.

The pig peered in after him. 'Nothing,' said the pig. 'Although you really don't expect this thing actually to fly, do you?'

'It's a masterpiece of Victorian technology.' Augustus made all-encompassing gestures that encompassed all there was. 'Look at it, it's wonderful.'

The pig did further peerings in. It was very smart, it was true. Two padded leather armchair jobbies, bolted to the floor. Lots of polished turncocks and dials with flickering needles. Heavy emphasis on the brass and the mahogany. Even a Constable landscape hanging over the fireplace. And all gas-lit and all just waiting for the off.

'I think I'll give it a miss,' said the pig. 'I have a "certain feeling".'

'I've a "certain feeling",' said Danbury, peeping down from on high.

'Keep this one to yourself,' said Sir John. 'Porrig is doing a fine job down there.'

The old bloke's old hands gripped tightly on the joystick. 'What news, doctor?' he asked.

Dr Harney shook his radio. 'The bastards have me on hold. They say that the top brass chap with the special key has gone off to the canteen. They've sent someone to look for him.'

'You've really shafted us,' said Danbury, turning and thumping the doctor. 'We're all going to be blown to dust and it's all your fault.'

'At least we'll have died in a noble cause,' said the old bloke. 'If the monster is destroyed, it will all be worth it.'

Danbury sighed and returned to the cockpit. 'Let's just hope then that Porrig can keep it confused. If the monster cops on, then—'

'Cops onto what?' asked Dr Harney. 'I was unconscious when Porrig outlined this plan of his. What exactly is he up to down there?'

Danbury sighed again. 'I really shouldn't tell you,' he said, 'you being such a double-dealing shit and everything. But as it looks like we're all going to die anyway, it can't hurt. The Porrig you see down there squaring up to the monster isn't really Porrig. It's Rippington. Rippington can hear the monster's thoughts, he can tune in to their wavelength, but he isn't affected by them. So, using Apocalypso's stage magic, Rippington is impersonating Porrig, while Porrig is running the other illusions. Fake chasm in the ground, fake bees buzzing, all that kind of stuff. Sufficient to slow up the monster until the nuke gets here. It's all very brave and very noble and—'

'Very far-fetched,' said the doctor. 'But as long as the monster doesn't cop on—'

'Exactly,' said Danbury Collins. 'As long as he doesn't cop on.'

Below the wasps stopped buzzing and the chasm ceased to be. Dilbert grinned a terrible grin. And Rippington said, 'I think he's copped on.'

Dilbert tapped at his swollen temple. 'Just listened in,' he said. 'To your chums in the helicopter. I could easily have killed them, you know, but I'm far too clever. I'm too clever for any of you and now I really must away.'

Squaring up his massive shoulders Dilbert strode towards his spacecraft. He swung a great hand at the pseudo Porrig, scattering rubbish and empty apparel. He stamped the lot flat and continued to stride.

'What now?' whispered Rippington to a shaking skulking Porrig, lurking down behind the spacecraft.

'Any suggestions?' Porrig asked.

'Only one obvious one.'

25

Dilbert climbed into his spacecraft. He lowered the dome and fastened his seat belt and reached out to turn the key in the ignition.

But the key wasn't there.

Porrig raced across the square, Rippington clutched under his arm and Dilbert's key in his hand.

'Now he's stuffed,' puffed Porrig.

'No I'm not,' said Dilbert.

He delved beneath the dashboard and brought out the spare. Stuck it in, gave it a twist and the engine caught first time. Rochets roared and the craft began to rise.

Porrig stopped short and stared back. 'Christ in a carwash,' he cried. 'The bastard's getting away.'

'The bastard's getting away,' cried the old bloke. 'Get out of the helicopter. All of you. Now.'

'What?' went Danbury. 'Just hold on.'

'Jump out now, just do it.'

'We'll be killed. Let me shoot him, this gunship is covered with—'

'No time for that. Just jump.'

'No,' said Danbury.

'Right,' said the old bloke, dragging back the joystick 'I'm sorry but you have to go.'

The helicopter rose with haste upon its forward rotor. Danbury and Dr Harney and Sir John toppled backwards and rolled towards the rear. The old bloke pressed a button or two and the cargo door swung open. With screams and cries and very bad language three men plunged down from the sky and fell into one of the fountains.

The old bloke forced the joystick forward and the throttle down.

'What's he doing?' Porrig asked, as the helicopter swept above his head.

'He's going to ram the saucer. Run some more.'

And as Porrig ran some more, the old bloke gripped the joystick in his ancient wrinkled hands and said what prayers he could before the impact.

Dilbert's eyes grew wider as he watched the helicopter come. He stomped his big foot on the accelerator pedal and flung mental pain at the kamikaze pilot.

The old bloke caught the agony. Caught it full force. The anger, the loathing and the disgust. The hatred of Dilbert for all the human race. He caught it and he screamed.

But he didn't let go of the joystick.

The helicopter smashed into the saucer, driving it backwards onto Nelson's Column. Right onto Nelson, in fact.

Dilbert opened wide his legs, as the huge bronze head of the great hero's statue burst through the bottom of his spacecraft and damn near through his own.

The helicopter, broken backed, its forward rotor gone to ribbons, swung in faulty circles, then crashed down to the square.

Porrig stared in horror and then rushed to offer help.

Smoke belched from the twisted hull and those little electrical sparks that always precede the explosion of the ruptured fuel tank fizzed and popped.

Porrig struggled with the cockpit door and strained to force it open. The door jerked back and Porrig stared within.

The old bloke was slumped across the instrument panel. Blood dripped from his left ear; his neck was clearly broken.

'Oh no.' Porrig climbed into the cockpit. 'Don't be dead. Please don't be dead.' He ran a shaking hand across the dog-eared tufts of snow-white hair. 'Please God let him be alive.'

The ancient's eyelids flickered and his mouth took in a gulp of air.

'Yes,' sighed Porrig. 'Come on, let me help you.'

'No!' The old bloke's voice was strong and loud. But it came not from the trembling lips. It came directly into Porrig's head. Into his thoughts.

'Go Porrig,' said the voice. 'Go before this thing blows up. You have work to do and I have done all I can. If now is my time to die, so be it.'

Porrig shook his now crowded head. 'I won't leave you here to die,' he said. 'And anyway, you can't die. Not until you've returned the angel's feather. That's what you have to do and I'm getting you out of here whether you like it or not.'

There was a blinding flash and Porrig fell back shielding his eyes.

'Get out,' called Rippington. 'It's going to blow, Porrig. It's going to blow.'

'No, not until I . . .' Porrig's voice trailed off as he opened his eyes. He blinked and he stared and he blinked and stared again. There was now someone else in the cockpit. He was small and he was naked and he perched upon the dashboard with his feathered wings outspread. A golden light flickered about him, glittered on his wings and perfect face.

'The angel,' whispered Porrig. 'The angel has returned.'

'Give him back the feather.' The voice in Porrig's head was just a whisper now. 'Give it back so I can be at rest.'

Porrig fumbled in the old bloke's waistcoat and pulled out the slim ebony box. He glanced down at the date engraved upon it. 1837.

Porrig sniffed away a tear and as he sniffed the smell of lilacs overwhelmed him. The odour of sanctity, the perfume of perfection. He held out the box and the angel took it in his tiny hand. The angel smiled at Porrig and Porrig sniffed another tear away.

'Come out,' called Rippington. 'Porrig, come out now.'

'Goodbye then.' Porrig gently patted at the old bloke's shoulder. 'And I hope you find perfection.'

'Goodbye Porrig.' And the voice, a fading whisper, then was gone.

'Porrig, quickly. Hurry now.'

There was another flash and this one came with flames.

Porrig leapt from the helicopter, snatched up Rippington and ran. The electrical sparks found the ruptured fuel tank and did what was expected of them. The helicopter erupted in a bristling bubbling burst of fire. Porrig flung himself down, shielding Rippington as shards of flaming metal span and fell about them.

'Rub a dub dub,' said the imp, raising his little bald head. 'That was a close thing, wasn't it?'

Porrig plucked something hot and painful from the seat of his pants. 'He's dead,' he said in a voice all cracked and broken. 'The angel came and took him and he's gone.'

'Oh,' said Rippington. 'That's that then.'

'What did you say, you little shit?' Porrig raised his hand to strike the imp. But as he did he stared him eye to eye. And there in the small blue cat-like eyes of Rippington he saw the tears.

'I cared,' said Rippington. 'I loved him too, you know.'

'Yes,' said Porrig. 'I know.'

Rippington pointed over Porrig's shoulder. 'That gobshite up there is still alive,' he said.

And indeed that gobshite *was* alive. Dilbert struggled from his mangled spacecraft and shook his verdant fist. 'Top of the world, Ma,' he shouted, all King Kong and raving. 'I am still the big boss here. Kneel before your God.'

And then the shockwave hit.

It came as a rumble and struck like a body blow. There was shuddering and grumbling of buildings that were shaken at foundations. Windows cracked and doors burst from their frames. Bricks and slates and lath and plaster ripped and shivered, trembled, tumbled, smashed and bashed and fell.

The ground rocked and paving slabs gave. The rumbling

became a roar; the roar increased in volume. Cracks shot across Trafalgar Square and Porrig dodged and ran.

But where can you run to, really?

Dilbert, one arm gripping Nelson, one fist in the air.

Danbury struggling from the fountain holding his groin for the very last time.

Sir John Rimmer kneeling, his hands clasped in prayer.

Dr Harney staggering this way and that, his radio lying some distance away, with a voice calling from it unheard that said, 'I can put you through now, caller . . . caller . . . caller . . . ?'

And then a second shockwave hit.

White-out. Blinding light and fireflash. Then up with a roar and a rumbling rush: Nelson's Column, with its lions and central plaza, up and up.

Nelson's Column with its raving sprouty bastard clinging to it up and up.

Nelson's Column.

Victorian monument.

Nelson's Column.

The secret escape pod.

'Up and away,' cried Augustus. 'I think we're going to make it.'

The column rose upon turbine jets, blinding light and fireflash. Porrig shielded his eyes and watched as it rose. And stared as it dwindled and dwindled and dwindled and dwindled away.

'Gone,' said Porrig. 'He got away.'

'Your dad too,' said Rippington. 'He was driving that thing.'

'Incredible.' Porrig shook his head. 'Look at it all. Look at it.'

Rippington looked at it. 'It's quite a mess,' he observed.

'Mess?' Porrig threw up his hands. 'Mess?'

'Well, you did your best. You tried your hardest, Porrig. You have nothing to be ashamed of.'

'But he got away.'

'This is true.'

'And the nuke . . .'

'Ah yes,' said Rippington. 'The nuke.'

★   ★   ★

263

'Ah yes,' said Augustus. 'I think we can definitely chalk this up as a success.'

'I'm quite glad I came,' said the pig. 'Even though I wasn't invited.'

'There's something up with the periscope,' said the man in the white coat called Albert.

'Stuff the periscope,' said Augustus. 'Let's open up the champagne.'

'Oh but, sir, I wanted to use the periscope. It's really clever, you can see out of Nelson's spyglass.'

'You do have to hand it to those Victorians. When they built an escape pod they didn't miss a trick.'

'Ah, that's got it,' said the man in the white coat. 'There was something blocking the spyglass. Oh shit!'

'Pigeon shit?' asked the pig.

'No. Oh dear, oh dear.'

'Let me look, you buffoon.' Augustus elbowed the white-coat-wearer aside and peered into the periscope.

A big black angry eye glared back at him.

'Aaaaaaaaaaaaaaaaaagh!' went Augustus. 'The monster's on board!'

'If you think that's bad,' said the pig. 'You should take a look out of this porthole here. There's something heading towards us on a collision course. It's coming very fast and I can't quite make out what it is. Oh yes I can. It's got the stars and stripes on the front. It must be the nuclear—'

26

It did make one hell of a noise.

Well they do, don't they, nukes?

But as it was very high up when it hit, there were few at ground level who heard it. There would be fallout, of course, but then what was a bit of fallout? The monster *was* dead. The Earth *had* been saved.

Of course there would be some explaining to do. An official explanation would be called for. Someone would have to own up to something.

And of course someone did.

He owned up to everything.

He took all the credit.

Because, after all, it had been a most remarkable feat. Remarkably achieved. Single-handedly achieved. Remarkable.

The President of the United States, in his speech, said just how remarkable he thought it was. The Prime Minister of England, who always agreed with anything the President said, agreed that it was indeed remarkable. And so did all those crowned heads of Europe and the new Pope and everybody else, really.

And as the motor cavalcade progressed slowly through the

crowded streets to Buckingham Palace, where he received a genuine knighthood, everyone agreed that what Sir Sir John Rimmer had achieved was truly remarkable.

Not only to have destroyed the incoming meteor that threatened to wipe out the planet, but in doing so to have eradicated the CONTAMINATION which had resulted in many deaths and the hallucination by millions that they had seen God on their television sets: that *was* remarkable.

Remarkable!

But then, Sir Sir John Rimmer *was* a remarkable man. So remarkable, in fact, that the British government had no hesitation at all in offering him a full-time job.

As the new head of the Ministry of Serendipity.

27

The wheel has come full circle for Porrig.

It is a month to the day since he lay in the gutter, not looking at the stars. He lay there then because he had spoken out of turn. Was politically incorrect. And for that he took a thumping and lost his fiancée.

But much can happen in a month. And much indeed has happened to Porrig. He is a changed man. A new man. A different man.

And yet here he is lying now in the gutter and once more not looking up at the stars.

So what has occurred?

And why, as we bid him farewell, most likely for ever, is he in this dire predicament?

He has blood on him, does Porrig, a gory nose has he. And there are rips upon his clothes and bruises upon his person.

Wherefore is this so?

Or is that whyfore?

A sorry business really, in a pub. And amidst so much in the way of celebration. Late extensions too.

What made him say it? What made him act in such a fashion? What?

The drink, perhaps. The drink and that television broadcast of Sir Sir John at the palace. That must have been it. The way he lost his temper and ranted at the screen. The way he screamed about cover-ups and conspiracies and people being pawns played in a callous game by a government department, and how he could prove it right there and then if he could only remember the special technique that seemed somehow to have slipped his mind.

Yes, it must have been all that. And the punch he threw at a transvestite. They had dragged him from the pub and beaten him up and dumped him in the gutter.

So now he lies there, bewailing his lot.

Not looking at the stars.

Porrig moans and groans and mutters and as he does so a hand falls on his shoulder.

No ordinary hand.

A small hand this is and most terribly small. It is grey and the fingers are bony.

Porrig jerks alert and covers his head for fear of further punishment.

But a voice speaks softly into his ear and Porrig uncurls at the sound.

A small grey head leans over him and two blue cat-like eyes go blink blink blink and the voice speaks again and says, 'Porrig?'

And Porrig's eyes go blink blink blink too and Porrig replies, saying, 'Rippington!'

And Rippington says, 'I've been searching for you, Porrig. I've been looking everywhere.'

And Porrig says, 'I thought you'd gone back to ALPHA 17 or somewhere. No-one believes a word I say. The Ministry has covered everything up.'

And Rippington says, 'Because now the monster is dead, everything's back to normal.'

And Porrig says, 'But you're still here.'

And Rippington says, 'Yeah, and I still don't like it.'

And Porrig says, 'If only I could remember how to sing the notes, I'd bugger off to a different reality.'

And Rippington says, 'And would you take me too?'

And Porrig says, 'Of course I would.'

And Rippington says, 'Guess what.'

28

And you can visit Porrig, if you want.

He still has his shop and he runs it with his best friend Wok Boy and a small grey companion who only comes out at night. The shop is pretty successful. Porrig wheels and deals in old comic books and he draws his own and prints them on his printing press. They're pretty odd stuff: all about alternate worlds and wild conspiracies.

No-one takes them seriously, of course. But they do have a big cult following. And Porrig even has his own fan club now.

People sometimes ask him where he gets his ideas from and whether he actually believes any of the stuff he draws and writes about.

Porrig always smiles when people ask him this. He shakes his head and he tells them no. Although he does say that such things might be possible, might even have happened, in a different reality.

But certainly not in the one that *he* lives in.

Which, of course, is the same one that we're living in.

Isn't it?

On 28 April 1998 Mornington Crescent Underground Station reopened after many years of 'extensive restorations'. It is interesting to note, however, that the station closes to the general public each night at nine-thirty.

Though perhaps not *that* interesting!